Cairo Kill

A bullet whistled past Dartley's ear like a crazed hornet as he pumped another shell into the chamber. The stinging impact of a dozen pieces of shot got across the message to Omar Zekri that his pistol was no match for a pump-action shot gun. The man turned and ran.

Dartley's voice was easy: "Omar, I guess you never heard the good advice never to be the bait in your own trap."

He loosed a blast from the gun which caught Omar in the chest and knocked him over like a soda bottle. He sat up in the roadway, an unrecognizable pulp of blood, hair and gristle. Dartley sent a second load into the half-butchered carcass. This time the bloodied torso fell back and lay still.

Dartley gestured to a terrified Abdel Ibrahim with the smoking barrel of the big gun. "You drive."

Also by Ian Barclay

The Crime Minister
The Crime Minister: Reprisal

Published by
WARNER BOOKS

THE CRIME MINISTER: REPRISAL

Ian Barclay

WARNER BOOKS

A Warner Communications Company

WARNER BOOKS EDITION

Warner Books, Inc.
666 Fifth Avenue
New York, N.Y. 10103

 A Warner Communications Company

Printed in the United States of America
First Printing: December, 1985
10 9 8 7 6 5 4 3 2 1

Chapter
1

Chestnut and oak leaves rattled down the road in scurries of an October wind. The young boy's mother called out the front window of their home for him to button his coat. She said it in French, so her eight-year-old immediately obeyed. Here in France he had taken to ignoring her when she spoke to him in Arabic or English. The family had never spoken French back in Egypt. Her husband was fluent in the language, and her son was already speaking in the local accent and using slang. Only she continued to have difficulties, and she knew that she was an embarrassment to her son before his friends here, a foreigner so barbaric she did not appreciate their precious language.

The previous day her husband received another of the phone calls at his lab in the Centre d'Etudes Nucleaires. It was a different voice this time, but again the man spoke in English with a strong Egyptian accent. They were to be made an example of, so that others equally reluctant to perform their patriotic duty might learn from their mistake.

When the Light of Islam fundamentalists suddenly overthrew the Mubarak government in Cairo, her husband happened to be at a conference in Brussels on the peaceful uses of atomic energy. An Egyptian civil servant at that time, almost a year ago, her husband had added his vacation to the conference and taken her and their son with him to Brussels. They had been lucky to be away. Her father and one of her husband's brothers had been killed in the bloodlettings and purges after the takeover. They would never go back. Both of them felt this way. No matter what they were offered to return. No matter how they were threatened . . .

Because of the phone call, she had walked the boy to school and picked him up in the afternoon. Now she was keeping a close eye on him as he played with a neighbor's dog in front of the house. She was cleaning the windows, shivering because she was unaccustomed to the raw October wind of northern Europe.

She noticed a black car pass the house. She couldn't tell one make of car from another, and she only looked because they had so little traffic on that road in the town of Saclay. The car seemed to slow a little in front of the house, and the driver glanced in and caught her eye for a moment before moving on. There was another man next to him in the front seat.

It was the same car a few minutes later, black, two men in the front seat—although this time the driver was on the side farthest from her since they were coming from the other direction.

The car was not traveling fast, and the driver deliberately swung the front in, so that its side was almost scraping the low wall of the tiny garden in front of the house. Her son turned and ran before it like a small frightened rabbit.

The front of the car struck him in the back and lifted him into the air. His light frail body smashed against the windshield, rolled rapidly across the roof, and dropped on the road in the wake of the car.

She dropped her cloth, leaped through the open window into a flower bed, and ran to the garden gate, which was ajar. She was screaming.

Before she reached the gate, the black car was backing up. The man next to the driver had his head out the window and was shouting instructions in Egyptian.

The rear wheel crossed over the child's body. The boy's head and shoulders were beneath the vehicle. His sneakers kicked as the tire sank a narrow lane across his chest.

"It's getting late, lieutenant," the gendarme said to Laforque. "You'd better go now if you want to see the body."

Laforque had a bony face and wore a dirty trenchcoat. No more than in his mid-thirties, he already looked soured on life. He said, "Any reason I need to?"

"No," the gendarme said. "I usually try to avoid dead kids myself when I get the chance."

The gendarme was at least fifteen years older than his superior officer and was not afraid to have his say.

The two plainclothesmen went to a bar and ordered Ricards.

"Maybe you think it was a waste of your time, lieutenant, having to leave Paris to come down here—"

"No, I don't." Laforque had forgotten the gendarme's name. "If they had listened to you in the first place, that scientist might never have caused all this fuss."

The gendarme was pleased. "I put in the call as soon as I heard what the child's father had to say about threats being made against them, especially because they were Arabs. I don't mind *our* Arabs, like the Algerians and Syrians. But the Egyptians weren't ours. Why didn't they go to England and bring their troubles there?"

"Because this Egyptian is an important nuclear scientist," Laforque said.

"Well, they have nuclear stuff in England too," the gendarme grumbled, lighting an unfiltered Gitane. "I still say they should have gone there and let us alone."

Laforque was undecided. So far Paris had handled things badly, and he didn't want to make bad worse by overreacting. The gendarme had acted professionally. As soon as the boy's parents had made the claim their son was murdered, he had notified Paris on an emergency basis. When no response came, the Egyptian pair drove into Paris themselves and somehow managed to interest Dutch television in their story. Government-run French TV had no choice but to pick up the story too. Which meant that what the Egyptian pair claimed had to be taken seriously. Like the gendarme said, because they were Arabs.

Lieutenant Laforque was liaison officer between the Gendarmerie Nationale HQ and its counterterrorist unit GIGN (Groupement d'Intervention de la Gendarmerie Nationale). GIGN was primarily an HRU (hostage rescue unit) and had sprung more than two hundred and fifty captives in its ten years' existence. But the unit was also on call as a SWAT team, unlike most HRUs in other countries. Every man in GIGN passed tests in endurance, swimming, running while laden with equipment, marksmanship, martial arts... fought full-contact karate with Black Belt instructors, warded off attack-trained dogs, attended parachute jump school at Pau and high-speed driver training at Le Mans... rappelled down the side of a highrise building, holding the rope in one hand and a pistol in the other, shooting at designated targets while coming down fast. GIGN's best known mission had been their rescue of a busload of French schoolchildren seized by terrorists on the border of Somalia.

Laforque had graduated from this school of hard knocks with a bullet lodged next to his spine. He had been taken off the active list and been given a commission. Lieutenant. If he behaved and made no big mistakes, one day he might make captain. He said nothing, but others remarked that he seemed less than thrilled at this prospect. It was rumored he had been recruited by one of the intelligence services.

The gendarme next to him in the bar knew none of this. To him Laforque was just another of those deskbound pen pushers from HQ who got irritable when asked to visit the outskirts of the city.

The lieutenant made up his mind. "I can't put a GIGN team on the house as things presently stand.

We don't even know if the pair will return here tonight. They may stay in Paris. Last I heard of them, they were on their way to see German and English reporters. They may be in New York by now, for all I know."

"Their child is in the morgue here," the gendarme said flatly. "They'll be back to bury him."

"You're right. I know that the initial medical examination backs up the mother's story of the car first hitting the child and then backing up to deliberately run over him, so we're probably not dealing with a hysterical story. I know that the parents may be in danger. But you have to understand that I can't call in a GIGN unit here and then tell the men to go hide in the bushes. There has to be a . . . a situation first. Someone for them to fight."

"I understand, m'sieu."

Laforque bought two more drinks. "All right, so I'm dumping on you. I've got no other choice." He made a smudge of water on the plastic counter. "Say that's Paris. Here we are in Saclay, to the southwest. Here's GIGN in Maisons-Alfort, to the southeast, maybe twenty kilometers away. Any sign of trouble, call this number I'm giving you and"—his index finger traced an inverted semicircle beneath the smudge representing Paris—"this place will be over-run in no time. I'll put in an alert. Can we depend on you to watch the house tonight?"

The gendarme nodded grumpily, making it plain he thought this was not how things should be done.

Laforque glanced at his wristwatch. "Got to go." He left a tip on the counter, shook hands, and took long strides out the door.

The gendarme surveyed the tip, decided it was too much and ordered another Ricard from it.

When the couple got back shortly after eleven that night, the gendarme got out of his car and stood in their headlights in order to reassure them.

"For a moment, we wondered who it might be parked outside the house," the man said.

"You were right to be cautious, sir," the gendarme said, peering in their car window, feeling that he was breathing the fear they gave off like a poison gas. "No need to worry. I'll be sitting in this car out here all night."

The gendarme had no plans to ambush terrorists or behave like a hero. He had placed his battered Citroen in a highly visible position directly in front of the two-story house. He sat behind the wheel and smoked cigarettes. Every half hour he got out and walked up and down the empty road beneath a single street lamp. The last lighted windows, in a house down the road, went dark sometime after one. The gendarme sighed and settled down to a long slow watch. What he disliked about all-night surveillance was how it raised gloomy thoughts in his mind, gave him time to brood, to go over wrongs done to him and all his disappointments. He could feel this despondent mood coming on and did not look forward to his own company during the long night.

A little after three he thought he noticed a movement in the garden to one side of the house. A shadow . . . for an instant. He could not be sure.

He stayed where he was in the car, looking intently at the place. He saw nothing further. Having slipped the door handle quietly, he eased out of the Citroen, his pistol in his right hand, a flashlight in his left coat pocket.

The gendarme sàt on the garden wall, raised his legs over it and stood again inside. The only sound as he moved forward into the dark was that of rose thorns catching the fabric of his pants leg.

Two figures behind the house—definitely!

"Stop!"

The gendarme fired. They disappeared.

He did not turn on the flashlight, not wanting to make himself an easy target. He stared into the dark, motionless, looking for any more signs of movement. Sticks snapped a distance back in the trees, as if someone stood on them. A window lit upstairs and placed an elongated rectangle of pale light on the ground in back of the house. The couple had been woken by his pistol shot; if they had ever managed to sleep.

Just then he noticed that a ground floor window was open. They had been inside!

"Come down quickly," the gendarme shouted up at the lighted window. "Come as you are. Fast."

He was still shouting when his words were drowned out by a roaring flash inside the house. The gendarme knew immediately what it was—an incendiary device, not explosives. He went in the open window and saw the staircase was in a sea of flames. The heat was intense, and the old timbers crackled like fireworks as the building started to burn. Dense smoke billowed everywhere, choking and blinding him.

Why hadn't they come to an upstairs window and jumped? Perhaps they had while he was inside the house searching for them. To see if he could get upstairs that way, he forged through the dense smoke into the front room, keeping his face next to the wall when he took a breath to make use of the thin layer of untainted air that always lay between smoke and a surface. He saw her on the floor of the room, lying facedown.

When he reached her, he saw her husband was lying not far away. They must have come downstairs just before the incendiary went off and been knocked unconscious by its force. A wall had protected them from being burned.

The gendarme slumped the woman over his right shoulder in a fireman's lift which kept his left hand free. He made for one of the closed windows in the room, then thought better of it. A window opened at this stage could feed the blaze a jet of oxygen which could explode the house in a fireball. He made his way back to the window he had entered in the back of the house, guessing he would never have time to come back for the man.

By the time he climbed through the window with his burden, laid her on the ground a safe distance from the house and returned, the whole interior of the ground floor was a raging inferno. He ran to the front of the house to see if he could get in a window there, but the room where he had found the woman was bright with flames. Her husband would be dead already.

She was on her feet when he got back, moving unsteadily and saying something over and over again in Arabic.

"I'm sorry, madame, I could not reach your husband. It was too late."

She stared at him as if he had said something so obscene to her she did not know how to react.

He went on gently, "We can't do anything now. I will take you into town where you will be looked after."

"My child! My husband!" she shouted in French and rushed toward the flaming house.

The gendarme caught up with her and stopped her from leaping through the fragmented glass of a window into the furnacelike interior.

"I want to die! Kill me! Let me die!" She beat desperately on his head with her small fists as he carried her, struggling, to the Citroen.

Keegan looked up from his desk at the State Department in Washington, D.C., and nodded to the Secret Service agent who entered his office.

"You're bright and early today, sir," the agent said.

"Early, but not so bright. It's never good news that brings me in early."

The agent went directly to the telephone scrambler in one corner of the office. The KYX scrambler was a big metal box, and the combination lock in its front made it look like a safe. The Secret Service man unlocked it and replaced an IBM punched card in it with a new one bearing the day's code. He left without another word.

Keegan glance at the off-green telephone connected by wires to the scrambler. It was only 7:30 A.M. The call from Paris was not due for another hour. He went back to his paperwork.

The call came through on time.

"Paris embassy. That you, John? Is the line safe?"

"Go ahead, Christmas Tree," Keegan said.

"Same shit today, John. Things as they stand now are like this: We've intercepted messages from the Israelis making open threats to the French of destroying the nuclear reactors the French are building in Egypt. The French seem to care only about the insolence of the threats, although they did put a mildly worded question to the Egytians on whether they might be making an atom bomb. The Egyptians, of course, denied it, and claimed that if the Zionist entity bombed their peaceful reactors, they'd launch missiles from the Sinai onto Jerusalem and Tel Aviv. The Israelis intercepted that message and told the French they were ready to nuke Cairo. All it would take was one Egyptian missile on Israeli soil and it was ashes-to-ashes and dust-to-dust. You following me?"

"Loud and clear, Christmas Tree," Keegan said, although the voice at the other end of the line sounded as if it were coming through a long tube. "You think they'd do it?"

"If you were in Cairo, would you order a missile to hit Tel Aviv?"

"No. But then I'm not a fundamentalist, Christian or Islamic. Tell me more, Christmas Tree."

"Big news is the French have continued to pull out their experts from Egypt. I'm pretty sure it's in direct reply to Washington's accusation of Paris being responsible for nuclear proliferation. When you people said equipment and fuel supplies might be effected, the French began to hear what you were saying. The Egyptians are trying to lure back their own technicians who fled when the mullahs took over, but so far they don't seem to be succeeding. Enough of the French technicians have left already to slow things down considerably. You might put this forcibly to the Israelis as a reason for them to delay any strike they might have in mind against the Egyptian reactors."

They went on to talk of other things.

The AirEgypt turboprop cargo plane touched down on the runway at Cairo International Airport. Two army Range Rovers waited at the cargo terminal, and an officer and four soldiers watched the ground crew set up to unload the aircraft. The temperature was in the high sixties, a sunny, pleasant October day, after a scorching summer that had made the asphalt runways and air laced with jet fuel fumes a more hellish place than any to be found in the Libyan Desert.

The officer climbed the ramp and pointed out two plywood crates, each about four feet square, marked London-Cairo/Al-Qahira with red serial numbers. He double-checked the numbers against those on a clipboard and shouted at the workers to handle the crates carefully because they contained sensitive, high explosives. The soldiers laughed and the workers grinned nervously.

They set the crates down gently on a small flatbed wagon attached to a miniature tractor, which towed them into a customs shed cordoned off by ropes. Paper signs dangling from the ropes read in Arabic and English: MILITARY INSTALLATION—KEEP OUT. The soldiers lifted the crates from the wagon and waited for the driver to leave the shed before they set about tearing open the crates. A bald man in civilian clothes took a stethoscope from his jacket pocket.

Inside the first crate were huddled a woman and a boy about five. The soldiers stretched them on their backs on the concrete floor. The doctor kneeled over each of them in turn to listen to their breathing, feel their pulse, lift an eyelid, look inside the mouth and place the stethoscope on the chest. He grunted and moved on to the next pair, two girls about seven and nine, obviously sisters.

When he rose to his feet, the doctor gave the officer a severe look. "I don't think much of this method. These people are fortunate to be alive. They should come out from under the effects of the drug in five hours or so. They'll be feeling groggy and nauseous for a while after that. Whose idea was this?"

The officer raised his eyes to the ceiling. "Not the Army's."

"I thought not. Well, you can tell whoever did think it up that, in my professional opinion—"

The officer gestured to the doctor to lower his voice and led him out of earshot of the four soldiers.

A cold drizzle fell on Cambridgeshire. The small, spare Egyptian physicist made his way through the centuries-old quadrangles of Cambridge University without a coat, seemingly heedless of the weather. He drew an occasional amused glance from students, who dismissed him as an absentminded prof for whom a raw October day was merely meteorological data.

But Dr. Mustafa Bakkush was not absentminded or

eccentric. He was in the middle of an emotional crisis so violent he was oblivious to his rain-soaked shirt, jacket and pants. He walked through deep puddles among the paving stones without seeing them or feeling the water spill into his shoes.

When he reached the research building, he walked past his lab door and on down the corridor to the director's office. Ponsonby was sitting behind his desk in his white lab coat, shaking his head slowly at a plastic model of a nuclear structure.

"We've got it wrong somewhere, Mustafa," he said without looking up, "and I'm damned if I know where."

Mustafa Bakkush was not deflected from his purpose. "Gordon, I want to resign. Immediately."

Gordon Ponsonby's eyebrows shot up. "Dammit, man, you just got here. You can't walk out on us like that."

"I have to." Mustafa sat on the edge of an upright chair, small, wet, cold, miserable.

Ponsonby stared at him. "Been on a bender, old boy? You look like something the cat brought in."

"Gordon, they tell me I've got to go."

"For God's sake, who? Buck up, man. Out with it. Those bloody Americans? They have no money for physics these days—don't believe a word they tell you. The Germans?"

"Home. Egypt."

Ponsonby was flabbergasted. "But the mullahs denounced you personally as a decadent Westerner. Who knows what would have happened if you and your family hadn't reached our embassy in time? And remember the fuss we had to smuggle you all out?

Now, hardly a year later, you walk into my office, looking as if you stopped to immerse yourself in the river on the way, and announce you want to go back. Homesick for the pyramids, I suppose."

"Gordon, I don't *want* to go back. I have to. They have Aziza and the children."

Bakkush told the director of the phone calls he had been receiving, culminating in the disappearance of his wife and children four days previously.

"You didn't go to the police?"

"The man on the telephone warned me not to. He said they would not be harmed if I kept quiet. I knew he was an Egyptian and not an ordinary criminal. This morning I received a phone call a little after five. He gave me a Cairo number and told me to phone it. It took more than an hour to get through. I asked for Aziza. She came to the phone and told me they were all safe and well. They allowed her to tell me what happened. Men came to the house with two crates. They put them in the garage, saying they were scientific equipment I had ordered. She could see they were Egyptian, and they explained that by saying I had contacted them because they were fellow countrymen and needed the work. They managed to delay until all the children were in the house, then they chloroformed everyone with a cloth over their faces. After that they must have injected them with a powerful drug and put them in the crates. Aziza overheard one man say they had been shipped out of Gatwick on a cargo plane."

"Gatwick! Good God, what's Britain coming to!"

"Much as I dread going back there, for Aziza and the children's sakes I have to."

"Yes, yes, of course you must. What rotten luck. We'll keep the journals open to you and expect to see you at conventions and so forth. . . ."

Mustafa shook his head. "I won't be working on the cutting edge of physics when I go back to Egypt, Gordon. They have a program I suspect they need me for, one that's become past history in more technically advanced countries."

Ponsonby averted his eyes. "When do you leave?"

"Tomorrow."

"Good luck."

There was nothing more to say. After Bakkush left his office, Ponsonby pressed the intercom to his secretary in an alcove farther down the corridor. "Mrs. Arthurs, I have to go to London today. What time's the next train?"

He held the phone in his left hand, and with his right removed a cassette from the tape deck concealed beneath a desk drawer.

John Keegan sat in the office of his State Department superior, F. Conrad Bigglesley. Like Keegan, he was a Princeton man and they got on well.

"Defense has gone too far this time," Bigglesley expostulated, his eyes bulging with indignation. "That whole department's developed a complex since Vietnam—it's like having to work with an emotionally disturbed person."

Keegan nodded. "They're always trying to play it too safe or too dangerously, never the happy medium. This time though, I think the CIA may be more to blame than the Department of Defense."

"It's Defense, with Treasury doing Defense's bidding. You don't see the whole picture, John."

"Maybe not."

That pacified Bigglesley enough to acknowledge Keegan's point. "I grant you this stuff is not coming from military intelligence. But neither is it originating with the CIA. They're just acting as messengers. And you know who for? Right. God's chosen people, our friends the Israelis. They and Defense are hand in glove. It's a known fact. Despite all our diplomatic work to ease tensions in the area, despite our numerous successes, our department gets little credit. You ask why. I answer, because peaceful discussion is less dramatic than violent confrontation. Don't you agree, John?"

"Absolutely, Conrad."

"That's what Defense relies on all the time—good publicity. They have no interest in settling things behind closed doors or in using the diplomatic touch— all they want is some playground stunt that will make them look good on the tube."

"You never said a truer word."

Bigglesley's indignation had subsided and he was now looking more pleased with himself. "Let me sum up our viewpoint for you. Ahmed Hasan is no angel. We'd prefer to have Mubarak back in power any day, but Hasan is a reality, and we can't get around that. If Hasan is deposed as president of Egypt, you'll almost certainly have one of those Light of Islam mullahs replacing him. Our friends in Defense and the CIA claim none of the mullahs could be any worse than Ahmed Hasan—that's what Israel wants us to believe. That's the whole ploy, you see?"

Keegan nodded. "If Israel can maneuver another Khomeini into power in Egypt, we will break relations with them and be all the more dependent on Israel."

Bigglesley looked pleased and surprised. "Very good, John, you hit the nail on the head. Now it's up to us to back Ahmed Hasan all the way, as the only moderate between us and the Light of Islam. We've got to save Egypt."

Keegan took a deep breath. "The CIA says Egypt's already lost, Conrad. I'm not saying I agree with that, but let me assume the role of devil's advocate for a moment. Ahmed Hasan is a butcher. He's very possibly insane—at the least he can be described as mercurial. And he's building an atom bomb with France's help because they are dependent on Arab oil. Defense wants to do something about it before it's too late—meaning before they put that bomb together. Our position at State is that this is all lies, fed to the CIA by the Israelis in collusion with the Department of Defense."

"Correct."

Keegan was a little taken aback by so ready an answer. "In spite of British intelligence's report that Mustafa Bakkush has gone back to Egypt under duress? I take it you saw the report from that physicist at MIT who said they don't need anyone else to make an atom bomb once they've got Bakkush. The Israelis didn't invent this."

"Let me spell it out for you, John. Where do you live and for whom do you work? Simple. Washington, D.C., the Department of State. You do not live in the eastern Mediterranean and you do not work for the Department of Defense. Therefore, you will support Ahmed Hasan until further notice."

"Clear as glass, Conrad."

"Great. I hope you and Alice can make it tomorrow night to the reception. Henry Kissinger will be there."

"I'm looking forward to it."

A sand-yellow Jaguar XJ-S drew up before the huge western gateway of Bab al 'Azab, into the Citadel complex, the high walls of which dominated the Islamic section of Cairo. The car's V-12 engine purred as it waited for the gates to be unlocked. This was the part of the Citadel which no tourists visited. Its purpose today was the same as it had been for centuries—a dungeon for political prisoners. The gates opened, soldiers with M16 automatic rifles peered into the sleek sportscar, then snapped to attention in a rigid salute. The Jaguar crept inside the walls of the Citadel, followed by a Jeep Cherokee, and the gates closed behind them.

The Jeep Cherokee had inch-thick Plexiglas in its windshield and windows. Heavy steel plates were welded inside the vehicle's walls, under the roof, and beneath the chassis. Eight men and women, hardly out of their teens, dressed in combat fatigues and toting Heckler & Koch MP5 submachine guns, spilled out of the Cherokee and fanned out about the courtyard. They assumed relaxed crouches, in contrast to the ceremonial bearing of other troops in the courtyard.

The Jaguar also had bulletproof Plexiglas windows, but no sign of armor plating was evident. Presumably, the plates were concealed beneath the fine leather upholstery, wood-trim paneling and plush carpeting.

The color of President Ahmed Hasan's military uniform exactly matched that of his car. He unfolded his long, lean, angular body out of the bucket seat and looked about him critically at each of the regular soldiers in the courtyard, standing chest out, chin in, eyes front. The president wiped the brass above the peak of his cap on his sleeve before placing the cap on his head. Then he crossed the courtyard and entered the old fortified building through a stone archway, preceded and followed by his bodyguards.

The jailers were expecting him and had the prisoner prepared. This man was flabby, middle-aged, and obviously American. He sat on a hard, upright chair until the army officer next to him poked him. Then he stood to acknowledge the president's entry into the large, high-ceilinged room.

Ahmed Hasan spoke in Arabic. "So you are the CIA spy."

The army officer translated this into English.

"Nothing of the kind, sir," the American responded in English with a strong Alabama accent. "My name is Wendell Ray Oliver and I'm a Baptist preacher come to bring the word of the Lord to sinners the world over. He who has ears to hear, let him hear."

The president smiled sardonically and continued in Arabic, plainly having understood the English. "In Egypt, eighty-five percent of the people are Sunni Muslims and most of the rest are Coptic Christians. I am told you speak neither Arabic nor Coptic. How do you hope to bring the word of anybody to them if you do not speak their language?"

"Through the gift of tongues," the Alabaman said confidently. "When the time is right, the spirit will descend upon me and all men shall understand my words."

Hasan nodded slowly. "This isn't much of a cover for an employee of the great CIA. Surely they can do better than ask their agents to pretend to be madmen. You were found in a zone in which foreigners are not permitted to travel without a permit. You made an effort a week ago to get this permit, and when it was denied, you traveled into the forbidden zone anyway. So you cannot plead ignorance. What were you doing there?"

"Bringing the word of the Lord to unworthy sinners."

A look of irritation flickered across Ahmed Hasan's face.

The military officer spoke urgently to Wendell Ray Oliver. "You are trying our great leader's patience. He is a busy man and has taken time away from the affairs of state to deal with your case. If you appreciate his effort and kindness toward you by cooperating immediately, he will be merciful to you. But if you continue to insult him with your lies and trickery, he will stomp on you as he would on a disgusting insect."

Oliver looked from the military interpreter to the uniformed president and said, "The Lord is my shepherd."

Hasan scowled. He produced a yellow, unsharpened pencil, tipped by an eraser, from inside his tunic and handed it to the American. "Read aloud what's on it."

"Eberhard Faber MONGOL 482."

"Anything else?"

Oliver looked at the pencil closely. "U.S.A."

"Precisely. An American pencil for an American confession." Hasan laughed harshly, and in one fluid, lightning movement whipped out a gravity knife and dropped open its fixed blade close to the throat of the startled American.

"The pencil, please," Hasan requested in a low, polite voice.

The American handed it to him with a trembling hand, glancing at the gleaming blade before his face.

As the president sharpened the pencil, the honed razor edge shearing away the wood around the lead, he spoke in a cold, commanding tone. "While I wait here to witness your statement, you will write a short summary of your association with the Central Intelligence Agency and the purpose of your mission here— particularly why you were in that zone where you had been denied admission."

He released the catch, folded the blade, and put the knife away. Then he held the pencil in his right fist, its newly sharpened point upward, and thrust it toward the American.

Wendell Ray Oliver stared back at him fixedly and made no move to take the pencil.

The military interpreter shifted uncomfortably in the silence that followed.

Not a muscle moved on Ahmed Hasan's face.

He drove the pencil in his fist up through the underside of the American's jaw, through the soft palate in the roof of his mouth, and deep into his brain.

Wendell Ray Oliver collapsed dead at Hasan's feet.

The president turned quickly and made for the door with his bodyguards scampering around him.

As he went, he shouted a single word in English over and over: "Spies! Spies! Spies! Spies!"

Chapter 2

Richard Dartley checked by phone from his room at the Beverly Wilshire. The TWA flight from Washington, D.C., was due on schedule at LAX, 3:15. Malleson had called previously. He had not been very informative. All he could say was that the man on the TWA flight was alone and presumably unarmed since he had to pass through a metal detector in order to board the plane. He was about twenty-five, athletic build, brown hair, no distinguishing features except for his strikingly fashionable two-piece suit of blue and white vertical stripes. He had no luggage, and so he presumably could not change clothes in midflight, unless this distinctive suit could be turned inside out to another pattern, which Malleson doubted. There was no way Dartley could miss him. One other thing—he had a Hertz car reserved.

A suit as eyecatching as a semaphore signal and a Hertz car reservation! Dartley wondered if any kidnapper could be that dumb. Yet the man had no reason to believe he had been detected and identified.

The victim had been grabbed in the parking lot of a swank shopping mall at Newport Beach, on the southern edge of Los Angeles. She was the daughter of a U.S. senator. The ransom call had come from a Washington, D.C., public phone to her father's Senate office, and one of his aides had put the caller through to the senator himself. A quarter mil. One week to raise it. Any tricks and the girl was dead.

The FBI, LAPD, California State Police and D.C. cops were all working twenty-four-hour days on the case. They made so little progress, the media never caught on that something had happened.

The second phone call to the senator's office on the Hill was also labeled a local call. The grab on the West Coast and the ransom demand on the other side of the continent broke all the kidnap patterns on FBI books. The senator was told to be ready to drop the money in L.A. The notes, none new, none over a hundred, were to be in a suitcase. The LAPD figured the senator would be told in some last-minute phone call to drop the suitcase from an overpass to the side of a freeway beneath. No date had been set.

Meanwhile, each day a Polaroid was mailed in a street box in a different part of L.A. The photo always showed a pretty nineteen-year-old with that day's issue of the *Los Angeles Times*, to prove to Pop she was still alive and well. The FBI were intercepting these envelopes now in L.A., but this brought them not one step closer to rescuing the girl.

There was something the senator hadn't told anyone. Like any good politician, he was wary of what he said. The first phone call had reminded him of something . . . The second made it clear. He knew who was calling him, demanding the ransom. The voice was disguised—yet it was the way the man had of speaking, the grammatical sentences, the way he paused to select the right word, which gave his identity away. He was an old boyfriend of his daughter's. The senator remembered that he hadn't approved of the young man as his daughter's escort, suspecting that he was on drugs. The senator now reasoned that if his daughter had been kidnapped by someone known to her, she could not be expected to survive the kidnapping after the ransom was paid.

The FBI would play this by the book. They would get their man all right, and in all probability he would lose his daughter. He had one other alternative. He could hold back on this man's identity and go after him by other means—with no holds barred, with none of the legal restrictions to which law enforcement agencies were subject.

The senator had once heard that his friend Charley Woodgate had a contact, some kind of paid assassin. He was careful how he asked so that this killer would not do a job on him for knowing too much. He explained to Charley Woodgate how he had heard disturbing stories and how he had used his senatorial power to quash them. He'd be pleased to do the same for the foreseeable future if Charley would do something for him in return. Money would not be involved. Charley was to regard it as an arrangement between gentlemen and friends.

Charley took the arm-twisting pretty well. His reply the next day was simple. His contact was happy to do the senator a favor. He would place himself in Los Angeles and have the suspect put under surveillance in Washington. The assassin's name was Richard Dartley. Charley Woodgate told the senator that he couldn't be of any more help except to pass on urgent messages to Dartley. The senator nodded his agreement, wondering secretly if this Dartley were imaginary—and if he were real, whether he was actually doing what Charley claimed he was.

Dartley was real and he was on the job. He hired outside help to do the surveillance, professionals who didn't know or care who they were watching. Malleson took care of information flow. Dartley himself bided his time in Beverly Hills.

Every kidnapper's great moment of vulnerability was the ransom pickup. That went wrong more times than anything else. Dartley's plan was to hit them before they psyched themselves up for the pickup. He had no idea how many were involved—at least two, one in Washington and one in L.A. to hold the girl. The trunk of his burgundy Lincoln Mark VII—a nicely anonymous car in Beverly Hills, hired under a false name—was loaded with gear he might need, from rope ladders, two M16 automatic rifles, smoke grenades through ten-gallon containers of fresh water and gasoline to gas masks and an inflatable rubber dinghy. He had only to phone down for the car and it would be waiting for him in the area between the old and new sections of the Beverly Wilshire.

The plane was due in at 3:15. He allowed himself plenty of time—he knew how a small unexpected thing like a traffic jam or minor accident, even a flat tire, could spike a whole operation if time had not

27

been allowed for unscheduled nuisances. He left his hotel, drove along Wilshire to Santa Monica Boulevard, and then the San Diego Freeway to the airport, exiting at La Tijera.

At thirty-seven, Richard Dartley was a little thick through the middle and his black crewcut was thinning a bit. His square-jawed face had prominent cheekbones and hooded eyes, which were gray-green, like a wolf's. His torso and limbs were muscular. He looked like—and was—the kind of man who ran ten miles a day, could party all night and work hard the next day, could come three times in a night with a hot chick.

He pulled the Mark VII to the curb where he could see the exit doors from TWA incoming flights. Things weren't busy and he guessed he wouldn't be hassled if he stayed with the car and kept out of the way. He passed the time flipping through the pages of a combat magazine in which jokers claimed to have single-handedly overwhelmed Cuban units in Angola and later in Nicaragua, decimated Viet Cong battalions and all the usual gung ho hero stuff that anyone who knew the real thing could see was plain bullshit.

Mid-twenties, athletic build, brown hair and of course the suit with the blue and white vertical stripes. He was easy to spot, like Malleson said. The subject knew his way and made straight for the stop for the rent-a-car courtesy trams. Avis and Budget trams came before the Hertz showed, and the subject let them go. He seemed relaxed and in no hurry.

After the subject boarded the Hertz tram, Dartley followed it at a distance, drawing close only when it stopped so he could see if anyone got off. No one did. When the tram left the airport area, he passed it and headed for the Hertz compound on Airport Boulevard, where he himself had rented his Lincoln a few days previously. He waited inside the compound until the subject found his assigned car, a blue Chrysler Le Baron. Dartley drove quickly to the exit and showed his Hertz agreement to the guard, who lowered the set of spikes in the road. He drove a short distance north on Airport Boulevard, pulled over, and waited for the blue Le Baron to appear.

While he waited, he drew his revolver from his shoulder holster and checked it. It was a Smith & Wesson M38 Bodyguard "Airweight" with a two-inch barrel. He spun the five-round cylinder and snapped it back in place. This short-barreled .38 was a backup gun rather than a main weapon, in Dartley's opinion, but more than adequate for his present purposes, where concealment and reliability were more important than firepower.

The blue Chrysler Le Baron turned south. Dartley made a U-turn, followed the subject west on Century and south again on Sepulveda, into the tunnel beneath the airport runways. Through El Segundo and past Manhattan Beach, Dartley hung back and let the Chrysler take a big lead. Dartley guessed he didn't have to be so cautious, since the subject seemed as carefree and unwatchful as before.

"This one's a total amateur or he's a genius," Dartley muttered out loud.

He speeded up when the subject pulled off at Hermosa Beach and located him again on a road parallel but nearer the water. The subject turned right into a narrow road. Dartley nosed the front of his Mark VII around the corner, saw the Le Baron parking, and reversed to the curbside where he was hidden around the corner. Then he nosed around the corner again and saw the subject walking farther down the street. The man in the striped suit crossed another street and entered a pedestrians-only walkway to the beach.

Dartley dumped the Lincoln, grabbed his combat magazine, and headed for the beach like he was looking forward to a peaceful read. The houses on each side of the walkway were tiny and squeezed together in a hodgepodge of architectural styles, each with its miniature but highly individual garden of flowering bushes and tropical flowers, or stones and cacti. Down a gentle slope, the peaceful blue sky hung over the calm Pacific.

The guy in the striped suit stopped outside a house, looked back, and saw Dartley. He froze. Dartley kept on, strolling casually, magazine in hand. It was no good, and Dartley knew it. The guy was now staring at him, standing stock-still, his mind racing.

As he neared, Dartley smiled in a friendly way at the man still staring at him. He twisted the magazine into a tight roll.

"Who are you?" the subject asked in a fearful voice, aware that somehow things were coming to pieces, but unsure in what way.

Dartley thrust the rolled magazine into the man's face. The top edge of the reinforced tube caught him at the base of the nostrils. His only sound was a whimper. Confused by pain, blinded by tears, swallowing his own blood, the man staggered.

Dartley slammed home a knuckles-up, straight right karate punch into his solar plexus, which knocked the air out of him with such explosive force, Dartley and the walkway behind him was spattered by blood.

When the subject half turned as his knees gave way beneath him, Dartley chopped him over the left kidney. The guy in the striped suit collapsed like a wet paper bag.

Something caught Dartley's eyes. A figure in the window of the house. A man with a big head had a big automatic pistol in his right hand and was leveling the barrel, steadying his right hand in his left palm... Dartley fell. Two bullets passed over him like crazed hornets a microsecond before he heard the shots and the window glass shattering.

He crawled the hell out of there, grabbing his magazine as he went. When he was clear of the house, he got to his feet and ran as hard as he could back to the Mark VII. His Smith & Wesson M38 Bodyguard "Airweight" was snug in his shoulder holster, but it was no good in this situation. Getting into a shooting war with that dude in the house would have led him into too many unknowns. First, he had no idea how many adversaries were in the house. Second, he had no way of knowing if the senator's daughter was in the house. If she were, he would be endangering her by opening fire. Third, he'd end in the hands of the LAPD no matter how things went and be hanging out in precinct houses for months on end, explaining who, what and why, his cover blown.

The fella in the house might have his problems too, Dartley decided as he ran. If he had the girl in there, he would have to surface soon and move out. The gunshots could be enough to have the place surrounded in ten minutes—though Dartley had noticed no bystanders and knew how things like afternoon gunfire often seemed to go unnoticed in residential districts, dismissed as something innocuous. If the girl were in that house, he had to move, knowing that a stranger was onto the place. Dartley looked back before he reached his car. No one was moving yet. The man in the striped suit was still face-down in the walkway.

Dartley opened the trunk, tossed the magazine in, and took one of the two M16s. This automatic rifle had a Laser Arms Corporation laser gunsight mounted on the rear sight. Now, if the girl was in the house and there was no back exit, he might be in business.

Sure enough, in half a minute the man with the big head came out of the house, pistol in hand, pushing a girl in front of him as a shield, his long hairy left arm around her waist.

Dartley set the rifle barrel on the top of a fence. He touched the remote button on the laser gunsight and angled the barrel about until the red laser dot crossed and recrossed the kidnapper and his captive. Dartley knew he would have to be careful, since the red dot projected by the laser gunsight was much harder to see in sunlight than in the shade or, of course, by night.

Dartley's advantage was that the kidnapper stood head and shoulders above his victim, giving Dartley some real estate to play with. He threw the red laser dot right on the middle of the man's large face. That should be exactly where the bullet would impact when he fired the weapon. He squeezed the trigger.

The small, high-velocity bullet cracked open the kidnapper's massive forehead. The lead projectile twisted into a shapeless mass and turned end over end through the brain tissue before bounding off the inside rear wall of the skull and plowing back through the brain again.

Sight faded from the kidnapper's eyes and his mouth dropped open. The dead nerves loosened his fingers and the pistol fell from his grip. Then he collapsed stone dead at the girl's feet.

She started to scream.

Dartley charged forward, grabbed her arm and shook her until she stopped.

"Who are you?" she demanded to know.

Dartley didn't seem to hear. He was looking at the man in the blue-and-white striped suit, who was lying facedown, unmoving but breathing regularly. Dartley raised his right foot and brought his heel down in a vicious stomp on the back of the man's neck.

The neckbone snapped with the crack of a dry branch.

The girl looked in Dartley's cold, wolflike eyes and started screaming again.

"Shut up, bitch, and move your ass," he said.

Awad and Zaid stood at a respectful distance from the president's desk, silent, keeping their eyes on the richly carpeted floor in front of them or looking out the window. They did not let their presence intrude on the president's consciousness as he sat working on papers. They could have stood like this for many hours without attracting attention to themselves. They had been summoned and they had come. That was enough. When Ahmed Hasan was ready to tell them what he wanted, that would be the time most suited to them.

Awad smelled of stale sweat. A sports shirt hung loosely over his big belly, and his baggy pants were held up uncertainly by a belt that went beneath rather than across his abdomen. His lips were thick and moist, his jowls unshaven, his teeth broken and green. Sunglasses hid his eyes.

Zaid was a walking cadaver. His sunken cheeks, hollow eyes, stooped shoulders, narrow bony hands, collapsed chest, and fleshless thighs made him look like a concentration camp victim or a hunger striker far gone. His tan suit looked as if it had been made for someone else, as it had, and one could easily imagine Zaid stripping it from a dead body for his own use, which he had. He had also killed the man, though not for the suit.

They waited quietly at a respectful distance from the president's desk, enjoying the air conditioning and the opulence of the office, which reminded them of pictures they had seen of the interiors of great sheiks' tents long ago, priceless carpets strewn everywhere, cushions, brasswork, scimitars... The president's office had all these, plus teak and mahogany furniture in Western style, a stereo, color television, video recorder, plus closed-circuit TV, electronic security devices and other Western things they hardly understood. Zaid had once said to Awad that being in this office with Ahmed Hasan gave him a feeling even more powerful than he got when he stood in Sayyida Al-Hussein, praying at the shrine that held the head of the Prophet's grandson, which had been carried to Cairo in a green silk sack. Awad saw what Zaid meant, but he himself was more inclined to Sayyida Zeinab, the mosque which contained the tomb of Muhammad's granddaughter.

It was another ten minutes before the president acknowledged their presence. He gestured to them to be seated on a leather couch, and they helped themselves to cigarettes on a glass table while Ahmed Hasan had coffee served. The three men sat together, exchanging courtesies over the thimblefuls of bitter black brew before Hasan got around to what he wanted them to do.

"I have a list of CIA dogs who do their master's bidding in Cairo and elsewhere. The Russian Embassy supplied me with the names of active CIA agents in the American Embassy here, and we watched which Egyptians and foreigners met with them regularly. So now we know who the Americans use to gather information in our country."

Awad and Zaid, like hounds sniffing blood, grew more alert.

Ahmed noticed this, smiled and held up a hand. "No, my friends, I must disappoint you. I am not ordering their wholesale slaughter. Not today anyhow. You'll have noticed I said these dogs gather information. It puzzled us that none of these CIA hirelings had sensitive government or military positions. What could they know that would be of value

to the CIA? But that was their only role—not to
provide information, only to gather it. We had them
watched and saw military officers, engineers, government bureaucrats, spies and traitors in all walks of
life come to these information gatherers. Rather than
make an American at the embassy conspicuous by
meeting with Egyptians outside diplomatic circles,
the CIA had these Egyptian traitors funnel their
information to one of these gatherers inconspicuously.
Are you following me?"

Zaid and Awad nodded eagerly.

"Good." Ahmed rang a brass bell for more coffee
and passed about the cigarettes. After they were
served, he continued. "Every system has its strengths
and its weaknesses. Only a foolish man fights against
another's strengths. The thoughtful man seeks his
opponent's weaknesses and strikes there instead.
The weakness of this CIA system is clear. The information gatherer is a node and thus a possible filter of
the information. They are Egyptians, and so without
American protection from our government. They are
traitors to their country and to Islam, so that no
penitence is too drastic for their sins. I say we must
strike them in the name of Allah!"

"May He always be praised," Zaid said reverently.

"We will disembowel the dogs," Awad promised
fervently.

Ahmed held up his hand once again. "Someday,
my friends, someday, but not at present. We have
other uses for these vermin. Only four have high
military contacts. I want you to persuade these four
men to give you the military information they collect
before they pass it on to the Americans. You in turn

will bring it to a certain colonel who will change what needs to be changed. In this way we will control the military information which is fed to the CIA without interrupting its flow and alerting them that anything is wrong. To ensure that the Americans suspect nothing, I want information on other subjects to go through untampered. This colonel knows what to change at the military level. Otherwise it will go to the CIA unchanged, even if we might prefer it did not. This is because one important secret must be concealed from the Americans without them realizing it. If they should discover everything else we do not want them to know, we must permit them to do so if it means we can keep this one secret from them." Ahmed paused and stared at each of them in turn to impress his seriousness upon them. "I tell you this only because I must warn you not to be too ambitious. Nothing matters except this thing, which you cannot be told. You must persuade these four men to cooperate in the next few days. Only the highest military levels are involved. You *must* let everything else through, even when it would be easy for you to prevent. You must practice restraint, in the expectation that the day of retribution will come. Everything is set down on these papers for you."

Ahmed Hasan looked after them as they left his office, mildly amused that he had to rely on "reformed" street criminals for highly delicate matters of state. They could be relied on to deliver exactly what had been requested, whereas intelligence officers and military men were so blinded by their own ambitions they were apt to bungle anything which involved judgment. Not Awad and Zaid. They knew for certain that they would never sit in parliament or be appointed an ambassador in London.

All the middle-level administrators in the military and security forces in Cairo knew Awad and Zaid, just as they made it their business to know everyone local with direct access to President Ahmed Hasan. So the two had no problem in getting immediate cooperation from the Tourist Police.

The Tourist Police knew where to find Omar Zekri. They picked him up at Giza, among the souvenir shops, papyrus museums, alabaster factories, camel and Arabian horse rentals, and the other stalls littered all around the pyramids. Zekri was one of the great horde of hustlers working the tourists—he was selling what he called "genuine Pharaonic artifacts" at the north side of the Cheops Pyramid.

He was still arguing with the officers who had arrested him when Awad and Zaid arrived, telling them that no charge against him for selling real antiquities would stick because everything he had for sale was fake, and that a fraud charge wouldn't work either because everyone knew that trinkets sold for a few Egyptian pounds, as his did, could not be genuine. Zekri was getting more indignant by the minute, even dismissing one officer's bribery charge with the claim that everyone in Egypt accepts a little baksheesh, including the police—until he saw Zaid and Awad. Then he grew pale and stopped talking.

Awad asked him quietly, "Where is Ali?"

Omar hesitated and then said, "I don't know."

Awad nodded to Zaid.

Zaid pushed the lighted top of his cigarette into

Omar Zekri's smooth cheek. Omar slapped his hand to his face and howled in pain.

"Where's Ali?" Awad asked again, as quietly as before.

"At the Chephren Pyramid," Omar sobbed.

Awad turned to the Tourist Police. "Take him with you so he can point out Ali, then bring both of them back to us. We'll wait for you a little way out on the Abu Roash road."

Abu Roash was a village about seven kilometers north of Giza. It had a little pyramid of its own, but the tourist mobs did not swarm out that way. When the Tourist Police returned almost an hour later, Awad leisurely checked both their prisoners against photos he took from a back pocket of his baggy pants. Omar Zekri had once been a handsome man, but now he was puffy eyed and bloated, obviously a heavy drinker. He was in his early fifties. Ali was in his early twenties, a pretty boy, probably not too bright or too honest.

Awad took the Tourist Police aside. "You never saw these two men today, no matter what witnesses say. You never saw us. You were never here. There's no paperwork or any record of this. Orders from higher up."

The Tourist Police didn't look too happy about this, being used to a softer line of work, but they had half expected something like this and had families to feed. They avoided everyone's eyes and drove quickly away.

Awad and Zaid frisked them. Ali had a knife. The Tourist Police had missed it or hadn't bothered to search him. Awad threw their "Pharaonic" artifacts in the back seat of the Ford, climbed in, and slammed the door.

"You two sit on the front seat with me," Zaid told Omar and Ali.

The two men exchanged a fearful glance and did as they were told.

Zaid turned off the road onto a winding track that became, in time, simply a double line of tire tracks across the desert. No one in the car spoke. Terrified, Ali and Omar held hands in the front seat.

Zaid pulled up at the ruins of an ancient tomb, which had probably been robbed thousands of years ago and had lain like this, half buried in sand, from before the time of the Prophet. The low swells of sand rose and fell all around them as far as the eye could see, their surfaces speckled with boulders and stones and occasional brown-leaved, stunted plants.

"Get out," Zaid said.

The two men did not dare look behind them at Awad in case he was pointing a gun at their heads.

As they climbed out, Omar asked, "Do you mind if we smoke?"

"Go ahead," Zaid said in a friendly voice, taking the car keys and going back to unlock the trunk.

The match held in Omar's hand shook so badly, Ali had difficulty in lighting his cigarette.

Awad opened the rear door of the car but stayed inside in the shade, although the October sun was not unpleasantly hot, even out here in the desert where the bare ground reflected the heat.

Zaid slammed the trunk door and came around the side of the car, carrying a Black & Decker power saw.

"Omar," Awad said from inside the car, "tell us what you do with your life."

"Well, I have no children and no wife." Omar smirked at Ali.

"Go on," Awad said patiently.

"I live just off the Sharia El Muizz and I do what I can to make a living. I used to be a schoolteacher, but no more. I have a degree in history from the American University in Cairo. What else?" He gestured into the car at the merchandise he had been selling. "You can see for yourself what I am doing these days. I buy for next to nothing and sell for what I can persuade them to pay. I speak excellent English and French and give friendly advice along with my sales talk. There's no harm in that."

"Go on," Awad murmured, still inside the car.

Omar glanced at Zaid, standing motionless with the power saw and staring at him with his deathbed eyes.

"I do anything for money," Omar said hurriedly. "You tell me what to do or not to do, and I will obey you."

A long silence followed this. Omar looked over at Ali and they smiled at each other. Zaid started the motor of the power saw. The sound bounced off the stones and naked sand.

Holding the moving blade of the saw in front of him, Zaid charged Ali.

"No! No! Not me!" Ali screamed, staggering backward across the sand. "Him! He knows! Not me!"

But Zaid paid no attention to Omar and kept after Ali. The young man seemed to lack enough common sense to take to his heels and run—he seemed too morbidly fascinated by the whirring blade being thrust at him. He put up his right hand to protect his face, and the saw sheared the fingers from his hand.

Ali looked for one horrified moment at his bleeding, digitless limb, then down at the fingers lying like fat worms on the sand. He began to howl piteously and to pray between his agonized, inarticulate cries, clutching his damaged hand to his stomach.

Zaid switched off the power saw and suddenly Ali's screaming and pleas to Allah were amplified in the still, desert air.

Awad spoke calmly from inside the car. "Tell us what we want to know, Omar."

"There's nothing more," Omar croaked.

Zaid started the motor of the saw. Omar stood petrified, staring with rounded eyes at the deadly implement. Doubled over and rocking back and forth, Ali seemed too far gone with pain to even notice that the power saw had been started again.

Zaid stepped quickly to Ali and began chopping on his stooped shoulders with the moving saw blade. The metal teeth ripped chunks of cloth and flesh out of the defenseless man. Ali staggered, raised his arms to protect his head, and was cut to the bone across both forearms.

Zaid kept chopping down at him, ripping globs of flesh from his body with every touch of the power saw. Ali rushed about, blindly trying to escape, somehow managing to stay on his feet, instinctively knowing that once he fell nothing could save him. Zaid was methodical, avoiding his victim's head while delivering quick chops that would maim but not quickly kill.

This was finally too much for Omar Zekri. He attacked Zaid by jumping on his back. The weight of the bloated man nearly knocked the cadaverous Zaid off his feet on top of the running power saw. Zaid regained his balance and flipped Omar over his shoulder so that he crashed to the ground on his side. Zaid then thrust down at Omar's face with the saw blade.

Zaid was too fast. There was no way Omar could escape. He cringed from the descending blade of devouring teeth.

Just as the metal spurs seemed about to rip open his face, Zaid turned the motor off. As the teeth came to a stop, they scratched Omar's cheek near the red welt left by the earlier cigarette burn.

"You know that you will have to tell us what we want to know," Awad pointed out in kindly tones from the backseat of the car.

Omar agreed. He rattled on about gathering information for an American at the embassy. He named names. He gave dates and times. He made promises. He was hard to stop.

Awad smiled in a pleased way at Zaid. Omar Zekri was coming along very nicely. Awad got out of the car and stretched lazily in the sun.

"Time to take Omar to visit the colonel," he said and got behind the wheel.

Omar climbed to his feet and looked across at Ali, bent over on his knees on the bloodstained sand, raw wedges hacked all over his body.

"What about Ali?" Omar asked. "We must rush him to the Anglo-American Hospital at Gezira-Zamalek."

"Forget your Yankee friends," Zaid spat.

"Well, then, the Cairo Medical Centre or El Salam Hospital."

Zaid laughed. "He can stay here and feed the vultures."

"Omar, don't leave me! Don't leave me!" Ali was lamenting, amazingly still conscious enough to know what was going on.

Omar made a decision. "Shoot him. Don't leave him to die slowly. Put him out of his pain."

Zaid shrugged and handed Omar the power saw.

"With this?" Omar asked, appalled.

"Sure," Zaid said. "You just press this here."

The power saw started in Omar's hands.

Zaid stepped back, well out of his reach.

Omar walked unsteadily over to Ali, who was now moaning and uttering incomprehensible words.

Omar hovered the power saw blade over the back of Ali's neck, tightly shut his eyes and pressed down.

As soon as the blade hit bone and the saw kicked in Omar's grasp, he opened his eyes and stared in disbelief at what he was doing.

Then he vomited over the butchered body of his companion.

Awad held tightly onto the steering wheel, and the massive rolls of fat around his middle shivered with his laughter.

Chapter
3

For Richard Dartley, it was always either feast or famine. At times he rushed from one mission to another, wary that the success he achieved on one assignment might affect his judgment on the next through overconfidence, or he went for seemingly long periods when no one apparently knew of his existence. Of course, he could not complain of that, since he had painstakingly set things up so that he had disappeared off the face of the earth. There was no such person as Richard Dartley—there was only someone living under the name of Richard Dartley, which was merely an assumed name at first. Then it grew to an assumed identity, and this assumed identity and name had in turn to be protected from the merely curious and others whose inquisitiveness was not so idle or so innocent.

Boredom was his greatest threat. So long as Dartley never knew where he would be from one month to the next, not even whether he would be dead or alive, boredom had no chance to wrap its scaly coils around his mind.

When he had long waits between missions, he ran, he exercised, he practiced with weapons on different targets, he looked up girlfriends, he waited, he waited, waited... Dartley did not regard the rescue of the senator's daughter as a full-blown mission. He had only taken it on because he knew he could not do what he did without the tolerance of Washington, D.C. They denied officially that he existed and condemned his actions in diplomatically phrased apologies when they had to, but they did not mess with him. And they did not mess with him only because he often was of use to them, directly or inadvertently. Now he had another senator in his corner, should he need him. Tears had welled into the senator's eyes when Dartley had returned his daughter to him. The girl was still claiming that Dartley was more dangerous than either of her kidnappers, which of course was the reason the senator had sought him out in the first place.

Getting back the senator's daughter had been too easy. Dartley did not feel like returning to a regimen of lifting weights, target shooting, running, reading— Southern California laid back, easy living was a pleasant change from the rigorous training he was accustomed to putting himself through between missions. Charley Woodgate was surprised to hear of this and wondered how long it would last. As it turned out, he never found out because he himself made the phone call that disturbed Richard Dartley's new, easygoing existence.

"His name is Jacques Laforque," Woodgate told

Dartley. "I've checked him out. As he says, he is a lieutenant with the French Gendarmerie Nationale—he was one of the star members of their SWAT team till he got hurt and was moved upstairs to a desk job. He came to me on the recommendation of one of our ex-ambassadors to France."

"What does he want?"

"Damned if I know," Woodgate said. "I just checked on his credentials. Whatever he wants, it's been ordered at the highest levels in France. I don't think I *want* to know. When can we expect you back?"

"He can come to me."

Charley laughed. "I suppose if he's crossed the Atlantic to see you, he won't refuse to cross the continent in addition. How do you want me to set up the meet?"

"There's a place on the north side of the channel into Marina del Rey—the Venice side—with seats, palm trees and guys fishing. I'll find him there tomorrow at four in the afternoon. I'll recognize a Frenchman."

Dartley spotted him there with no trouble. Laforque had the typical, fastidious mannerisms of a Frenchman abroad, looking about him with a curious yet disapproving air. The bony-faced Frenchman spotted Dartley almost as quickly as Dartley had identified him. Laforque strode without hesitation toward him and shook his hand.

"Mr. Dartley, it's an honor and a pleasure to meet you," Laforque said in strongly accented English.

"I'm Paul Savage," Richard Dartley said. "Dartley told me to deal with you."

"Impossible!"

Dartley shrugged. "That's what Dartley said I was to do. He said you were to deal through me."

"This is very frustrating!"

"Listen, I'm going to be the one who does whatever job you want done, so you got to talk with me sooner or later. That's how it works. I do the job, Dartley gets the credit."

"All right, Mr. Savage, I will explain my problem to you. First, however, I wish to register my protest at how this is being handled, and I insist that Mr. Dartley be made aware of this displeasure."

Richard Dartley shrugged and left the Frenchman wondering if he even fully understood what had been said. They walked by the edge of the channel for a while in the October sunshine. Small sailboats were tacking this way and that in the channel, while bigger boats left their masts bare and ran on their engines. Fishermen sitting on rocks watched their lines placed at the outflow of dirty water from pipes. Both Dartley and Laforque scanned the faces of people sitting on benches, standing next to parked cars, walking on the embankment.

Laforque stroked his bony jaw and began to talk in a disillusioned way, like someone who knows he must live with some disappointment.

"Mr. Savage, you probably love your American homeland as I do mine. Some of the things I feel called upon to do for love of my country you may judge improper—perhaps only because your country has not the same needs as France. France has no fuel. Winters are cold and most of the people depend on industry. We found that we were becoming hostages of some of the same countries who had once been our colonies. And those people had not forgotten us from those times—or I should say that they had not forgotten the wrongs we did them and had completely forgotten the benefits we brought them. France was hit much harder than America by the OPEC oil embargo. Our answer was to build nuclear reactors all over the country so that we would be less dependent on oil for electric power. And that led to unexpected developments."

He walked along with Dartley for a while, and both of them watched two pretty blondes in bikinis expertly handle a small sailboat.

Dartley said, "I don't think we're going to get a chance to rescue them."

"More likely they could rescue us," Laforque said dryly, then went on. "France found herself in a new position with nuclear technology. Countries which had been refusing her oil at bargain prices were practically willing to give it away for nothing if France would build a nuclear reactor for them or one of their allies. When Ahmed Hasan overthrew Mubarak in Egypt, the Iranians committed enormous oil supplies to us at low cost if we built Hasan several reactors and supplied fuel. They guaranteed us that they would use nuclear power only for peaceful purposes."

"Like the Iraqis and Pakistanis," Dartley said sarcastically.

Laforque shrugged. "The Israelis and South Africans seem to have gotten nuclear weapons from someone also. I wonder who. Certainly not France. Anyway, the Arabs can see no justifiable reason why they too shouldn't have nuclear weapons."

"Perhaps because they would be only too willing to use them if they had them."

"That's what the Israelis say." Laforque grinned. "The Western nations blame France and say we will cause the end of the world by giving nuclear capability to desert sheiks. Typical imperialist racism."

"Not even the Russians are dumb enough to give nuclear equipment to that part of the world," Dartley pointed out

"Ah, yes, they are, Mr. Savage. They sell off any outdated equipment they can get them to take. However, the Arabs don't want that stuff. They have the money to buy the newest and best, which happens to be French these days."

"What do you want me to do?" Dartley asked.

"Mr. Savage, we want Richard Dartley to save France's good name by going into Egypt to discover if Ahmed Hasan is really making an atom bomb with French technology."

"And if he is?"

"To stop him by any means necessary."

This amused Dartley. He was not naive enough to believe that he was being asked to do something which French intelligence operatives could not achieve themselves. If Hasan was making a bomb, French intelligence already knew of it. And if they wanted to stop Hasan, they could do so more easily than a lone American in a hostile country could.

Dartley had no doubt that Jacques Laforque was a member of one of the branches of French intelligence. His background was perfect, along with the fact that gendarmes were not ordinary cops in the American sense of the word. The Gendarmerie

Nationale was a highly militarized force, run along army lines and with military spirit and discipline. They were enough to make FBI agents seem like hippies.

Dartley also wondered if Laforque had seen through his guise of claiming to be Paul Savage. Or did Laforque not really care whether he had Dartley or Savage, so long as he had an American agent doing France's dirty work in Egypt? Why? Dartley knew it would be a waste of time for him to ask questions. Laforque would already have answers prepared for them—answers which would only let him know what Laforque wanted him to know. In all likelihood, Laforque had been told very little himself. In every country's intelligence services, information was rationed carefully, on a "need to know" basis.

"Go in," Dartley mused. "Find out if he's making a bomb. If he is, stop him. By any means necessary. Keep France's name out of it. Any complications?"

"Israel."

"I see. So neither France nor Israel can find out if Egypt is making a bomb. Yet you believe that I can. Amazing."

"French intelligence has reached its own conclusions," Laforque said loftily. "We will use your findings as confirmation of ours. As for the Israelis, France has no wish to collaborate with them against our Arab friends."

Dartley grinned. "In case those Arab friends of yours find out? That's right, I mustn't forget: You need oil. Sure, I'll go. You know my fee? A million. In U.S. dollars."

Laforque did not bat an eye. "Where can we deposit it?"

Dartley wrote for him an account number and the name of a bank in Panama.

Charles Stuart Woodgate was Richard Dartley's uncle and lived on a fifty-acre farm near Frederick, north of Washington, D.C. Charley had taken a bad leg wound at Monte Cassino in the slow climb up the Italian peninsula against the Germans. Since then his career had been a mystery to some and a marvel to others. A few knew he was a gunsmith and had a large collection of rare and unusual weapons. Very few were aware that he made special guns to order, with no questions asked, for those who knew exactly what they wanted and could afford the heavy expense involved. Certain of his guns could be taken apart and fitted into aluminum crutches or specially designed bicycles. Silencers were another of his specialties. Ammunition, too. With new advances in surgical techniques, increasing numbers of people were surviving assassination attempts. Bullets that exploded on impact or those with poisoned tips were beyond the reach of the most advanced physicians. Charley supplied them all.

Charley had more or less taken his nephew in after the youth's father had been murdered. Now Dartley still didn't have a place of his own. As a base, he used a studio apartment over what had once been a horse barn on his uncle's farm. It was when he stayed there between missions that he put in long hours of target shooting and practicing combat with various weapons. Charley very often had something new to show him, and Dartley was more than happy to break in new weapons by firing the thousands of rounds from them necessary before they could be judged fully accurate and trustworthy.

This was how Richard Dartley was these days—cold, efficient, merciless, one of the very top hitmen in the world. But Richard Dartley hadn't been born that way. In fact, he hadn't even been born Richard Dartley.

Charley Woodgate often looked at him now and wondered. He wondered if it mightn't have been better if he had never helped the youth. But he knew for sure that the damage had already been done by the time he arrived on the scene. Without Charley's help, there would not have been a Richard Dartley. There would just have been someone else with another name, but equally deadly, equally driven. So Charley told himself.

Dartley was born Richard John Woodgate, son of Richard Woodgate and Martha Dartley Woodgate, in 1945 in Washington, D.C. Even that was not true. His mother told him when he was twelve that he had been adopted. Just that, nothing more. If he had known earlier, he could have grown up with the knowledge. Since she had waited that long to tell him, Richard only wished she had held off even longer.

It wasn't until much later—when he was twenty-two—that he found out who he really was. If that was who he really was anymore. Through illegal access to court records on adoption, he discovered that he was the son of teenage parents, both the offspring of prominent Washington attorneys. His birth name had been Paul Savage.

He was raised by his adoptive parents in a big old house with a veranda in Chevy Chase, Maryland, went to Bethesda-Chevy Chase High School, went to Episcopal church and didn't particularly excel at anything. Richard knew that his adoptive father worked for the government—"something in the State Department," he wasn't sure what. When an ex-CIA agent, disillusioned with America, named names, the family was astonished to find the head of the household high on the list.

Woodgate was in Buenos Aires at the time and may never have known he had been exposed. As he got into a car on September 11, 1976, outside the American embassy, he was hit in the forehead by a Kalashnikov AK-47 bullet. The family had thought he was in Florida. The *New York Times* referred to him as "an American security advisor," and the vice president of the United States, in an oration at his funeral, called him a "courageous warrior."

The man who was to become Richard Dartley realized, in a sudden rush, that he knew nothing about anything—he had not known his adoptive father as a real person, he decided.

When all this took place, his head was already messed up by what he had done in Vietnam; and what it had done to him. He did his share of butchering there, but also lost some good buddies to the Cong. The thing that really broke him was falling for an almond-eyed beauty, really going for her in a big way. It was only when she tried to kill him that he realized she was Cong. He had asked her to marry him! He killed her by crushing her skull with the heel of his boot.

His father's murder was the thing that made him get his act together. In the months after his father's death, he moved to one room above a store on K Street in Georgetown, ran for hours every day along the C&O Canal, quit smoking and drinking, went on a special diet... He became fit again, sinew and muscle, tough in mind as well as body. And he was ready then to face a couple of facts—he was thirty years old and he didn't have a job.

Charley Woodgate gave him advice. Go in his father's footsteps. Join the CIA. But the CIA didn't want anyone with his confidential Army record, which besides the death of the Viet girl, included a fragging and other stuff he tried never to think about anymore. The CIA wanted to train nice kids to be killers; they had no program to train crazies to be nice CIA men. So that was out.

It turned out that so too were other government jobs. He was only an ant on an ant heap, but word traveled. He leveled with his Uncle Charley. By this time he knew that Charley was cast in the same mold as his adoptive father, who was, of course, Charley's brother. The man who was to become Richard Dartley did not share their genes, but he felt he sure shared their way of looking at things.

Charley scratched his head when Richard asked him to find a job as an assassin. Charley said, "You better change your name. Make a fresh start. Born again, you might say."

Richard John Woodgate became Richard Dartley, after his mother's maiden name. It wasn't untraceable, it wasn't clever—but it was as far as he had been willing to go at that time. His sense of identity was shaky enough already. Totally dumping everything and assuming a one hundred percent, strange new identity made him panic deep down inside. He needed something to cling to.

His next trouble was that a paid assassin is not born overnight. No one wants to hire someone unless they hear he has done a clean job for someone else they know. It was a word-of-mouth business. A man might want someone dead and be willing to pay well for it, but his greatest fear had to be that the assassin he hired would turn out to be an amateur or a psycho, and in either case bungle the job and perhaps reveal the money man's identity. This was the kind of position where they took "experienced only."

Dartley would have gotten nowhere had it not been through Charley Woodgate. A man who made weapons to order occasionally was asked if he knew a skilled, professional shooter. Even so, it took a year before Dartley drew a pro job.

By 1980 Richard Dartley was known to the select few as one of the two or three best hitmen in the world. Once he had accepted an assignment, he had always gotten his man. Besides this, he had managed to keep his identity unknown. In 1981 he first asked for a fee of a million dollars. Now he rarely worked for less.

He had been careful all the way—and moral too, in his own peculiar way. He had never assassinated anyone who hadn't deserved it. That was his most important rule. Dartley could honestly say that, to the present time, he had never deliberately harmed an innocent person in his life.

For Dartley to take him out, the target had to be real scum. Dishonest was not enough. The man had to be certified garbage in the worst way before Dartley would agree to touch him.

Although Dartley admitted he had become hardened and maybe cold-bloodedly vicious and calculating because of the work he did, he never lost sight of that one thing—each of the cockroaches he took out had to have lost the right to go on living.

Dartley sat at a table in the farmhouse with Charley Woodgate and Herbert Malleson. Malleson was doing the talking. He had neat columns of lists before him and was adding to them. Occasionally he pulled a photocopy from a large manila envelope and tossed it to the others to illustrate or back up what he said. His arch mannerisms and Oxford accent had earned him in America the nickname "the Viscount."

"Interior Minister Ahmed Rushdi, Foreign Minister Esmat Abdel Meguid and Speaker of the Parliament Rafaat el-Mahgoub and their families are in the American Embassy in Cairo with ex-President Hosni Mubarak and his family. There's almost a hundred more lesser lights of the previous administration taking shelter there also. All have been condemned to death by the Light of Islam mullahs for their so-called pro-Western, pro-degeneracy stance. I've had it on the highest authority that President Reagan has warned President Hasan in person, over the phone, that if the American Embassy in Cairo is stormed, the USAF will saturation-bomb every military installation in Egypt, land, sea, and air. Since then Hasan has been cooling it so far as Washington is concerned, and in return the State Department presently seems to be going to all sorts of diplomatic extremes to avoid confrontation with him."

Charley Woodgate shook his head in disagreement. "That's not how certain acquaintances of mine feel about things, and I assure you they have a lot of say in this administration."

Malleson smiled. "Charley, you talk with the wrong sort of people—always a fault of yours. These dreadful Pentagon types and spooks from Langley. I wish you'd go to some fashionable cocktail parties on the embassy circuit instead of talking to such troglodytes."

Charley shot back, "The trouble with people at the embassy cocktail parties and State Department receptions is that they can't imagine people who are not like themselves. People like Ahmed Hasan, for instance. I bet Hasan has never been to a cocktail party in his life. I suppose that's why he's such a mystery to them."

Dartley could see that the two older men were getting into one of their interminable arguments again. Charley and the Viscount could pass three hours pleasantly disagreeing with one another on just about any subject. The only rule of the game seemed to be that neither must give an inch in concession, no matter how good a point his opponent made.

The Viscount was a graduate of Oxford and Harvard Law School. He served as Dartley's data bank. Malleson's computers had information on every country and its most important citizens. It was the unique quality of this information which made it useful to a hitman. It could be used to blackmail as well as for other purposes.

"Herbert," Dartley said to him, politely cutting short the two men's argument, "how do I get into Egypt?"

"I can give you a choice," the Viscount replied. "As an archeologist or an expert on short-stemmed, disease-resistant wheat."

"I'll take the wheat."

"Good choice," Malleson confirmed. "Those pharaohs' names are the deuce to memorize in correct order. I hear that's why the CIA rarely uses archeology as a cover these days. They find it easier to finance the dig and have *real* archeologists do stuff part time for them. Right. You fly to Athens, change planes there, then to Cairo. You're one of these Green Revolution types they love to see. Every time they welcome your sort, they see big World Bank loans just over the horizon. Those papers explain everything for you. You work for the International Maize and Wheat Improvement Center—you call it CIMMYT after its title in Spanish. That's based in Mexico, but you're coming from the Botany Division of the Indian Agricultural Research Institute and you're arranging to ship in several thousand tons of some of the wheat varieties which have done so well in India, Pakistan, Nepal and Bangladesh. They're all based on semi-dwarf varieties developed in Mexico. You'll have no trouble getting in, even as an American. Just remember to say you've never worked at any time for the U.S. Agency for International Development."

Dartley couldn't tell wheat from barley or barley

from oats, but he wasn't worried. He knew that Malleson would have explained clearly and concisely what he needed to know in the batch of papers. The Viscount was meticulous about details and could generate thousands of words on anything in a very short time. From previous experience, Dartley knew that everything Malleson gave him was worth studying closely. It could even be interesting, since the Viscount was an award-winning historian who had written several bestsellers on such unrelated subjects as the true identity of Jack the Ripper, the Gloria Vanderbilt custody case, Josef Stalin, Huey Long and Nazi sympathizers in the 1930s British aristocracy.

Why was such a talented, wealthy man working for a paid assassin? For the same reason that Richard Dartley *was* a paid assassin. To escape from boredom. Except that in Herbert Malleson's case, being an armchair assassin was sufficient. The intellectual excitement was enough to satisfy him. Dartley enjoyed this, but he had to have the physical thrills too.

After Dartley had gone through his other requirements with Malleson and his uncle, he left them to continue their arguments, fueled by a quart of Jack Daniels. Dartley knew that Charley had a weapon delivery to make later on that evening, and he offered to do it so that Charley could enjoy some drinks with his old friend. Charley could not risk being pulled over by the D.C. cops for impaired driving and having them find a sophisticated weapon in the car. No one could claim they needed the kind of gun that Charley Woodgate put together so they could shoot possum.

"I got a date with Sylvia tonight," Dartley said. "Why don't I deliver your package and you go attack that bottle of sour mash with the Viscount?"

Charley beamed at the prospect.

The weapon to be delivered was a bolt action sniping rifle. The Remington 700 action chambered for .308 was fitted with a fiberglass stock. Its Schmidt and Bender eight-power scope had a 56 mm objective. Under conditions of good moonlight, this scope could detect a man at five hundred yards. Charley had test-fired and adjusted the piece until it was as accurate as could be expected under night conditions. This yardage was important to a sniper, because he used the moments of confusion after the shot to escape and thus every added yard between him and his target increased his chances of leaving the scene undetected.

Charley had picked a bolt rifle over a semi or full automatic because the average bolt rifle can consistently shoot ten rounds in an eight- or nine-inch group as compared with a semiautomatic's fourteen- or fifteen-inch group. A gunsmith can get an ordinary bolt rifle consistently shooting 1.5 inches at three hundred yards and well under a minute of angle all the way out to one thousand yards. In addition, the bolt action has fewer things to go wrong.

He had chosen a .308 cartridge over a .223 because of its better bullet weight velocity combination, which made it very stable at long ranges, with good wind backing ability and lots of power on contact.

The stock was made of temperature-stable fiberglass with glass bedding between the receiver and the stock. These materials did not alter with changes in temperature and pressure, thus providing that little extra in accuracy which can make all the difference to a sniper, who may be limited to a single shot.

Dartley had first started to deliver his uncle's handcrafted or altered weapons not as a convenience, but out of necessity. Not all of Charley's customers were reliable people to do business with. Especially when it came to their having to pay in cash. Once it had been a case of the customer wanting secrecy so badly he decided to silence Charley too when he made the delivery. He never saw Dartley behind him and died before he knew what hit him.

Tonight Dartley had no such concern. The customer was a military attaché with the Australian Embassy. The Aussies came to Charley for special guns when they didn't want the Brits and Canadians to know what they were doing—an inebriated first secretary had once told Charley that at a Christmas party.

The Australian attaché knew Dartley by sight, though not by name, from previous deals. The only thing Dartley disliked was the place set for the meet by his uncle—outside the White House gates. That was Charley's idea of a joke.

It was already dark when the attaché caught Dartley in his headlights for a moment and pulled into the curb.

"Those Secret Service guys are giving us a good looking over, mate," the attaché remarked cheerfully. "Where's your car parked?"

Dartley directed him. He did not open the thick

envelope the Australian handed him. The money would be there to the last dollar.

Dartley had left his car on a ghetto street a few blocks from the White House. As they approached, Dartley spotted three figures in a doorway near the car.

"Drive on slowly," he said to the attaché, who had also seen them.

Dartley got a close look as they passed by. The three black youths in the doorway were about twenty years old. They were making no effort to conceal themselves, and obviously had not, as Dartley first thought, put his car under surveillance.

"They're okay," Dartley said. "Probably local guys. Park here and walk back with me. I'll cover you on your way back to the car."

The pickup went off without incident. The three men in the doorway watched curiously as the two white men opened the trunk of the car. One threw a thick envelope in and pulled out a long cardboard box, which he gave to the other and slammed the trunk down. Then the dude with the box walked back to his car, while the other one watched his back. The one with the box drove away.

"Hey, you," one of the three shouted to Dartley, "why don't you mess with that shit on your own streets, 'stead of bringing it down here?"

"We don't need your fucking garbage, man."

"You dumping enough shit on us as it is."

They were moving from the doorway toward him, fanning out, looking for action.

"It's not what you think," Dartley said in a calm voice, making no effort to dash inside the car.

"Hah, man, you come down here to deal your dope and piss on us 'cause you think nothing matters down here."

"You're right, bro."

"This muffa think he something."

Dartley wasn't armed, if it could be said that a man with Dartley's skills in the martial arts was unarmed, simply because he was not carrying conventional hardware.

The first of them came at Dartley, assumed an exaggerated stance, and kicked sideways at his head. The guy was all show and had about as much speed as a slow-motion demonstration film. Dartley stepped barely out of range of the kick, clamped his right hand on the upper side of the man's shoe and pressed his left hand powerfully upward on the inside of his heel. The anklebones shattered and the foot hung, loose and floppy.

The guy whimpered as he fell, and scratched the sidewalk with his fingernails to ease the pain.

Dartley moved from his first to his second assailant in a blur of continuous motion. He dodged the long narrow screwdriver the man tried to sink into his stomach, grabbed the steel shaft of the screwdriver and bent it back into the V formed by the man's thumb and index finger, thus twisting the tool out of his grasp.

At that moment Dartley took a heavy body punch or kick—he couldn't tell which—from the third man, and then a sharp rap across the forehead from his fist. Dartley felt the stone in the man's ring tear his skin, and warm blood leaked into his left eye.

He had seen this blow to his forehead as it was

coming and rode with the punch. He couldn't have avoided it and also have sidestepped the far more deadly rabbit punch being delivered by the man he had just disarmed of the screwdriver.

Dartley stood apart from the two men for an instant, brandished the screwdriver and then drove its long steel stem into the ribcage of the man he had taken it from. He thrust the screwdriver upward at a forty-five degree angle, to fit between the slats of the ribs. He left it buried to the handle in the man's left side.

The third man stood and stared, transfixed with shock. Dartley let him be. He knew the fight had gone out of this one and he bore him no personal grudge. As the body of the stabbed man crumpled to the sidewalk, his uninjured companion felt an instinctual urge of self-preservation and took off down the street.

Dartley made sure the fleeing man did not turn to look at the number on his car's registration plate. Then, using the victim's own shirt, he wiped his prints off the handle of the screwdriver still buried in the dying man's side.

The one with the broken ankle still lay groaning, too immersed in his own problems to have noticed what went on around him.

Dartley looked up and down the empty street. He got in his car, started the engine, and drove away, waiting a couple of blocks before he flicked the lights on.

He had arranged to meet Sylvia Marton at National. She was taking the shuttle in from New York and so couldn't be sure exactly which plane she would be on. She had been there since early morning, making a TV commercial for a pantyhose company. This was a bit of a step down for a movie star—but then she had been a star only in Yugoslav films, never on this side of the Atlantic.

"Every twenty-nine-year-old woman needs an ego boost regularly," she had told Dartley a few days previously. "If the ad agency for the pantyhose company thinks my legs are more shapely than those of all the young bimbos they've got in New York City, who am I to argue with them? Of course I couldn't refuse them!"

While he waited, Dartley mopped the blood from his forehead with Kleenexes and covered the red furrow gouged by the ring's stone with a Band-Aid. He knew Sylvia wouldn't ask questions. She would merely raise her eyebrows to let him know she had noticed.

She was not averse to excitement herself. To his amazement, Dartley discovered she was a crack shot, and on several occasions she had been his getaway driver. She knew nothing, asked no questions, wanted no money—she just went along for kicks. Which made her Dartley's kind of woman.

"Darling, I'm exhausted," she cried when she saw him at the airport. "Those brutes made me pose nearly nude all day in all sorts of lurid positions. My little tush is numb from the effort."

Several men who had been eyeing this blonde, blue-eyed, sexy lady smiled when they heard this. It was plain that any one of them would have given a lot to trade places with Richard Dartley as she threw her arms about his neck and kissed him full on the mouth.

The taping may have been exhausting, as Sylvia claimed, but it sure had acted as a turn on for her also. As Dartley drove to her Georgetown apartment, he felt her undo his belt buckle and unzip his pants. Next he felt her soft palm caress his lower belly until he got a monstrous hard-on.

She massaged his dick and gave him some tender strokes that made the car fishtail. Then she went down on him, and he felt her moist lips and tongue on the head of his cock. This wasn't making the car any easier to steer.

Finally, he pulled into the parking lot of her apartment building and eased into a remote corner beneath a tree. He turned the car engine off and let his body's motor run at full throttle in Sylvia's throat.

Chapter 4

Omar Zekri was having bad dreams. They'd start out good, with Ali smiling and everybody happy. Then Ali's face would begin to disintegrate, in the middle of a smile, and the contents of his skull would leak like those of an overripe melon. Or worse would happen. Omar had taken to staying awake, sitting up all night in an old armchair, taking cat naps, trying never to allow himself to become immersed in deep sleep and those horrible dreams.

He even eased up on booze and coasted all day on beer, to calm his nerves. With the lack of sleep, he hardly had enough energy to be nervous anyway. He just went from place to place, doing what he had to do, too sick to sorrow, too tired to think.

Awad and Zaid came around every day. Sometimes several times. He would bump into them in unexpected places. Sometimes they would greet him and shake hands, as if they were very old friends or even cousins who had not seen each other for a long time.

Other times they would pretend not to know him. He could never tell what they would do. The only thing he could be sure of was that no day would pass without his seeing them. Deep in his mind, he knew they were a more immediate threat to him than his scary apparitions of Ali. The dead did not harm the living. Omar kept telling himself that. It was the living he had to fear more than the dead. He was not afraid of Ali. The dreams were what he was afraid of. . . .

He could not sleep.

Omar had expected to be tortured and killed when he admitted to Zaid and Awad that he collected information for the Americans. Instead, the two men had given him three bottles of Scotch and a hundred Egyptian pounds. All he had to do in the future was to pass the information from some of his contacts through Egyptian military clearance before he gave it to his American contact. As they explained, he was now working *with* his own government instead of against it. He had nothing to fear now about getting caught for treason. Why then did Awad and Zaid keep circling him like two sharks? Did they think he might be tempted, for more money, to tell the Americans how some of the information was now being monitored by the Egyptians? Of course, Omar had considered this opportunity. He had dismissed it as being too risky, considering what would happen to him if he disobeyed Zaid and Awad.

He wondered what Pritchett would do to him if he found out what was going on. Pritchett seemed pleasant enough, but so were all American Embassy spies—or at least the two who had been his contacts before

Pritchett. They were trained to be pleasant and inconspicuous. No doubt they were trained also to deal with Egyptian informants who double-crossed them. Pritchett would shoot him and push his body in the Nile. Which was not so bad, really, when he thought about what Zaid and Awad said they would do to him.

"Thank you, ladies and gentlemen," John Keegan said to the assembled reporters from the dais with the State Department seal, signaling that the news conference was over. "I only have time for one or two questions."

He pointed to a black woman.

"Sir, can you tell us why Defense seems to be going along with State these days on President Ahmed Hasan? Has President Reagan told them to shape up?"

"Not to my knowledge, Charlayne. I think I am free to say that we are beginning to hear some heartening things from Egypt. That is not to say that everything has changed overnight for the better, but there are definite, encouraging signs...that is all I can say. I think that everybody sees now that we must be patient—that we must give President Hasan a chance. It would be tragic if we prematurely withdrew our support for him and by so doing denied him the opportunity to return Egypt to a more democratic society. Thank you."

"Sir!"

"Sir!"

"What about Israel's claim that—"

John Keegan smiled and quickly walked away.

* * *

Dartley had no trouble at Cairo International Airport. He was required to change $150 into Egyptian currency at the official rate, since he did not have a visa (Malleson hadn't wanted to stretch things by applying for a genuine visa with Dartley's fake credentials in the name of Thomas Lewis). As Dartley passed out of customs, he picked up a map to the city at the Tourist Office desk. He was not being observed. Then he took a black-and-white cab to the Nile Hilton, where a room had been reserved for Mr. Lewis.

So far he hadn't noticed any anti-American displays, and certainly the Hilton, Sheraton and other American investments had not been seized like they had in Iran. Dartley's problem was that he now had to make a move, but in what direction he couldn't tell. There was no reason why doing one thing was better than another, so far as he could see.

Egypt was a signatory to the Nuclear Non-Proliferation Treaty, and thus was open to the inspectors of the International Atomic Energy Agency, the United Nations' body charged with halting the spread of nuclear weapons. The inspectors checked nuclear inventories, affixed seals to prevent diversion of material for unauthorized use and scanned millions of photos taken by sealed automatic cameras they installed in the plants.

But there were ways around these inspectors. For example, Iraq was thought to have made plutonium for bombs secretly from its big stockpile of natural uranium. Natural uranium in the form of yellowcake was not something the agency inspectors kept track

of. The yellowcake had been secretly refined in a
hot-cell laboratory that Iraq had bought from Italy.
The refined uranium was then irradiated in the reactor, between agency inspections, to produce weapons-
grade plutonium. Israeli warplanes interrupted that
project. France had supplied the reactor and fuel to
the Iraqis, and they were supposed to have technicians on the spot to stop all irregularities. Dartley
could sympathize with the French. They had been
made to look like fools on two scores—first, the
Iraqis had apparently tricked them, and then the
Israelis had showed themselves to be more alert and
more decisive.

Since those times Iraq had gotten bogged down
financially in its war with Iran; the revolution in Iran
had more or less put an end to nuclear research
there; and Libya was still unsuccessful in its attempts
to buy readymade atom bombs. Dartley could see
the Egyptian point of view. There were no longer
ties between Egypt and Israel, and if Egypt could
develop a nuclear capability, the country would re-
gain its leadership of the Arab world. That was an
understandable aim, and even an acceptable one had
it not been for the fact that this would put the
near-ultimate weapon of destruction in the hands of
Ahmed Hasan and the Light of Islam mullahs.

The Viscount had done his homework all right.
Dartley's head was now filled with facts, but facts
were one thing and what to do with them was
another. He had been immediately attracted by the
list of Egyptian scientists who had recently returned
from abroad. Malleson identified one among them as
by far the most important, a Mustafa Bakkush. If he

could be located, the bomb would not be far away. He was an internationally famous man and would not be so easy to hide. There would be talk. Certainly, asking around for a man would be easier than for a bomb.

Dartley lay back on the bed in his luxury room at the Nile Hilton and wondered how to start. It had been easy to use his bogus identity as a wheat expert at the airport, but it might be quite difficult with knowledgeable people. His best bet would probably be to pass as a tourist, keep his mouth shut, and hope people wouldn't spot him as an American—a wild hope, he knew.

The phone rang.

It was a Mr. Pritchett to see him. Dartley knew no one by that name, yet had him sent up to his room. Whoever this turned out to be, Dartley wanted to face him behind a closed door.

"Pritchett, from the embassy." The stout, red-faced man with blue eyes shook Dartley's hand and flopped into a chair. "Got anything to drink?"

"No," Dartley said in an even voice to the sweating man. "You didn't say which embassy."

In reply, Pritchett produced a plastic-encased ID card.

"I'm not here on American business," Dartley snapped.

Pritchett shrugged. "You know, before Hasan kicked out Mubarak, the U.S. was making long-term, low-interest loans to Egypt to buy American wheat. Two hundred and seventy-five million bucks' worth."

"You afraid I'll teach them how to grow their own so they won't want any more from the Middle West?"

"Naw. I was just showing off my knowledge. I couldn't give a shit about wheat." Pritchett mopped his brow with a large red handkerchief. When he saw that his host still was not going to offer him a drink, he went on, "Mr. Lewis, I want you to keep your eyes and ears open wherever you go and report anything unusual to us at the embassy."

Dartley cursed silently. Contact with the American Embassy was the last thing he wanted. He said, "I'd certainly be pleased to help any way I can. However, I can't jeopardize my work for the United Nations by seeming to be an . . . agent or whatever for the American Embassy. Even talking to you here would probably be enough to have me expelled from the country."

"You don't have to approach me directly," Pritchett said hurriedly. "We needn't ever talk again. It would be better that way. Here, memorize the name of this Egyptian. You will find him at that location at that time every day of the week. He is very dependable. Write what you wish me to know. Verbal messages become confused. Sign it with a code name. How about N. Hilton?"

"Great," Dartley said. After some small talk, he eased him out the door.

Pritchett wasn't such a fool as he pretended to be. After all he had known of Dartley's arrival in Egypt within three hours. Somehow he had learned that his name was Thomas Lewis and that he worked for CIMMYT. Obviously Pritchett had an informant in Immigration, and obviously Pritchett was CIA. He hadn't pressed Dartley to collection information, just left it to his patriotic duty. CIA method of operation.

Dartley made up his mind. Thomas Lewis was going to disappear from the Nile Hilton that very night.

He would get moving right away. That Egyptian would be a start. He looked at the piece of paper Pritchett had given him. The Egyptian would be there in about an hour. Outside the Mahmoud Khalil Museum, opposite the exit gate of the Gezira Sporting and Racing Club, on Zamalek Island in the Nile. The man's name was Omar Zekri.

"No, no, it is enough that I pick up messages for Mr. Pritchett," Omar Zekri was saying in his high-pitched voice and unusually accented English as he and Dartley walked along a dusty residential street. "I see no reason for me to have talks with people. It is not expected of me. You give me your message. No more. It is not reasonable."

Dartley let him go on complaining so long as he kept moving. The big houses along this stretch of the roadway were behind walls, and they walked beneath fragrant trees which leaned out from behind the walls, giving shade. They were alone.

Dartley interrupted the Egyptian's complaints. "I want to know where the scientist Mustafa Bakkush is located."

Omar paused and looked at him in surprise. "At Cambridge University in England. That gentleman considers himself too important to stay among us humble Egyptians."

Dartley shook his head. "He's been back now for a while. That's common knowledge. You make money from knowing what's going on. I'll pay."

Omar began uncertainly, "I will make enquiries—"

"No, you won't," Dartley barked.

"Why not?"

"Because you're not going to get the chance to. Either you tell me where I can find Bakkush or you die right here where you now stand."

"No!"

Dartley grinned. "Why do you think I brought you down to a quiet, lonely place?"

"But Pritchett—"

"Fuck Pritchett," Dartley said. "Pritchett works for me. He'll just have to find someone new after you're gone."

Omar's lips were trembling. "Don't hit me! Mustafa Bakkush works somewhere out in the desert, no one knows where or what he is doing. I have heard he is working on a nerve gas."

"That's not his technical background."

Omar gestured. "I do not understand these things well, but I think you are right. He is more splitting the atom, right? Who knows? What I can tell you is this, and no more: He comes into Cairo two days a week and meets with scientists and engineers from here and Alexandria. They all gather at the Citadel. I stay away because it would be dangerous to be seen lurking there. I am too shaky in my present position already. But I do more than this for you. Yes, I think I can." He waited, looking at Dartley expectantly.

Dartley took out a wad of American bills, peeled off three twenties, and handed them to Omar.

"I think this is worth more," Zekri said politely, unable to keep his eyes off the wad of paper in Dartley's hand.

Dartley peeled off two more twenties and handed them to him.

"An engineer who works at a government plant down in the Delta has attended some of these meetings. He helps me with things. But he will want much money. Here? At this place? Tomorrow? I will bring him. His English is bad. At this time? But remember you must pay for everything he tells you."

Dartley nodded and looked after him as he waddled off into the evening along the dusty street, nervously glancing back over one shoulder from time to time.

The block was smeared with glistening blood and three right hands, severed at the wrist, lay on the cobblestones at its base. Dr. Mustafa Bakkush had not seen Islamic justice in action before. He had wondered why he had been seated on a wooden bench in this courtyard inside the Citadel instead of going to one of his scientific meetings. No one had said anything to him. The military officers just pointed. And he had done what he was told. As usual. He sat in the shade on one of the benches. Two of the benches were filled with fierce looking, righteous mullahs. Their fawning attendants stood along the rear wall. Charges were read against three men. They were accused of theft. Bakkush recognized none of them. They were riffraff from the bazaars. What had this to do with him? Why was he forced to sit here?

The cutting off of the first man's hand had been the worst. A brutal looking, overweight man had chopped it off on the block with a ceremonial ax. The hand

had dropped to the cobblestones. A doctor and two
nurses had rushed to staunch the bleeding from the
man's stump.

Mustafa vomited on the ground at his feet. When
he recovered, he looked around him in an embarrassed
way. Some of the mullahs were looking at him. One
gave him a small smile of contempt.

After those three, charges were read against three
more men. These three were foreigners—two Pal-
estinians and a Jordanian—and they had been
condemned to death for smuggling a large quantity of
heroin. Two soldiers forced the first man, his hands
tied behind his back, to kneel at the block. The
heavy brute hacked off his head with three blows of
the ax. The soldiers carried the executed man's body
out of the courtyard, but they left his head behind,
along with the three right hands and a few liters
more of fresh blood. The head lay on its left ear, eyes
and mouth open, a vacant look on the face.

Mustafa Bakkush could not say why, but somehow
that first hand which had been chopped off had
affected him more deeply than this decapitation. It
must have been the initial shock. Of course, he had
known this was going on since Mubarak had been
deposed—he just hadn't realized the barbarity it
entailed.

The second man to be executed—like the first—
seemed so groggy and disoriented by fear, he hardly
resisted and was slaughtered without protest. The
third man shouldered aside the two soldiers, walked
to the block, said something to the executioner which
made him scowl, knelt, stretched his neck across the
block, and died without displaying shock or fear. The

mullahs murmured angrily among themselves at this display of defiance.

While this man's body was being removed from the courtyard, a movement in a grilled window some twenty feet up the courtyard wall caught Mustafa's eye. The sun cast diamonds of light through the grill onto a man's face observing them while remaining concealed. The eyes, nose and mouth were caught for an instant in a single diamond of sunlight—and Mustafa recognized the face of President Ahmed Hasan.

They had brought out another prisoner and charges were being read again. He too had been condemned to death. Mustafa wanted to blot everything out. Then he heard a name. He focused his eyes and looked. It was not possible! They couldn't do this! With a horrible sinking feeling in his stomach and another surge of nausea, Mustafa Bakkush realized why he had been brought to this courtyard.

He was on his feet. Shouting. What was he saying? He was telling them they could not do this, that this man was a genius, the greatest electrical engineer the Arab world had produced, a credit to Egypt, there was a mistake, it could not be allowed...Mustafa realized he was walking across the courtyard to the man, standing between him and the executioner at the block. Mustafa knew it was no dream. He could feel the baleful stares of the mullahs on him. He did not care. He was rescuing his old friend. They had been students together, had achieved worldwide fame together in the sciences. Mustafa heard the charges and did not care. He would see that everything was all right.

No one stopped him when he led the condemned man, whose hands were bound behind his back, out of the courtyard and through a dark archway into an old building. Mustafa did not know where the passageway led. He felt the cool air of the interior on his skin. He was still shouting—but had no idea what he was saying.

He saw tears running down the cheeks of the electrical engineer.

Thirty minutes later, Mustafa Bakkush found himself, calm and fearful, bowing in respect before the reigning mullahs of the Light of Islam, the very ones before whom he had disgraced himself in the courtyard, first by vomiting in the presence of an Islamic legal edict and then by disturbing the proceeding by his irrational behavior. The mullahs sat along one side of a very long table—for one offbeat moment Mustafa was reminded of a King Farouk banquet—and he stood alone on the other side of the table. President Ahmed Hasan sat among the mullahs, not at their center or in any place of honor, simply among them. Yet it was he who spoke.

"Mustafa Bakkush, I have spoken on your behalf with these men who have devoted their lives to the honor and glory of Allah and to respect for the message of His Prophet. Islam is merciful. You have spent years in the degenerate world of the West and your values became corrupted. Now you are again in the Islamic fold, but it will take time for you to purify yourself. These great mullahs whom you see before you, men who tread in the footsteps of the Prophet, have decided to be patient with you. Bow your head in gratitude and humility."

Mustafa bowed his head and kept it bowed until Ahmed Hasan, apparently satisfied, began speaking to him again.

"Word was brought to me, Mustafa, that you expect your scientific colleague can be persuaded to work under your direction."

Mustafa had sent no such message, not having been able to communicate yet in private with the electrical engineer. His eyes met with those of Hasan and he saw the look of warning there.

"Yes, indeed, honorable President."

"I am pleased to hear it. Up to this point, he has refused to cooperate in achieving the goals of our Islamic republic. We will all depend on you to steer him toward the true path of enlightenment."

"I will," Mustafa said. He suddenly realized that this was a continuation of the spectacle put on in the courtyard, and that it was being put on for the mullahs by the president rather than for himself. In fact, Hasan was now making him part of his show.

This was confirmed by Hasan's next line of talk.

"Some of the holy men present here doubt the value of Western technology along with its immoral ideas. Some see how we can further the aims of Islam by using the weapons developed by the West against itself. Others—and I number myself among them—go farther. We say that if Islam is to survive in this hostile world, we must arm ourselves against our enemies. Muhammad knew the power of the sword! Today we must not shrink from the power of the atom!"

The bearded faces of the mullahs passed comments among themselves. They showed no fear or respect for the president seated among them in his military uniform.

Mustafa met Ahmed Hasan's eyes. Again there was that warning look.

Hasan spoke quietly and slowly. "Dr. Mustafa Bakkush, a humble and devout man, our fellow countryman, will now explain to us what is involved in Egypt making a bomb. He will remember that we are not scientists, yet he will explain the processes involved and how we may achieve them. I know that, like me, Dr. Bakkush will never forget that the Zionist entity has full nuclear capability. The Christian, Jewish and Hindu civilizations possess this capability. Communist powers also have it. Only the Islamic civilization is without it. You may say to me, Pakistan has the atom bomb and Pakistan is Islamic. I would say back to you that Pakistan is not Arabic! Pakistan is allowed to have the bomb because the Russians are in Afghanistan and because its enemy, India, has the bomb. Pakistan does not care for us! There is no Arab bomb! Now Dr. Bakkush will speak to you."

They sat in silence for a time and looked at him. Mustafa did not know how to begin. Then he remembered a talk he had given science students at Stuyvesant High School in New York City. He didn't know how to talk about Islamic or Arabic bombs, but he did know how to give a simplified technical explanation of the manufacture of atomic weapons.

"The radioactive element uranium occurs more than ninety-nine percent of the time as uranium 238, which is a relatively harmless form or isotope. Less than one percent occurs in a lighter, unstable isotope called uranium 235. It is called unstable because its atom can be fairly easily split by a beam of electrons, and this splitting causes the chain reaction that results in the nuclear explosion."

Mustafa cleared his throat and went on. "It is very difficult to separate these isotopes from one another in naturally occurring uranium ore. The process is called 'enriching' the uranium, and a number of complex techniques have been developed by Western industrialized nations. Also, things are complicated by the designs and knowledge possessed by the makers of the bomb. A simple bomb might need about twenty kilograms of enriched uranium. This amount is known as the critical mass. The new designs used by the Americans today have a critical mass of less than eight kilograms. We would need less than twelve to develop a bomb here. That may not sound like much, but it is a great quantity when you consider the difficulties involved."

Ahmed Hasan growled, "If the Zionists can do it, so can we."

"Well, they probably didn't use this method," Mustafa said. "I'll come to what they did in a minute. However, the Pakistanis are believed to have used this method. A Pakistani scientist working for a firm in Holland is believed to have smuggled home the plans for a cascade of high-speed ultracentrifuges which work through a spinning action. They are available on the market today. So is uranium ore, and at a very reasonable price, too. That represents one way we could do it."

Hasan snarled, "I want to hear what the Zionists did."

"The Israelis simply bought a French reactor for generating electric power and contracted for them to supply fuel, just as we have done. To work such a reactor, fuel rods or a blanket of fairly harmless uranium 238 are bombarded with neutrons, which causes some of the uranium to turn into plutonium, an element that is not found in nature. This artificial substance is highly unstable and is ideal for bombs. This kind of bomb can have a critical mass, even for us, as low as five kilograms."

Mustafa shifted about on his feet. "The problem with this method is the danger in handling the plutonium. It has to be extracted by chemical means from the spent reactor fuel, and elaborate precautions must be taken to protect the workers from irradiation. Even the smallest—"

"There is no problem!" Ahmed Hasan boomed. "There are a thousand martyrs for Islam who tomorrow will use their fingernails to pluck this plutonium from the spent fuel! They will sacrifice themselves and be rewarded by Allah!"

Mustafa stared at him speechlessly.

Hasan sneered. "Don't worry, Dr. Bakkush. You will not be required to show your devotion in this way. Unless, of course, your work elsewhere becomes unsatisfactory. Yes, we will soon have our bomb! Get us that plutonium!"

"I'm afraid it's not going to be that simple," Mustafa said apologetically. "The bomb must be designed."

Hasan glowered. "I am not a fool, Bakkush. I too know of events in the outside world, although you may think I am nothing but an ignorant Arab who has never left his homeland. I have heard that university students can make bombs. They say that revolutionary groups in Europe and America will soon make their own atomic bombs and hold cities like New York for ransom. If these people can have bombs, I want to know why can't Egypt too?"

"We will have a bomb, honorable President," Mustafa said placatingly. "But only after the work has been done. You yourself have spoken of exploitative Western journalists. Here is another point to back what you said. While students or terrorists might have an understanding of how a bomb works, and could find many calculations in technical journals, these things would not enable them to make a bomb—in spite of what Western TV and novels claim. For example, one of the very important things is the shape of the charge. There are literally scores of factors which must be exactly right or the bomb will not work, and no one except an experienced man in the field would know what to do without years of trial and error." Mustafa smiled sardonically. "After all, that is why you brought me back to Egypt. You have many bright young men who know everything theoretically. Yet you needed a knowledgeable old-timer like me to put the nuts on the bolts."

A look of cold fury spread across Ahmed Hasan's features as the scientist stood up to him opposite the mullahs.

"I will speak with you later," the president grated, frustrated that he could not have this insolent dog shot immediately because of his value to the nuclear program. "You may leave."

Mustafa Bakkush left, looking pleased with himself
and far more confident than when he had entered
the room. He seemed oblivious of the president's
anger toward him.

"I do not like that man at all," a mullah with a
huge white beard announced.

There was general agreement to this.

"But you do understand what he said?" Hasan
asked eagerly, forgetting his rage. "You understand
how this bomb is now within our grasp?"

The white-bearded mullah answered, "I understand that we play with the Devil."

Hasan was clever enough to keep his mouth shut
at this point. He let the mullahs discuss the fine
ethical and theological points among themselves, and
watched anxiously for who would show themselves to
be his supporters and opponents. When he saw that
fully three-quarters backed him, he spoke in a humble voice.

"All of us here know that I am a mere figurehead,
only a tool to achieve the will of the Light of Islam.
You are the true rulers of Egypt and I live only to
obey your commands. At one word from you, the
mob would tear me from limb to limb. And yet a
nation needs a figurehead. Within the privacy of
these four walls, I ask you to tell me what to do.
Shall I go ahead to achieve an Islamic bomb?"

More than three-quarters showed their hands in
support, and Hasan took to bowing and thanking
them profusely. He deliberately did not ask those
against him to declare themselves. But this did not
stop one thin-faced man with a glistening black,

pointed beard and the sharp eyes of a desert warrior from standing up and gesturing for quiet.

"Fear not, brothers. I do not intend to fight your majority on this. You know that I think Ahmed Hasan holds too much sway over you and that he is a dangerously deluded man." The fierce looking mullah paused to stare boldly at the president, who avoided his eyes. "It is not that I and my supporters in this are less dedicated than you. Perhaps each one of us have different reasons for feeling as we do. But, as I promised, we will not spend time discussing our dissent. Yet we will ask something in return for not opposing you vigorously on this. A small thing. Something of benefit to you as much as to us."

He looked about to make sure each man was listening. When he spoke again, it was with a different voice. No longer was his tone friendly and reasonable.

"We have detractors overseas, Egyptians who insult their homeland with false stories, who shame us before the world, who insult our Islamic values. These men are embittered by their material losses when the corrupt reign of the dog Mubarak was overthrown. I need not name these individuals for you, and others join them daily when they see it is safe to do so, that no retribution is visited upon the heads of these wrongdoers who are an insult in the eyes of Allah and His Prophet and a scourge to the worthy mullahs of our homeland."

He pointed a long finger in Hasan's face. "We want you to open a training camp without delay to train young men to go out in the world and silence these infidels."

Hasan looked genuinely pleased and relieved that this was all that was being required of him. "Tell me what to do," he shouted to the others. "Is this your wish?"

This proposal was even more popular than the one for the atom bomb.

After dutifully escorting the mullahs to their waiting limousines in another inner courtyard, Ahmed Hasan retired to a private room deep in the fortress. There he drank tea and smoked two pipes of hashish. He needed time to think. Ahmed was acutely aware that he was now dealing with types of men he had previously been unaccustomed to. His whole adult life having been spent in the army, he knew the military mind, and over the years—out of necessity—had become acquainted with the political mind and the business mind. However, military men, politicians and businessmen were simple and straightforward, babes in arms in comparison to mullahs and scientists. The religious mind and the scientific mind were ones he would have to familiarize himself with before he could get the better of them. Ahmed liked to divide men into compartmentalized types according to their calling in life. He noted each man's behavioral eccentricities within his own group and remembered them. But to Ahmed, a man was first what his job proclaimed him to be—a soldier, a politician, etc.—before he was an individual. (Ahmed put all women into only two types: pretty ones and ugly ones.) Yet each man had a fearful peasant streak in him, no matter how high and mighty or intelligent and enlightened he had become. He had only to be trapped within his own nightmares and be pressured in exactly the right way, in exactly his weakest place, and he would howl in anguish like any backward member of the fellahin. Ahmed's problem was that he was not quite sure how to go about bringing mullahs and scientists before him on their knees.

They too were greedy men, but theirs was an intellectual greed. Their lust for power was cloaked, often from themselves as well as others, by their much praised strivings for and benefits to mankind. Ahmed always found it easier to manipulate men who were aware of their own weaknesses. When a man wanted land or gold, that was what he got. But when a man's greed was for respect and fame instead of land or gold, Ahmed found him a trickier adversary to subdue. And all Ahmed wanted was to subdue them—not degrade them into mindless yes-men who would be useless to him in their fields. He needed these mullahs and scientists. He felt he needed them as beasts of burden. To use them as that, he would first have to break them, domesticate them.

Little Mustafa Bakkush had surprised him with his performance in the courtyard. The scientist had showed his own strange kind of courage—after having previously displayed his cowardice by vomiting at a simple decapitation! A strange man... Ahmed had looked down on the scene from a barred window high in a wall. It gave him pleasure to witness his enemies meet their end. The mullahs had condemned these felons, and Ahmed saw this as a new beginning in their relationship with him, in which they would function as a tribunal to pass judgment on those who offended him. Dr. Bakkush had nearly ruined everything with his unexpected outburst and rescue of the engineer. Ahmed had merely wanted to frighten the little scientist by having him see the execution of a colleague. It turned out that Bakkush too had an unpredictable side, like all these scientists. The electrical engineer had been the same! Ahmed had forgotten now what he had done to cause the man to rebel—there had been some incident, and the engineer refused to cooperate any further, regardless of penalty. Now Bakkush had saved this man's life in an unexpectedly reckless move. Ahmed could not let the engineer think he could defy authority and be saved by Bakkush. He could not let Bakkush think so either. The engineer would obey or he would die, and Ahmed would teach him this. Even if he was a scientist and behaved in strange ways.

Ahmed Hasan put aside his tea and hashish pipe, sent for an army officer and told him: "That electrical engineer will be important to us if we can get him to work for us again. I don't want him injured or too badly treated. Is there a prisoner here he knew before they both came to the Citadel?"

"Yes, sir. A chemist we caught spying for the Americans. They often walk together in the yard. The engineer also knows most of the other technical people under confinement here, sir."

"He does? Of course. Is this chemist important to our military effort?"

"He's a soil chemist, sir."

"Useless! I'll use him. Bring them both here."

The officer left and Hasan wandered out of the room into the corridor. Two privates pushed a load of supplies on a two-tiered metal table with wheels.

"Get rid of that stuff and bring the table in this room." Hasan commanded. "Bring some rope too."

The two privates returned with the table and in a while the engineer Mustafa Bakkush had saved was brought in. Hasan ordered him bound in an upright chair close to the metal table. When the chemist arrived, Hasan had him stretched on his back on the table, his wrists and ankles bound to the four table legs.

"Did you know that this man was a spy for the Americans?" Hasan asked the engineer, indicating the chemist spreadeagled on the table. "At least you did not do that." Hasan took a length of nylon fishing line from one pocket. He said to the engineer, "You refused to work in your country's nuclear program. I suppose that may be negotiable. But spying for a foreign power is unforgivable." He beckoned to one of the two privates and turned to the man on his back on the table. He gripped him under the chin with one hand, his thumb on one side of the mouth, his fingers on the other, and by squeezing his grip, he forced the man's mouth open. He said to the soldier, "Catch his tongue. It's slippery. Use both hands, pull it right out of his mouth all the way it will come, hold on to it."

The man on the table, who had said nothing until this point, now began to gurgle, but could not enunciate any words because the soldier held his tongue extended from his mouth. Hasan wound the nylon line tightly around the roots of his tongue, knotted the line, and cut off the loose ends with a knife. Hasan nodded to the soldier to release the man's tongue. This done, the man on the table began to talk desperately, but only one word in ten was understandable. Hasan covered each of the man's nostrils carefully with a Band-Aid. His tongue swelled slowly and still fewer of his words made sense. Hasan placed another upright chair next to that of the engineer's and sat beside him to watch the man on the table, whose tongue was now bluish purple and filling his entire open mouth.

"I'll go back to work," the engineer suddenly offered. "Let him go."

"It took you long enough to make the offer," Hasan observed.

"Because it's sincere. Let him go before it's too late. I promise. I'll work."

"We will consider your case," Ahmed said judicially, turning the tables on him by treating the engineer's bargaining as if it were a plea for mercy for himself.

The president then lapsed into silence and stared stonily at the man choking on the table. As his tongue swelled more and almost completely blocked the airflow through his mouth, the man tried vainly to snort off the Band-Aids sealing his nostrils. He struggled wildly against his bonds, but they were secure. He quieted down and tried to wheeze air into his throat and lungs around his swollen tongue. His eyes were popping. His head turned to one side and he gave the engineer a desperate, pleading look.

The engineer struggled against his own bonds in the upright chair. "What can I do to save him?" he begged Ahmed, next to him.

The president ignored him.

The man on the table choked, gasped, struggled, coughed and shuddered. The engineer looked away.

Hasan gazed straight at the man until his last movement ceased and he lay staring from protruding eyes up at the ceiling, his large purple tongue bloated in his mouth.

Hasan stood and cut loose the engineer. He spoke to the officer: "Have him wheel this punished traitor to all the cells where there are technicians and scientists. He may describe what has happened in any words he pleases."

The officer nodded to the privates, and they jostled the engineer toward the table. They followed him as he trundled the table out the doorway.

Ahmed Hasan had a final word with the officer after they left. "Make sure he pushes the table himself and tells what happened to everyone. When he's finished, give him a week in solitary confinement and then ask him if he wants to work. If he does, free him. If he doesn't, shoot him."

The officer saluted and left.

Chapter
5

"No one can work in a vacuum," Richard Dartley muttered aloud to himself as he walked along the corridor of a modern office building in Cairo's New City. He had told Omar Zekri that Pritchett at the American Embassy worked for him, which should take a rise out of the CIA man. Dartley did not worry about being harassed by the CIA in Cairo—they had more than enough on their hands already, from what he had heard, in trying to deal with Ahmed Hasan's administration. He didn't expect to learn anything more from Zekri himself or anyone he produced as an "informant," now that Zekir had time to consult and organize. Yet, for better or worse, the Egyptian and the embassy CIA man were his only contacts in Egypt—his only escape from the vacuum—not counting the man he was on his way to see in the office building. He found a frosted glass door with a legend, beneath Arabic script, in English: NILE VALLEY ENTERPRISES.

There was no one at the receptionist's desk inside the office. Dartley caught sight of a man through an open doorway. He was sitting at a desk, bent down in intense concentration over something in his hands. Dartley stepped quietly in and looked. The man was fixing a pair of horn-rimmed spectacles, snapped across the bridge. When he heard Dartley, he picked up one half of the spectacles and held the lens over one eye like a monocle.

"Who are you?" he asked in English. He was dark-skinned, chubby, not at all apprehensive.

"Mr. Yahya Waheed?"

The chubby Egyptian scrutinized him through the lens and nodded.

"Herbert Malleson in Washington, D.C., told you I would be coming."

Waheed smiled and waved to a chair. "Yes, he did. Make yourself comfortable and I will be with you in a minute." He spoke English with a noticeable American accent, but said nothing more as he went back to fixing his spectacles with a small tube of super glue.

Dartley watched him work in the manner of a very nearsighted person, with the broken rims and tube of glue almost next to his eyes. Waheed shook his right hand. He shook it again, then tried to separate his second and third fingers.

"Bonded," he said. He picked up the tube and read, " 'Warning: Bonds skin instantly. Contains cyanoacrylate ester. Avoid contact with skin and eyes. If eye or mouth contact occurs, hold eyelid or mouth open and flush with water only and GET MEDICAL ATTENTION. If finger bonding occurs, apply solvent.' " He put the glue down thoughtfully and tried to separate his fingers again, without success. "I don't have any solvent."

Dartley fixed the spectacle frames with the glue. Waheed put them on and walked agitatedly around the office, looking at his bonded fingers. Dartley observed him. If it had been anyone but Malleson who had put him onto this arms dealer, he would have left there and then and taken his chances on a street purchase. But Malleson had never steered him wrong. Yet . . . Dartley put a lot of importance on the source of his weapons. A dependable source was essential to the success of a mission, and at the same time it represented one of its greatest security risks. It was often through the arms dealer that work leaked about an upcoming operation.

Dartley never carried weapons across a border, seeing it as a foolish risk. He liked to enter a country in a business suit or dressed as a tourist, and travel by scheduled airline or whatever would not attract attention.

There was no way around the vulnerability of a weapons pickup, and when he had the weapons, he became open to all sorts of charges if he were caught in possession of them.

Availability of the latest and best guns, even in relatively isolated places, presented no problem. Anywhere in the free world, if you had the cash to buy the best, someone found them for you.

Yahya Waheed didn't look the wheeler-dealer sort that Dartley expected a gun merchant to be. What worried Dartley was that he looked incompetent— was he to trust a harmless fuck who couldn't even fix his own spectacles to do a weapons deal with him in a country where the government claimed all Americans were agents of the Devil? Dartley couldn't afford to have anything go wrong for him in a place like this. Certainly not on the level of buying hardware from a jerk...

"Did you get everything Malleson asked you to get?" Dartley inquired.

"Yes, everything. We'll go down now to my car and I will show you."

They took the elevator down to a garage in the basement of the office building. Waheed led him to a green Mercedes parked off in one corner away from the other vehicles. But they weren't going anywhere. Waheed opened the trunk and gestured to two leather suitcases.

Dartley liked this less and less. He unzipped one case—it wasn't even locked—and lifted a light blanket that served as packing for a field-stripped Heckler & Koch MP5 submachine gun.

"I want to assemble it," Dartley said. He looked around. The garage was deserted. "All right here?"

Waheed nodded in a relaxed way and put a cigarette in his mouth.

Dartley put the gun together. It was new and in perfect condition. So far so good. This weapon was what he would depend on if he was going to take out Hasan. This was a Model SD, the silenced version of the MP5. He had thought of an assault rifle, such as an M16, but decided on a submachine gun for its easier concealment and quick action.

When people thought of submachine guns, they thought of the Uzi. The U.S. Secret Service used the Uzi—all the world saw the agent holding one on videotape when President Reagan was felled by a psycho's bullet. The tough guys—good and bad—on TV dramas carried Uzis. But everyone in the know used the Heckler & Koch MP5; the Coast Guard, DEA, Special Forces, Rangers, SEALS, the FBI counterterrorist team . . . in the United States alone. And they had one good reason: The MP5 was the only submachine gun which fired from a closed bolt. This meant that when a shot was fired, the only part of the mechanism which moved was the hammer, and this, of course, greatly increased the gun's accuracy.

The gun's method of operation was delayed blowback. The delay in the unlocking of the bolt after the firing of a shot was caused by rollers. This delay allowed the bullet to leave the barrel, and thus the gas pressure to drop, before the breach could open. The cartridge case acted as a piston during recoil in this roller lock system. The cartridge case pushed the bolt backward while being floated in the chamber by the powder gases. The system was therefore a combination of recoil activated and gas operated, but without a gas system to clean.

The semirigid bolt was locked by two side-acting rollers that bore against notches in the receiver. When a shot was fired, the rollers pushed into the bolt head and exerted pressure on the firing pin extension. This extension became separated from the bolt head and was pushed back. The rollers left the receiver grooves and withdrew into the bolt. By then the bullet had exited from the barrel, causing the gas pressure to drop. Only the return spring was now holding the bolt in place and thus it was easily driven backward by the recoiling cartridge case. As the case ejected, the return spring forced the bolt forward again, stripped a new cartridge from the magazine, and pushed it into the chamber.

Everything looked in good order to Dartley. He loaded some thirty-round detachable box magazines with 9×19 mm parabellum ammo. He hefted the weapon—it weighed a little less than six pounds, and felt nicely balanced, a little heavier toward the front.

He replaced everything in the suitcase, ready to use, checked other items, then replaced the packing and zipped the suitcase. Dartley went through the second suitcase much more quickly. He took out a miniature spray can, filled it from a plastic bottle of Clorox and dropped it in his pocket.

Next he took out what looked like a pen. Using only one hand, he flipped off the top to reveal a short, double-edged blade. The base of each side of the blade was serrated to cut through nylon line and plastic tape. This was the new Tekna T-6000 Micro-Knife, the blade of which was formed from a single billet of moly-vanadium stainless steel—it was tough metal and didn't lose its edge being hacked around. He replaced the top of the pseudo pen and dropped that in a pocket too.

"I'm not going to chance carrying anything else," he said to Waheed, "in case I get taken in or searched."

"I have arranged a pickup for the bags," the Egyptian said. "You have a hundred-dollar bill?"

Dartley peeled a crisp one from his roll and handed it to him.

Waheed tore it in half along a zigzag pattern. He

gave one half back to Dartley and said, "That will be your hatcheck. That is what you say?"

"Sure."

"I leave these suitcases in the Pensione Cornwall at this number on Adli Street in the New City. You give the desk clerk that half of the bill so he can put it with this half to make himself very happy. You will have your two suitcases. What could look more natural than an American leaving a hotel with two suitcases?"

"Sure." Dartley made to walk away across the garage to an exit door.

Waheed called after him. "The Pensione Cornwall is on the seventh floor of an apartment building. Mostly the elevator is not working, I am sorry. But it keeps the place very private."

"Sure."

When Omar Zekri told Awad and Zaid about the American who claimed to be Pritchett's boss and was looking for Dr. Mustafa Bakkush, they checked on him at Immigration, noted his phony "agricultural expert with the UN" status, thought nothing much about it and filed a routine report. Which got them hauled in on an emergency basis. Find this man. Take him alive if possible. At all events, take him out of circulation even if the crudest means were necessary. But only as a last resort. Go. Do it. Now.

Yes, sir.

Like that.

Zaid and Awad were used to such mistreatment from their bureaucratic superiors. They hardly bothered to wonder why this was such a big deal. They just drove out and hit on Zekri again, had him show them the exact place where he was to meet with the American along with the other informant he was supposed to bring. They didn't have to tell Omar he was not to show up as arranged.

They set things up calmly, paying no attention to the screams and demands of the pen pushers giving them orders, collected good men and allowed themselves plenty of time.

The black van turned off the Sharia El Sheikh Marsafy on Zamalek Island in the Nile and continued down the dusty, tree-lined, residential street.

"Here," Awad called, and Zaid pulled the van to the side.

Zaid climbed out and opened the rear doors. He said to the four men who emerged, "Remember, take him alive. That's why there's four of you."

The van waited until the men had disappeared over the wall and then drove slowly on down the empty road. The men had a wait of three hours in front of them, so they settled themselves comfortably in the shade behind the wall, with one posted as a lookout in the branches of a tree where he could see up and down the road.

Dartley showed a little before time. At least the lookout figured it had to be the American they were waiting for—he had a description and this Westerner fitted it—and what other American could be expected to be walking along this particular high-class, residential road at this particular hour, not even with a limousine or taxi? He called down softly from the branches to the three other men.

It was Dartley all right. He was expecting the

worst as he walked along the deserted road with its high walls, big gateways into hidden residences and tropical shade trees. Omar Zekri would have gone to Pritchett at the embassy, and Pritchett would have said keep away or play him along without giving him anything or chase him out of town, maybe worse. Omar wasn't capable of doing any of these things except keeping away, and so it was no surprise to Dartley not to find the Egyptian at their arranged meeting place.

Dartley looked at his watch. He was ten minutes early. He'd give Omar or whoever was going to show an hour. In the meantime it made no sense for him to stand out like a bowling pin in an empty alley. He took a short run, gripped the top of the stone wall with his fingers, hauled himself to the top, rolled over and landed on his feet on the other side.

Dartley found himself standing among four startled Egyptians, strong-arm types not given to conversation.

"Masa' al kheir." Dartley wished them good evening. They said nothing. But their muscles were twitching. Any moment now, their brains would be working.

Dartley's hands came from his pockets. He flipped the top off the pen in his right hand and sprayed Clorox in the faces of the two nearest men from the can in his left hand.

As those two staggered about, yelping and wiping their eyes, Dartley advanced fast on the next man. Holding the penlike handle of the Tekna Micro-Knife between the first two fingers of his clenched first, he punched at the man's throat. He missed the first time. The second time the man's arm took the blade and he clutched at the wound, leaving his neck open. The third time Dartley hit home.

He punched the short blade into the man's throat just to one side of his windpipe. Then he thrust sideways and the blade's serrated edge ripped through the windpipe, artery and veins, leaving his neck looking like a ripped open phone cable, not counting the blood.

Dartley lost his grip on the knife and had used up the spray can on the first two men, so he had to take the fourth man with his hands. The guy must have been slow or had been doing one thing and took the time to change his mind and try another. He was still in the act of drawing an automatic pistol from his shoulder holster. He nearly had the weapon drawn— Dartley could see it was taking him an extra second because of a silencer which extended the length of the barrel and had maybe gotten delayed in the holster.

The man was right-handed. As he drew the pistol from under his left arm, Dartley checked his right arm with a left-hand pressing block. Simultaneously, Dartley delivered a right vertical flatfist to the back of the Egyptian's gun hand.

Keeping his grip on the man's right arm with his left hand, Dartley grabbed the right side of his collar with his other hand. He wrenched his head and neck downward, positioning him nicely for a right knee kick to the groin.

The knee in the balls seemed to knock the joy of life out of his opponent. Dartley grabbed his right wrist with both hands and used a reverse twist throw to bring him down on his back. He freed the gun from the holster and put a bullet between the Egyptian's eyes at point-blank range, like putting away a sick animal. The guy kicked and stiffened. That was all.

The two Clorox customers were still blindly thrashing about and complaining. They didn't even see Dartley put the gun to their heads to relieve their discomfort.

He glanced at the gun out of interest. It was a 7.65 mm Manurhin, which was the French licensed version of the German Walther PPK. The silencer was big and clumsy, but effective. Dartley was tempted to keep the weapon. He decided against it, wiped his prints from it and carefully replaced it in its dead owner's shoulder holster.

Knowing there was nothing to learn from the four bodies, Dartley searched for the spray can, the knife and its top. When he pocketed them, he pulled himself to the top of the wall and spotted a black van traveling slowly, too slowly, in his direction some distance down the road.

He jumped down inside the wall again, crossed some more compounds, found another road and waited until dark before slipping out of the area.

The meeting was going badly for Aaron Gottlieb. The Russian contingent was giving him the most trouble. The bastards had barely learned Hebrew and eased off moaning about the beauties of Mother Russia when they were trying to take over the kibbutz already. Aaron Gottlieb was a Sabra. Born right here on this kibbutz. Father and mother both American citizens. Grandfather and grandmother well-to-do German Jews prominent enough to be forced out by the Nazis in the 1930s before the ovens were built. He, Aaron Gottlieb, had fought for the entry of these Russian refugees into the kibbutz when they had no where else to go and neither spoke Hebrew so you could understand it nor knew how to work the land. Couldn't tell a chicken from a pigeon—of course they might be the same thing in Russia. Anyway, he had helped them—and now that they had found their feet, they turned on him, accusing him of ordering them about and calling him behind his back "the kibbutz commissar." Truth was, he had a brain and was not afraid to use it. A lot of the other young people with brains had left the kibbutzim for the city. He had stayed, when he wasn't away on missions. . . . One old Russian—who, God forgive him, Stalin should have liquidated—was droning on in his weird accent.

"For this we come to the Promised Land? We return to the soil. We should have cows and orange groves and chickens. We should irrigate the soil, make the desert green. We should give thanks to God, humbly, and labor in the fields under the open sky. This is what we are told we will find. Is this what we find? I ask you that. Is this what we find? I say to a stranger who does not know this place, 'Would you believe alligators?' He says to me, 'Like crocodiles?' " The Russian shook his backside and snapped his teeth. "Alligators in freshwater ponds, crawling around among the palm trees and bougainvillea. This is a kibbutz in Zion! 'This is not all,' I tell this stranger, whose mouth is already hanging open because he cannot believe such things about the Jewish home-land. 'You think we show you temples the prophets may have preached in? No, we don't care about those! We dig up a Roman theater and build a museum for a pagan culture and other Jews *pay* to see how these godless butchers sacrificed our people to wild animals.' And the stranger says to me, 'Leave this crazy place, go to another kibbutz.' And I say to him, 'Where? In Givat Haim they have Arabian horses, breeding horses for the sport of kings on a kibbutz, if you can believe it. In Haon they have ninety members and eighty ostriches.' For this we come to Zion? To raise show horses for aristocrats and pluck ostrich feathers for showgirls?"

The Russian sat down and the others slapped his back and said things to him in Russian, obviously pleased with his performance.

Aaron Gottlieb stretched wearily to his feet. As he did so, a figure outside the south window of the kibbutz community hall caught his eye. It was Nabel. Looking a year older, unshaven, his gut hanging out over his belt, the scar a livid white across his tanned cheek. Nabel saw him look out and nodded to him.

The kibbutzniks knew Nabel and no one came up to ask him what he wanted, waiting outside the hall. Everyone knew he had served his country from the days with Menachim Begin against the British to more recent times with Ariel Sharon against the Arabs in Gaza. They also knew that he came for Aaron Gottlieb maybe once or twice a year and that Aaron went with him and would be gone often for weeks on end, to come back quiet and touchy, wanting to lose himself in hard work at the kibbutz. No, no one said anything or wanted to know anything about Nabel, and were happy when neither their sons nor daughters wanted to know either.

There were times when Nabel's unannounced appearance at the kibbutz had caused Aaron's heart to sink, and other times when his arrival was a clear trumpet note in his dusty, workaday existence. Today Nabel was all trumpet.

Aaron's resentment at the Russians had ebbed completely in the time it took him to get to his feet. "I think we should listen closely to these objections and decide on them. We all know that we raise alligators for their hides as we might raise sheep for their hides. It's true that at Givat Haim they raise Arabian horses which only rich people can buy. Why do they do this? Because they have the special conditions and skills to supply a special need which rewards them with a better income and allows the young people on the kibbutz to use their education from agricultural colleges. Some of the old people do not like to see the young with things they never had and do not now understand. We raise alligators because we have free water from Lake Kinneret and young people who want to learn new things. You know what a friend at Haon told me? One ostrich egg makes thirty omelets. But we are here to talk about" —he wiggled his ass and snapped his teeth in imitation of the Russian—"alligators in Zion. Before we had alligators, we depended mostly on turkeys—and they came from America, too, along with alligators, and I never heard anybody claim there was something non-Zionist about turkeys. I have to leave now and, as you know, I'll abide by any vote you take. I'm willing to go back to milking cows and feeding turkeys, if that's what you want. But ask yourself one question before you vote: Which is the outside world more likely to be willing to buy from us, alligator hides or more Israeli cheese and frozen kosher turkey meat?"

"Egypt?" Aaron said to Nabel.

"Egypt," Nabel confirmed.

"Why me?"

"You're the best available on short notice," Nabel informed him.

"You could find someone better if you had a little more time?"

Nabel twitched his mouth to one side, which was his gesture toward a smile.

They walked over the dusty ground toward one of the big ponds.

Nabel gazed at the alligators sunning themselves shoulder to shoulder along the bank, with the tips of their tails stretched back into the water. He said, "I remember when you people used to tend sheep in the hills like Arabs."

"Those were the good old days," Aaron observed. "Before my time."

Nabel looked once more at the alligators and shook his head in disgust. "What's wrong with ordinary farming?"

Aaron said with an edge to his voice, "Let's talk about something you *do* know about. What's in Egypt?"

"This one will be easy. Bloodless. A CIA agent with their embassy in Cairo has an American there with false ID who said to someone he was CIA. He's looking for an Egyptian nuclear physicist who's presently making an A-bomb for the meshugannah who seized power there. You should know that we've briefed the Americans on what is going on. The CIA and the Department of Defense agree with us. Their State Department doesn't. What the Agency man in Cairo wants to know is, who's this Yank working for? State? Defense? Some game the CIA is playing on its own agents? The Agency's men are stretched thin these days in Egypt, and besides, they want a non-American to approach him."

"A Lebanese banker?"

"The Egyptians believed you were that every other time we sent you in," Nabel said.

"You believe this story the Americans handed you?"

"I think so. Pritchett is the one I talked with and you can see him if you need to." When Aaron Gottlieb shook his head, Nabel went on. "I agree. No unnecessary contact. But Pritchett will be there at the American Embassy if you need backup. I don't have to remind you the Egyptians have closed down our embassy and I'm not going to put you in touch with any Mossad people in place there. I think Pritchett's only covering his ass—as the Americans say—by finding out who this operative is. And we're helping him because it's to our advantage when the Americans listen to their own intelligence agency on Egypt. Find out who he works for in Washington. Help him if you can. Nothing more."

"When do I go?"

Nabel pointed at his car and glanced at his watch. "Hurry. Get your things. We're late."

Dr. Mustafa Bakkush started nervously at the sound of steel-tipped boots on the stone floor behind him.

A private he had seen before in the Citadel came to a halt with a final rasp of his boots. The soldier nodded to Dr. Bakkush with disrespectful familiarity. "He wants to see you."

The soldier did not have to say who it was that wanted to see him. Mustafa asked, "Is something wrong?"

"They don't tell me."

"All right," Mustafa said. "Wait a few minutes and I'll be with you."

The private grinned. "I pick up a lot of people to come to President Hasan, and that includes cabinet ministers and generals, and they all drop everything and come at a run. You're the first who's ever had something more important to do than answer the president's summons without delay."

Mustafa stiffened in anger at this soldier's leering informality. "Leave now, if you must. You may inform the president that I had to complete an essential task before coming."

The private was awed. No one had ever dared say such a thing before. "I'll wait, sir."

"Then wait outside. You're distracting me."

"Yes, sir."

Ten minutes later, they left Bakkush's office in the Citadel and walked down a staircase instead of along the series of corridors that led to Hasan's quarters. Mustafa was surprised that the president was not already at the Citadel. He asked no questions, merely followed the soldier down the staircase which he knew led to a courtyard where Jeeps were parked. He guessed they were on their way to the presidential palace. This would be his first time there, and he wasn't looking forward to it. They climbed in a Jeep, and the driver wove through the Cairo traffic at a speed that suggested he was trying to make up for lost time. They were stopped at two checkpoints on the way into the palace and then had to pass sentries and metal detectors in the entranceway. Mustafa was searched twice, each time courteously. His driver was left behind in the palace lobby and Mustafa was led by three soldiers past many doorways, then up a staircase, then told to follow a long corridor alone and go through a door at its end. Before he reached the door at the end of the corridor, he heard shouts and laughs coming from behind it. The sound of laughter came as a relief to Mustafa, although it occurred to him that this indeed might be some truly diabolical scene. Certainly something was happening on the other side of that door. What had it to do with him? He tapped timidly on the heavy wood, realizing as he did so that they would be unable to hear him. He looked back and saw that his three-man military escort was still standing there watching him. One of the soldiers stabbed his finger forward several times, meaning for Mustafa to go through the door. He put his hand on the brass handle, turned it and pushed the door inward.

Mustafa Bakkush had never before seen any woman entirely naked, except his wife. And he had never seen her dancing without any clothes. To now see five naked women—beautiful women with large breasts that bounced as they moved, with narrow waists, swelling hips over smooth-skinned thighs, little black triangles at the base of their bellies, and inviting eyes heavily outlined—five naked women who all gave him alluring looks and gyrated their full, voluptuous bodies at his own thin delicate frame, made him wonder whether to cover his eyes or run back through the doorway. He did neither. He stood unmoving as a lizard trying to escape the eye of a hawk and he watched them as they came closer to him.

"Come in! Come in!" Ahmed Hasan boomed. His tall, spare body was naked also, and he sat on a big cushion next to a large hookah pipe.

Mustafa stepped forward. The five dancing women parted to let him through and then formed a circle to cavort obscenely around him. Mustafa felt dizzy and he could not feel the floor under his feet—though this might have been caused by the extra thick pile of the carpeting as much as his mental state.

"This is the famous scientist, Dr. Bakkush," Ahmed announced. "He has returned to us after being abroad. I think he may have picked up some corrupt Western customs. I feel sure he has a taste for Scotch. Someone get him a glass of whiskey."

Mustafa did not drink alcohol, even when he had been at social gatherings in Cambridge. He saw one of the president's bodyguards—this one fully dressed in combat fatigues, bush hat and jungle boots with submachine gun strapped over his shoulder—approach him with a bottle and a tumbler. Even Mustafa knew that whiskey wasn't sloshed into a big tumbler like beer, but he watched impassively as the youth emptied a third of the bottle into the glass. He put the tumbler to his mouth and tried to keep his face from puckering up at the smell and taste of the foul, burning liquid. The attention of Ahmed Hasan had already wandered elsewhere, perhaps out of disappointment at Mustafa's seeming lack of outrage or protest against what he was being subjected to. Mustafa had little doubt that Ahmed would get around to him again in good time.

Apart from the five dancing women, who to Mustafa's relief were now over on the other side of the huge room, everyone else present seemed to be Ahmed's bodyguards, including the two playing guitars. Three remained dressed and combat-ready; one of these had given him the whiskey. The rest were in various states of disarray, both mental and physical. Six of the bodyguards were women and they, like the men, were half disrobed or fully naked. Aside from himself and Ahmed, Mustafa decided that no one in the room was beyond his or her early twenties, and two of the female bodyguards looked to be fifteen or sixteen. Most were smoking marijuana and drinking from beer bottles. Unable to bear the reek of the straight whiskey in the tumbler, Mustafa put it on a side table. He loosened the knot in his necktie—then tightened it again immediately in case his action might be misinterpreted as a gesture that he too wanted to shuck his clothes. That would be going too far! In spite of the close atmosphere in the room, he intended to keep his jacket on. He even buttoned one button to show his determination.

He stood by himself, close to one wall, trying to make himself as inconspicuous as possible. None of them paid him any more attention. He gathered from the relaxed atmosphere that he had arrived shortly after some climactic stage in this orgy and that everyone was presently resting. Except, of course, the five crazy dancing girls, who were probably hired for the occasion. Mustafa considered that Ahmed had summoned him as some kind of butt for their jokes. He was pleased that, so far, he had not satisfied their expectations.

To Mustafa's alarm, one of the women bodyguards broke away from a group and cruised past him, giving him the eye. She was dressed only in a camouflage shirt, unbuttoned down the front, and held a joint in her right hand and a beer bottle in her left. Her long black hair tumbled to her shoulders, her sensuous mouth smiled at him and the brown tips of her titties peeped through the open army shirt front. After she had passed him once, she came by again. She was less than half his age and everything his strict upbringing had taught him to despise—yet he could see how a man other than himself might be attracted to her. She had soft feline movements and, yes, Mustafa had to admit, she had certain things about her which could appeal to him were he not a happily married man who disapproved of women like this. Mustafa was not able to keep his eyes off her, and he saw the knowing smile on her face as she came up to him. When she offered him her joint and he shook his head, she dropped it in the neck of the beer bottle and put that next to his whiskey glass on the side table. Then she placed her left hand on his right wrist.

When Mustafa tried to stop her taking off his necktie, she put pressure on his wrist which almost immobilized him. Then she relaxed her crippling grip. He moved in protest again when she unbuttoned his shirt, and he felt her fingers tighten on his wrist until he changed his mind. She peeled his shirt and jacket off him and pressed her bare breasts and belly against him, her thighs against his, then tried to insert the tip of her tongue between his lips. Mustafa was virtuous and would not allow her to invade the privacy of his mouth, but in spite of his strong will, he could not prevent his erection from forming. She felt it against her and gave him a triumphant smile as she reached between them with one hand and unzipped his fly.

Mustafa felt his belt being unbuckled and then his pants drop around his ankles. He tried to push her away from him with his left hand—and she used his own force against him to flip him on his back on the floor. She ripped down his jockey shorts, bobbed her mouth a few times over the head of his distended member. Then, still holding him almost immobile by her stranglehold on the nerves in his right wrist, she mounted him, slid his member deep inside her and rode him with powerful thrusts of her hips.

Mustafa, even in his least pious imaginings, had never dreamed Arab womanhood could ever have come to this.

Richard Dartley was pleasantly surprised by the Egyptians he met each day. They seemed to hold no hatred for him as an American, despite the almost constant diatribes against the United States over the government-controlled TV and newspapers. The ordinary people reminded him of people in the Soviet Union in the way they did not take seriously anything their political leaders said. Religion was another thing. Dartley took care to stay away from mosques and anywhere he might run into fanatics.

He was totally unaware that he had anything to

fear from the Egyptians. He knew nothing of Awad and Zaid. He assumed that Omar Zekri had sent the four men to Zamalek Island to lie in wait for him and that Omar was obeying Pritchett's orders. He had checked out of the Nile Hilton and was now staying in a small hotel in the New City, only a few blocks from where his weapons were stashed (he hoped). The place was shabby, none too clean, and badly run—so badly run, in fact, that the desk clerk had not bothered to demand his identification, which suited Dartley fine.

Believing that it was his fellow countrymen who had set the trap for him, Dartley set himself one rule for survival in Cairo: keep away from mullahs and Americans.

He had no idea he was the target of a manhunt led by Awad and Zaid, who combed the ancient monuments and museums for him, circulated his description at luxury hotels and expensive restaurants, and questioned car hire people and taxi drivers.

Dartley hid himself in the anarchy of the city streets. At first the crowds, noise and exhaust fumes bothered him. After a few days he hardly noticed the traffic-clogged streets and accepted that cars often ignored traffic lights, that pedestrians were responsible for their own safety and could not reasonably expect a driver to slow or swerve to avoid them. He too, like any Cairo resident, walked casually into the stream of cars, donkey carts and bicycles, dodged, ran and jumped, breathing the polluted air, half-deafened by the honking of car horns.

He practiced his rudimentary Arabic and learned many new words. He kept out of tourist spots and ate in quiet neighborhood restaurants. He knew enough to avoid the food offered by street vendors, because no matter how tempting and good it looked, an unacclimatized Western stomach could not handle the bacteria that came with it. So he picked out clean, quiet places and feasted in them with no ill effects. The food was not hot and spicy, as he had expected. Instead, it was rather bland. He ate kebab, beef or mutton chunks grilled on a skewer, served with a salad, pita bread and tahina dip. He also ate what seemed the two most popular dishes with Egyptians, fuul and kushari. Fuul was brown beans with occasional pieces of egg or meat, and kushari was a mixture of lentils, macaroni and rice in tomato sauce; at least that was what they looked and tasted like.

Not knowing that Egyptian government agents were searching for him made him take many of the wrong precautions. Besides, he was almost entering the lion's den by hanging around the Citadel so often. Awad and Zaid operated from the Citadel, sending out men to search for him, while he observed the Citadel to wait for Mustafa Bakkush. Dartley positively identified the Egyptian scientist and was putting a plan into operation when disaster struck.

One of Awad and Zaid's men decided to question Dartley. This did not alarm Dartley. He had been questioned on the street a number of times, as he had seen other foreigners, including other Americans, questioned briefly. On previous occasions he had shown his papers in the name of Thomas Lewis, employee of the International Maize and Wheat Improvement Center. The papers and some baksheesh soon overcame whatever doubts the policeman or government agent had about him. This time it was different.

The man was short, immaculately dressed in a cream colored, Western-style suit, with close cropped hair and a neatly trimmed mustache. He spoke English and showed Dartley his official ID. Dartley hardly glanced at it because he knew that Egypt had a tangle of security enforcement agencies, including nine different police forces of more than a quarter million men in a country that had very little crime.

Dartley showed him his papers in the name of Thomas Lewis. When the man in the cream colored suit saw the name, he suddenly became agitated. His mustache twitched as he struggled to calm himself. It was clear to Dartley that this man had been startled to find so easily what he was looking for, and that it was the name of Thomas Lewis rather than Dartley's appearance which had struck him so forcibly.

"You must come along with me," he said to Dartley, holding his passport and entry papers. "There are irregularities."

"Certainly," Dartley said agreeably. "But I suppose I should sign this before I go."

He reached for one of the papers from the man's hand and took the top off his pen.

Dartley hit him with the miniature blade of the Tekna Micro-Knife in the left eye. The razor-sharp steel punctured the eyeball, it popped, and the fluid inside ran down the man's cheek.

That was enough. Dartley had no need to butcher the man. He picked the passport and papers up from where the stricken Egyptian had dropped them as he staggered backward, clutching his head.

In a few moments Dartley was walking down the street unhurriedly, as if he'd had nothing to do with the man in the cream colored suit, who was now leaning unsteadily against a building with a palm clasped over one eye. But Dartley was out of luck. He had been seen by two men prepared to do something about it. They jumped in a little yellow Fiat and speeded after the American until they drew level with him. As the car stopped, Dartley saw a long-barreled revolver in one man's hand. He himself had no gun.

Dartley ran. The first bullet bit stucco out of a building wall above his head and whined off in a ricochet. Dartley used passersby as cover, trying to keep them between him and his pursuers. This didn't faze the gunman, who shot at him regardless of innocent bystanders, using the revolver's long barrel for accuracy in aim. In all, six bullets smashed into walls or windows in front of, behind and above the weaving, running American.

After the sixth shot, Dartley heard the roar of the little Fiat's engine as they closed the distance again between them and him. Only one was shooting. Right now he would be reloading as the other one drove. The Fiat screeched to a halt no more than twenty feet from him.

There was no place for Dartley to go except through a large gateway that led into a courtyard. He might be trapped in there or he might not—but it was his only alternative right now to dodging bullets at a few paces' range on an open sidewalk.

The gunman stepped out of the Fiat and raised the revolver's barrel at him. Before Dartley could reach the courtyard and before his pursuer had the gun leveled on him, someone in a gray business suit at the edge of the sidewalk shot the Egyptian. He slumped back against the Fiat and slid down into a sitting position on the road, his head nodded onto his chest, his big pistol lying now in a slack hand.

This new gunslinger sent three rapid shots through the open door of the Fiat, and the driver fell forward onto the steering wheel.

Dartley saw the tall man in the gray suit—he looked to be in his late twenties or early thirties and was not Egyptian—run around the front of the car, open the door on the driver's side, pull the dead man out and discard him on the street. He beckoned to Dartley.

A crowd was gathering about Dartley on the sidewalk. They looked frightened, but also unhappy at the sight of foreigners gunning down their fellow Egyptians. Dartley was not in a position to explain. He made for the car.

Chapter
6

"Have you contacted Mustafa Bakkush?" his rescuer in the gray suit asked Richard Dartley. These were the first words the man had spoken to him, apart from some comments about the traffic and the suggestion that they have a coffee.

"Bakkush?" Dartley said, apparently unfamiliar with this name.

The young man smiled. "From what I hear, you've been asking all over town for him. Let me introduce myself. I am Pierre Giraud, a Lebanese banker. Maronite Christian, I should add."

"A banker," Dartley said in open disbelief.

"In much the same way as you are a wheat expert."

That shut Dartley up. They had driven across Cairo and dumped the Fiat some distance from where they now sat at a cafe table. This man had been as careful as Dartley to wipe his prints from the car as they left it.

Dartley was already considering how best to kill

this man because he knew too much. It mattered nothing to Dartley that the man had in all probability saved his life. Dartley knew that this action had not been a heroic gesture, but the impersonal, calculated move of a trained professional. Dartley owed this man nothing. Especially not information.

The stranger probably sensed from Dartley's demeanor that it might be dangerous to tease him further with his mysterious knowledge. He said, "Pritchett said to help you."

"Pritchett is the one who hires these hitmen," Dartley snapped, acknowledging at least that he knew who Pritchett at the American Embassy was.

"Look, I'm Aaron Gottlieb, Israeli intelligence—Mossad. You've heard of us, I believe. Now you level with me."

"Savage. Paul Savage. CIA. Pleased to meet you."

"How come Pritchett doesn't know who you are?"

"I'm on a special job," Dartley said. "Don't want to stir up mud for the men posted here."

"Seems like you've raised quite a bit of mud already."

"Not my fault. That fool Pritchett hit on me first day I was here and stuck me with one of his Egyptian contacts named Omar Zekri. If it wasn't Pritchett who called out the hounds on me, then it had to be Zekri."

"Those two I killed back there, and the one you disabled further back on the street, are all government agents. I know the type."

"Which means that Pritchett's man Zekri is a double agent," Dartley said. "You might mention that to him when you tell him to stay out of my way."

"I will," Aaron Gottlieb agreed mildly. "You want help on Bakkush?"

"I work alone."

"It doesn't make sense for you to turn down help offered by an experienced man," Gottlieb pointed out. "Do you want to hear my background in Egypt?"

"It'll help pass the time," Dartley grunted, making it clear that that was all it would be. He knew that Gottlieb had not bought his story about being a CIA agent as easily as he pretended. The Israeli's strategy now would be to hang as close as he could to Dartley in order to find out what was going on. Dartley himself was reasonably sure that Gottlieb was a genuine Mossad agent—perhaps even a CIA agent. Either way, he didn't give a damn so long as the Israeli did not interfere or continue to ask questions which could not be answered.

"First, I think you should know about Israel's first intelligence operation in Egypt, back in 1962, when I was in elementary school. Nasser, who was the Egyptian president then, launched four rockets. Two of them had a range that could have reached Tel Aviv. As could be expected, the Israelis were worried, since Nasser had promised to drive the Zionists into the sea. When the Mossad discovered that ex-Nazi German scientists were developing these rockets in Egypt and were working on nuclear warheads for them, they had a strong suspicion in which direction the rockets would be aimed. Instead of going after the hardware or the Egyptians, the Mossad decided to concentrate on the German scientists. One bomb that arrived in the mail killed five people. There were other deaths and maimings from booby-trapped

devices. Threatening letters to the Germans promised more of the same. Their children were threatened, in Egypt, Germany and elsewhere. These
scientists and their families knew who was after
them, and that didn't give them much comfort either.
Most quit. With their departure, Nasser's rocket
program collapsed. There were a lot of complaints
about Israel in the world press, but no nuclear
missiles on Tel Aviv."

Dartley nodded noncommittally and sipped the
bitter black coffee from his tiny cup.

Gottlieb went on, "You may wonder what this has
to do with what's happening today. I think Ahmed
Hasan learned his lesson from what happened back
in 1962. This time he is seeing to it that it is the
Egyptian president who is applying the pressure on
the scientists." He told Dartley briefly how Bakkush
had been forced to return through his wife and
children being shipped in crates from London to
Cairo. "So that when you meet with Dr. Bakkush and
try to turn the screws on him, you will find he is
already under maximum pressure and has no more
give. It is the same with most of the other scientists
working on Hasan's nuclear project, so far as we
know. Apart from some inexperienced junior scientists who are enthusiastic because they are fools, all
the senior men have been bullied or blackmailed into
joining the project."

"You seem certain that Hasan has a nuclear bomb
in the works," Dartley observed.

Gottlieb laughed. "If that's all you want to verify,
your task will be easy. Is that all you need to know?"

"Just a few details," Dartley said, to keep Gottlieb

thinking that the bomb was the chief purpose of his mission rather than the bomb's maker, Ahmed Hasan. "You were going to talk about your background here in Egypt."

"I speak Arabic fluently. I happened to learn it from someone brought up in Beirut, so that I speak it with Lebanese overtones, just as I speak English with American overtones. I also speak fluent French and spent two miserable years working in a bank. So here I am, a Lebanese Maronite Christian, who are bankers to the Arab world today, just as Jews were once bankers to medieval Christians. Needless to say, I am welcome in Egypt. Ironically, on previous visits, I have arranged actual loans for Egyptian businesses with Beirut banks through Mossad contacts."

"You risk this cover by openly telling me you're an Israeli agent?"

"You'd hardly speak to me about Bakkush if you thought I was a Lebanese banker, would you? I can help you. But you say you want to work alone. Very well. I like to do that where it's possible. For you, an American in Cairo, it's impossible. How can I help? First, I can find out who is hunting you. If it's at a high level, this information will cost very generous baksheesh. Can you spare five hundred dollars?"

Dartley peeled off five notes under the table and slipped them to him, well aware that by doing so he was accepting Aaron Gottlieb as an accomplice and possible back stabber. But Dartley knew he could not afford to turn down his help at this point. He decided to make a gesture toward him.

"Can you meet me tomorrow at noon?" He described a little cafe almost in the shelter of the

Citadel wall, only a few streets away from where the Egyptian agents had confronted him earlier.

Gottlieb raised his eyebrows. "I can't say I'd have chosen that area myself."

Dartley got to his feet and left an Egyptian pound on the table. "Don't be late."

The Israeli made no attempt to follow him.

Dartley was unshaven and wore a straw hat and dark sunglasses. He looked like a hungover tourist the morning after a big night in the fleshpots of Cairo. At least he looked different than he had the previous day, and the hat concealed his American-style, short-clipped hair. He carried no weapons.

He reached the cafe about ten minutes before noon, having taken a taxi within several hundred yards of it to cut down on the chance of another sidewalk incident. Gottlieb was already there, sitting before a coffee and leafing through an Arabic newspaper. Dartley ignored him, sat two tables away, ordered coffee and glanced through the *Cairo Press Review*, a government-controlled, English-language digest of newspaper articles, these days mostly devoted to abuse of the West and what was described as "the lair of the Devil," otherwise known as Washington, D.C.

At twelve precisely, Dr. Mustafa Bakkush entered the cafe and sat at a table near the two men. Dartley was amused at the startled look on Gottlieb's face, and it was clear that the Israeli agent knew who Bakkush was. The Egyptian scientist had hardly glanced at them and now ordered a coffee with an abstracted air. Then he sat staring out into space without touching it.

Dartley had observed before how the mullahs herded what looked to be a group of scientists and technicians several times a day out of the Citadel to a nearby mosque, presumably to point their heads toward Mecca and pray. Bakkush was adept at giving the group the slip before it reached the mosque and slipping into this cafe for a spell. Dartley could have spoken to him on the street, but saw no reason for not doing it in more comfort.

Dartley kept his voice low. "What process are you using?"

The Egyptian nervously twisted his head toward Dartley at the sound of English. "Pardon?"

Dartley wasted no time. "A while ago your wife and kids were put in big boxes. I'll chop 'em up and put 'em in cans if that's the way you want it."

"What do you wish to know?" the scientist asked in quiet desperation.

"What method are you using?"

"Plutonium."

Dartley had his answer. Ahmed Hasan was making a bomb and using French reactors to process the nuclear charge.

"Forget you ever talked to me," Dartley told him and left the cafe.

Gottlieb followed him out after a minute, got in a small gray Peugeot, and stopped to pick up Dartley farther down the street. "What now?"

"Nothing."

"That's it? You're ready to return to America?"

"Mission complete," Dartley confirmed.

*   *   *

Gottlieb and Pritchett sat on wooden chairs in a nearly bare, one-room apartment in an odorous Cairo slum. They could hardly hear each other with the noise from the street.

Gottlieb looked about him at the floorboards and unadorned green walls. "I didn't want to have to set up a meet with you, but I thought the information on your middleman, Omar Zekri, was worth our getting together. When will he get here?"

"In a few minutes."

After a pause Gottlieb asked, "How good is your source on the wheat expert?"

"Good. The best. Langley says he isn't one of ours."

"Have they any reason to make you want to think so?"

Pritchett shrugged. "Maybe they have. But if so, why tell me to track him down and okay my working together with you?"

"I admit it sounds like he's not CIA," Gottlieb conceded. "I'd place my bet on the Pentagon then."

"No. They'd have come clean with us. I tell you he's State Department. And it pisses me off that they send him in right under my nose and think I'm not going to notice."

Pritchett was genuinely mad about this, Gottlieb decided. In fact, the embassy CIA man seemed a great deal more upset about this mysterious, so-called wheat expert who went by the name of Thomas Lewis and claimed to be CIA than he was about the treachery and double dealings of Omar Zekri. Pritchett had surprised Gottlieb when he had suggested a meeting with him by calling him back right away on a secure line and telling him that the CIA had cleared their cooperation with the Mossad already. Pritchett had been waiting for his call. Gottlieb knew that if permission for them to work together had been granted, there was probably a coded message already waiting for him at his drop-off point. He would check tomorrow. In the meantime, he'd help any way he could.

"You checked all exit points?" Gottlieb asked.

"He certainly hasn't left Egypt under the name of Thomas Lewis. I wouldn't be doing all this if I didn't think he was staying on. Now that he knows the bomb is to be made with plutonium, his next move could be anything. Except go home, like he told you he was going to. By the way, I should add that your people have denied he's one of theirs."

Gottlieb grinned. "I was beginning to think of that possibility."

There was a rap on the door. Gottlieb pulled a ski mask over his face. As he went to the door, Pritchett wondered idly where in Egypt the Israeli had been able to obtain a ski mask.

Omar Zekri stood in the doorway with a nervous, ingratiating smile on his face. He shook Pritchett's hand with a soft, damp palm and tittered at the sight of the man wearing the ski mask. Pritchett looked out into the stairwell, then closed the door and bolted it. The American left the Egyptian to stand uneasily before the masked man sitting on a wooden chair in the bare room. He pulled the wooden shutters over the windows, which caused the street noise to lessen and the room to grow dim. Then he came back and sat in his wooden chair and stared at Zekri. The Egyptian looked about him. There was no third chair. He took a cigarette from his pack, then thought to offer the pack to the two seated men. They shook their heads, but said nothing. Omar touched the flame of his lighter to the cigarette tip and anxiously eyed his surroundings.

Pritchett spoke one word: "Talk."

"What about?" Omar flicked some ash from his cigarette and waited.

Pritchett climbed to his feet and went to a back corner of the room. He turned on the single faucet over a deep porcelain sink and plugged its drain with a wadded paper bag.

Omar moved toward the door.

"Come back!" Pritchett barked.

Omar stopped.

The man in the mask spoke for the first time. "We want to hear all your dealings. Everything you've been doing. Name everybody."

"Only Mr. Pritchett and the contacts he knows about," Omar said. "No one else."

Pritchett looked behind him. The big sink was nearly full. He nodded to Gottlieb.

The two men moved swiftly toward Zekri, seized him by the arms and dragged him to the sink. Pritchett forced his head under the surface of the water, which ran over the sides of the sink onto their shoes and the floorboards. Pritchett seemed to be counting to himself. After about a half minute, he let Omar raise his head, exhale and gasp air into his lungs before pressing his head under the water again for another half minute. The CIA man allowed Zekri to fill his lungs each time he raised his head and did not lengthen the periods during which his head was under water. All the same, it wasn't long before the Egyptian's gasps and rasping intake of air became louder and more desperate.

Then he vomited half-digested food onto the surface of the water. It splattered on all their pants legs. Pritchett displayed no anger or disgust as he calmly forced Omar's face into the floating vomit and down into the water beneath.

The next time up, Omar threw up clear water between hysterical sobs. Pritchett allowed him a few deep breaths before ducking him under once again.

This time Omar began to struggle wildly in their grip, heaving his shoulders from side to side and attempting to force his head up into the air. Pritchett let him struggle until he panicked.

Then he dragged the Egyptian's head out of the water for a little more than a second and splashed it back under as Omar was taking a breath.

A few seconds later, Pritchett nodded to Gottlieb, and they released the Egyptian. Omar lifted his head from beneath the surface and leaned against the sink for support as he upchucked water, wheezed from the water in his windpipe and lungs, tried to swallow huge mouthfuls of oxygen for his starving blood. He did not have to be told again to start talking. As soon as he was able to, he began chattering on at length about everything he knew.

The fact that the Egyptians were previewing and presumably altering military information from Omar's informants before he passed it on to the American Embassy was news to Pritchett and Gottlieb. They had been careful not to press Zekri for specific information or give him any opportunity to limit what he need tell them. Omar knew that if he held back anything they knew about, he was headed for the sink again—or maybe something worse.

He told them about Awad and Zaid, what they had done to Ali, how they had told him they would wait for the American on Zamalek Island.

"I want you to apologize to Thomas Lewis," Pritchett said.

"Where is he?"

"Find him."

Omar nodded. He was good at finding people in the vast mess of the city. "You want me to learn more about him?"

"If you can," Pritchett agreed. "The main thing is for you to locate him. Warn him about Awad and Zaid, but not about me."

The soaked Egyptian beamed with gratitude at this definitive sign he would not be killed. "I can do it," he said cheerfully.

"As for this Egyptian military censor," Pritchett continued, "pretend to go along with the arrangement. But before you take stuff for him to see, bring it to us first, then take it to him so he can change it, then bring it to us again as if we knew nothing."

Omar laughed and wrung water from his shirt. "That makes me a triple agent," he said with satisfaction.

Getting to Ahmed Hasan, president of Egypt, was going to be a bigger job than cornering Mustafa Bakkush. Although Richard Dartley had no particular plan in mind and had no knowledge of Hasan's movements—which he assumed would be deliberately made unpredictable for the president's safety— he was not feeling overwhelmed by the difficulties. Experience had taught him not to make too much of difficulties. In the first place, things never worked out as planned and unexpected opportunities usually cropped up, which if taken could change everything.

When Dartley had first started out as a professional assassin, he had been a meticulous planner down to the last detail. He still made detailed plans when he could, at the same time realizing he would only rarely be able to predict and plan an operation with blow-by-blow accuracy. The chance encounter, the unexpected coincidence, the lucky break or persistent bad luck, an unforeseeable event . . . in Dartley's experience these were the things which rendered any but the simplest plans into wishful thinking—daydreams.

But just as the unexpected usually upset a complex plan and made it useless, so too could unexpected events be relied on to make what looked nearly impossible happen. What it took was persistence and readiness to move at an instant's notice when the opportunity presented itself. From what Dartley saw of the chaos around him in Cairo, he guessed that Ahmed Hasan and his administration were hanging loose rather than buttoned down. Anything could happen here. And it probably did several times a day to Ahmed Hasan. Richard Dartley was determined to make himself one of those unexpected things that happened to Hasan. In the very near future.

He saw the president fairly often, since the country's leader seemed to rush back and forth from his presidential palace to the Citadel in a demented way at all hours. Dartley never saw him as a person because his guards and assistants stayed close to him when he traveled through the streets. The president was most vulnerable when he traveled in his yellow, two-seat Jaguar—there he had to be either the driver or the passenger. More often he simply piled into an army Jeep or Range Rover, or even a truck, along with everyone else. Occasionally he used a black Mercedes limo.

Whatever vehicle Hasan used, it was always preceded and followed by open Jeeps or closed Range Rovers, loaded with teenagers in camouflage battle fatigues. Some were pretty girls who somehow evaded the dress code for women that the mullahs were demanding against much resistance. Occasionally, one of the presidential guards fired his or her automatic rifle into the air to help clear a traffic jam. When the presidential cavalcade was underway, the sirens screamed, the flags fluttered and the drivers performed high-speed maneuvers through the city streets.

This setup was hardly an assassin's dream.

Dartley could now find his way around Cairo with ease. He kept to overcrowded thoroughfares, where he would be hard to spot in the throngs of people and crazy traffic. It wasn't hard to find these streets in Cairo. He avoided all the places that foreigners and tourists frequented. Each day he was stopped by police, usually in plainclothes, who asked to see his passport. This never happened less than three times a day, and on one day he was stopped eight times. He took to leaving a five-pound Egyptian note folded inside his passport. The note was always gone each time he got the passport back.

Dartley assumed that, like government agencies everywhere, the Egyptian police forces did not properly communicate with one another because of rivalries and so forth. While one group was hunting him, others were letting him slip through their fingers several times a day. He came to depend on such bureaucratic fumbling for his freedom.

In addition to interdepartmental foul-ups, the cop on the street often had no way of knowing the priorities of his superiors. The man on the street had his own realities and his own problems, which were usually very different from those of highly placed administrators. A man whose job consisted of watching for pickpockets and motor scooter thieves at the suqs, bazaars and marketplaces could not readily tell one foreigner from another. He was not about to mess with foreigners in the first place because they spelled trouble. Their consulates would complain about police brutality, dirty cells, lack of food, demands for bribes—there was no end to what foreigners thought they could complain about and raise hell to try to change things, sometimes bringing all sorts of unwelcome attention and pressure from superiors who pretended not to know what went on. A man who brought these kinds of things down on his colleagues through his mistake of an unwise arrest would be a man without friends. Why take the chance with these unknown foreigners? Let them be. Pickpockets and motor scooter thieves played by the rules.

So Dartley reckoned he had little to fear from regular cops on the street. Yet his trained eye kept watch for special squads. His run-ins before had not been with regular cops. These men were secret police or members of an intelligence group. They looked no more like cops than a CIA operative resembled a cop on a beat. All the same, they shared one thing with policemen everywhere in the world— the habit of always scanning their surroundings with watchful looks. Every cop and intelligence operative developed this habit unknown to himself. The really good ones were careful to conceal their watchfulness.

It was the watchfulness of two men on the street which attracted Dartley's attention to them. Most passersby gave a foreigner a look of frank curiosity, then lost interest. These two men each gave him a fast appraising look and then studiously avoided looking at him again. Danger. At first Dartley could not be sure they were together. They were walking toward him, one maybe ten paces ahead of the other. They both fixed him for an instant with the same piercing look, followed by studied indifference as they passed by.

Dartley walked on. He knew that if he looked behind him now, he would see that both of them had reversed direction and were following him. But to look back at them would be to acknowledge their presence and invite arrest. Were they following him? Or was he becoming paranoid? Paranoia was a risk for everyone in his line of work. While paranoia was taking suspicions too far, a hitman who did not take his suspicions far enough would not survive long.

Were they following him? He turned into a narrow side street and followed it across several major streets intersecting with it, walking purposefully but unhurriedly and never looking behind him. Three hookers stood in a doorway. As he neared them, they twisted their hips, batted their eyes and said hello in English.

Dartley pointed at the prettiest one, said, "You," and pushed her in the door ahead of him. Surprised at his sudden response, the two left behind made loud remarks in Arabic, which made the girl he was with giggle. Dammit, Dartley thought, I should have taken all three of them.

He pushed the woman out of his way in the dark, smelly hallway and ran up a flight of stairs to a window looking out on the front. He waited and watched, ignoring the woman's demands for money. She grew curious, quieted down and watched also.

Dartley wasn't getting paranoid. His two tails had worried looks on their faces, looking this way and that, alternately hurrying and slowing down. They were on opposite sides of the narrow street, on sidewalks so narrow they had to step off when they met someone else. Occasional cars shot by at sixty miles per hour, grazing the pedestrians' shoulders in typical Cairo style.

He saw the two women in the doorway withdraw inside. They too knew cops when they saw them, and the law had been hard on female prostitutes since the Light of Islam mullahs had gained power. Dartley had read about how some mullahs were demanding that they be stoned to death.

The men stopped outside the door. The near one beckoned the women out. They reluctantly obeyed. Dartley watched the man's mouth moving as he spoke to the women and he saw the nodding of their heads. One pointed farther along the street, and the two men moved on fast.

The woman next to him giggled. Dartley sent her downstairs with a twenty-pound note for each of them, knowing that it wasn't him they wished to protect, but their colleague, yet figuring that a bit of generosity hurt no man.

As he waited for her to return, he measured his own reactions to the incident. He felt cold and rational. If the women had given him away, he would either have escaped or walked away after having left both men dead. He was not sure how he would have killed them, but he was calmly convinced he could have done so if necessary. Dartley was pleased with his own attitude. Any man could psyche himself into thinking he was ready to handle any situation; Dartley knew that it took an actual confrontation for the truth to out. Pressure was the only test. Any wimp could feel he was a hotshot when there was no threat on the horizon.

She was with him again, demanding money. Dartley couldn't follow her backstreet Arabic, but she made it very clear that if her two friends got twenty pounds each for not having to move their asses, she expected considerably more if he hoped that she would move hers.

"May Allah chop off the hands of all those who help the evil foreigners!" Ahmed Hasan shouted in a rage.

Everyone grew quiet in the room at the presidential palace.

"The mullahs are right—a tide of evil sweeps

through our country!" Hasan shouted, beginning to stride up and down now, his hands clasped behind his back, wearing a khaki military uniform with all his decorations. "The bringers of this scourge upon Egypt must be rooted out. Painfully! They must atone for what they have done with their blood!"

The people in the room tried not to move and listened urgently for a clue about who or what the president was condemning.

Hasan saw no sign of their puzzlement. He saw the evil right before his face, everywhere he looked, weakening, corrupting, undermining . . . He went on shouting, and they listened. His eyes blazed and his pace quickened as he thought about his enemies, the ones who could not be permitted to exist a day longer in Egypt.

When he ran out of steam, he sat beside a water pipe and lit the hashish in its bowl. He inhaled the tranquilizing smoke deeply and its sweet smell spread through the room.

As yet no one had figured out what he had been ranting about. They gave him surreptitious looks now to see whether his mood would improve while he smoked the dope.

Their glances irritated Ahmed Hasan. He cursed them silently for always watching him, for being weak and fearful, too timid to stand up to him. That was what he needed—someone he could talk to, have reasonable discussions with, use as a sounding board for his ideas instead of all these cringing toadies who timidly said whatever their tiny brains calculated he wanted to hear. Either they were like that or they were gun-waving maniacs who had trouble understanding anything longer than one-word commands. Here he was, a great Arab leader, perhaps the most important Arab of this century, surrounded by cringers and maniacs. Allah, grant him patience . . .

Along with the cringers and maniacs came spies. Everywhere! These enemies of Islam insinuated themselves close to him and his government ministers, watched, listened to everything, then reported back to their foreign masters. These dogs should be skinned alive. He had already ordered the ears, nose and tongue cut from some of them, intending to set them loose on the streets as a warning to others. However, they all died on him before he could turn them out. A pity. He would try again, with medical surgeons next time.

Meanwhile, an American devil was wandering the city streets. This monster had killed four loyal Egyptians on Zamalek Island and put out the eye of another. A second foreigner with him had killed two more government agents. Hasan had sent a strongly worded note of protest to the American Embassy, and they, of course, had denied all knowledge of this wrongdoing. So long as they went on sheltering Mubarak and other ministers of the overthrown government, they were his enemies. Those who were not his friends were his enemies. They sent spies. Everywhere . . . Would Reagan bomb him if he stormed the embassy? Yes. It was unfortunate, but that was the clear answer. If he broke off diplomatic relations with the Americans, they would almost certainly seize the Suez Canal with active European support. Better to live on with them as one would with a thorn in one's flesh, yet ready always for a chance to pluck it out.

But he did not have to live on with the traitorous dogs his men had captured in the act of betraying the Islamic revolution. And he would not!

Hasan jumped to his feet and began pacing again. The murmur of conversation in the room which had gradually risen now died away again. They kept an eye on Ahmed Hasan.

The president was beyond being annoyed by such trivialities at this point. He had decided to take action! He snapped his fingers and pointed to a door. At this signal, his armed bodyguards in their battle fatigues peeled off walls, grew out of corners, clustered around him, and suddenly moved with him like a small swarm of angry hornets out of the room.

A military officer in the room phoned the Citadel. "He's on his way." He smiled when he heard the groan from the other end of the line. He replaced the receiver and joined a group in the room, which now was filled with conversation and laughter.

Ahmed Hasan jumped from one of the Range Rovers that came to a stop in an interior courtyard of the Citadel. He and his bodyguards stormed through a stone archway into one of the buildings. Some plumbers working on a pipe in the hallway squeezed against the wall to let them by.

Hasan stopped and grabbed a ten-pound monkey wrench from the plumbers' tool box.

"Where are the traitors?" he shouted at the desk sergeant. "Take me to the traitors!"

The frightened sergeant dithered for a moment,

not daring to ask the president who he meant. He grabbed a bunch of keys and left his desk, with the president and his guards right behind him. The sergeant unlocked a steel door and pointed at four men behind the bars of the first cell they came to. The four were wan and emaciated, their muscles withered from malnutrition and extended lack of activity, their skull and arm bones revealing the skeleton beneath the skin.

The president gestured toward the lock on the barred door. The sergeant fumbled, found the key, turned it in the lock, and pulled open the door.

Hasan rushed in with the heavy wrench raised in his right hand.

"Traitors! Hand servants of foreigners! Dogs! Spies!" the president shouted.

He staved in the top of the head of a squatting prisoner with a single blow of the wrench.

The three other prisoners jumped to their bare feet and scampered around the cell in their rags as the uniformed president chased them. The sergeant slammed shut the barred door.

Hasan brought one man down with a wild blow that caught him on the back. Before the man could rise, Hasan beat him to death in a frenzy of blows while screaming about the Devil.

The two surviving prisoners watched, cowering against a wall and whimpering for mercy.

A female guard asked the sergeant, "What did these four prisoners do?"

The sergeant looked at her for a moment to see if she was serious. He shrugged.

Ahmed Hasan rushed at the two prisoners, sending them both to the floor with a few blows of the reddened wrench. He beat each of them in a series of dull thuds until their bruised and bleeding bodies stopped moving and they lay inert as sacks of wet clay at his feet.

He threw the wrench across the cell and made for the door. The sergeant held it open for him. A female bodyguard handed him a large white handkerchief, which he used to wipe the blood from his hands and arms

She pointed to blood spatters on his pants. "They've ruined your uniform."

"No," Hasan declaimed. "Any loyal Egyptian should be proud to wear a traitor's blood upon his clothes."

Chapter
7

Dr. Mustafa Bakkush did not dodge away from the prayer group for coffee anymore. He had not said a word about being waylaid by the American in the cafe, fearing that, sooner or later, Hasan would make him pay for his betrayal with his blood if he ever came to know of it. There was safety in numbers, and Mustafa now liked to bury himself in the midst of the group of engineers, scientists and other technicians that was ushered from the Citadel to the mosque by the mullahs. On one occasion, while the others were prostrating themselves on the mosque tiles, a mullah Mustafa had never seen before clasped him by the arm and led him away from the prayer area. He took him to a large room with a vaulted stone ceiling and decorative tile walls. The floor was covered with a magnificent thick carpet. There was no furniture. The mullah pointed to the carpet and Mustafa sat, tucking his stockinged feet beneath him. The mullah left without ever having spoken a word to him. Mustafa waited.

Then two mullahs, whom Mustafa had seen before, entered the room and sat near him on the carpet. They all exchanged the polite pleasantries customary for Arabs before a serious word was spoken. Mustafa had seen these two when he had explained nuclear technology to President Hasan and the mullahs at the Citadel. One had a huge white beard. He remembered this man's striking appearance, although he had left the meeting before this mullah accused the president of playing with the Devil by depending on advanced Western technology.

Mustafa remembered the second mullah as the hawk-faced desert warrior with a glistening black, pointed beard who had stared unblinkingly at him with dark, contemptuous eyes. Mustafa had also left the meeting before this mullah had forced the president to set up a terrorist training camp in exchange for his not opposing Hasan's nuclear program.

The desert warrior said, "What progress are you making on the bomb?"

Mustafa tried to be vague. "All goes well, in sha 'allah."

"You blaspheme by suggesting that Allah might wish us to mire ourselves in the Devil's plan to destroy the world."

"That was not my intention," Mustafa said firmly, determined to avoid matters of religion with these two fanatics.

"We are opposed to Ahmed Hasan's plan for an Egyptian atom bomb and we make no secret of our opposition," the one with the white beard said, bringing them back to the matter at hand. "You will therefore realize that we do not view your role in all this very kindly."

Mustafa said nothing.

The white beard continued, "You might have excused yourself by saying you are not here of your own free will. We have heard about how your family... arrived at Cairo airport before you made your decision to come. We sympathize with your position."

The desert warrior mellowed a little and added his piece. "We have not brought you here to abuse you."

Mustafa waited in silence.

The white beard picked up the conversation again. "There are zealots who wish to harm you because they feel you alone can achieve this bomb for Hasan."

Mustafa suddenly got the uncomfortable feeling that the desert warrior was the main zealot that the white beard was talking about. Maybe they were doing what the Americans called a "good cop-bad cop" routine on him. Mustafa was a devoted reader of detective novels. He kept his mouth shut.

"I myself have pointed out to them that personal harm to you would merely delay the project, not halt it," the white beard said.

"Killing me wouldn't even delay it," Mustafa explained quickly. "All the basic processes are already set up and some are even in production. The president would have adequate time to find a replacement for me for the final steps in arming the weapon." Mustafa was making it sound easier for Hasan than it really would be, hoping this was being taken in by the desert warrior. "I am not a vulnerable point in the chain of production."

The pointed black beard glistened and the hawk's eyes bored into him. "What then is the vulnerable point?"

"There are more than one," Mustafa said, turning on them suddenly with the defiance they had seen him display to the president. "The vulnerable points vary with your ability and willingness to act. For the French they are different from those for the Americans."

"We are mullahs," the desert warrior said dryly.

"Simple," Mustafa said airily. "France supplies Egypt because of oil. Egypt does not have the oil resources to pressure France. Who then is Egypt's ally in pressuring France for an Islamic bomb? If you could persuade them to withhold their support, France would laugh at Hasan's demands."

Though no names were mentioned, all understood that Mustafa was talking about Iran. The cheap oil on long-term contracts being given to France was all from Iran. It was commonly rumored at high levels in the Citadel that Hasan had promised Iran two bombs for use on Israel, but refused them one for Iraq. It was even rumored that King Hussein of Jordan was deeply concerned, since his country was next to Israel and could expect to be ravished by nuclear fallout. Hasan had questioned Mustafa closely on fallout patterns under conditions of a moderate east wind.

Mustafa had taken the bull by the horns by saying that any bomb dropped on Israel in an east wind would deposit fallout on Egypt's second largest city of Alexandria. A bomb dropped in a west wind would affect Jordan's capital, Amman. In a south wind, the coastal cities of Lebanon and Syria would be affected, and in a north wind it would be the Egyptian and Saudi coasts of the Gulf of Aqaba and probably the Red Sea coasts also. Mustafa had added that, besides this, wind patterns and directions were unpredictable and changed with altitude, so that fallout could in reality occur in any direction.

This slowed Ahmed Hasan until someone told him about small bombs with low radioactive yields. Use four small ones instead of one big one. This approach had the added advantage, from Hasan's point of view, that even if they brought down one plane, there were still three more on the way. Mustafa was now working on small bombs, which greatly increased the technical problems and delayed the delivery schedule.

Mustafa had now begun to hope that a change might occur in Hasan's unstable regime before he would be called upon to complete a workable nuclear weapon. All he had to do was keep quiet and pretend that all was going well—and hope that Ahmed would destroy himself before he gained the capacity to destroy millions of others. But Mustafa had no intention of explaining this to these two mullahs, who would probably misunderstand what he was saying and wildly misquote him, with dire consequences for Mustafa himself.

When Mustafa hinted to the two mullahs that if they wanted to stop Hasan their best way was to stop Iran, they were stung by his words. Iran was controlled by mullahs. What could be easier for them?

The white beard answered him. "The Persians are not Arabs. They share Islam with us and so we are bound together under Allah. Remember too that they are Shiites and we are Sunnis. These Persians consider Ahmed Hasan's plans to be in their interest. What do they care if the Mediterranean is devastated by nuclear weapons? Not at all."

Mustafa decided to take a chance on these two mullahs. He had to, since the desert warrior was likely to order him killed on the offchance that it might delay the program in spite of what Mustafa claimed.

"A working nuclear device is still in the future," he said with insolent confidence to the two mullahs. "I will warn you well in advance of the time these bombs become a physical reality. Until that time, all you hear is merely empty words. In sha 'allah"—this time he very deliberately repeated the phrase that meant God willing—"that time will never come while we three are here to prevent it."

The mullahs nodded, smiled, touched his arm and left the room in that slow way they had of moving, which showed their dignity and power.

Fuck them all, Mustafa thought, I wish I were back with my wife and kids in the cold English rain.

Jacques Laforque left his crumpled trenchcoat in his room at the Hotel des Roses on Talaat Harb Street—he would not be needing it in the mild Cairo autumn. The hotel was modest but pleasant. He always stayed there on his frequent trips to the city, which he supposed made things a little easier for his opposite numbers in Egyptian intelligence. They didn't seem to care and had ignored him for years. Never flattering for an intelligence operative, yet a fact of life for most. You got classified as middle level, and no one these days could afford continued surveillance on all the attachés, visiting businessmen and tourists who fitted into this category. It was because of the French government's tight purse strings that he stayed at the Hotel des Roses instead of the Nile Hilton, the Marriot Hotel or one of the other expensive places.

Paul Savage, the man Richard Dartley had sent instead of himself, had cabled his coded message to Paris: Hasan was building a bomb; Savage would now kill Hasan. Everything was going as agreed. Which was enough to make Laforque's Paris superiors nervous. They didn't like this lone operator out in the field with no strings attached for them to pull. No, no, they had no change of mind, they were pleased with how things were going. But... if Laforque would not mind... they would feel reassured if he would go to Cairo himself just to make sure everything was in place. Yes, they realized that Laforque had no prearranged way to contact this American Paul Savage—which they regarded as a serious weakness in the plan, as Laforque conceded—but even though Laforque did not know how to find him, they felt sure that a man with Laforque's talent and resources would discover a way... How could he refuse?

Laforque had a simple way to locate Savage all right. He would pay Omar Zekri to find him. Omar knew the name of every rat in the sewers.

The Frenchman found Omar at one of his usual places, where he tried to be on time every day so that his numerous informants and contacts could trade with him on a regular basis, and besides all that there was his "ancient artifact" business aimed at the tourists. Omar was a constantly active man. There were rumors he had a Swiss bank account. Others said he spent everything in wild flings.

"I am looking for an American," Laforque told Omar. "His name is Paul Savage, or so he says." He went on to describe Richard Dartley in detail. "Look for him around the nuclear technicians at the Citadel when they make their frequent trips in from the desert." He passed a wad of Egyptian bills to Omar. "You'll get the same amount again when you put me in touch with him. You know where to find me—at the Hotel des Roses."

Omar said, "The American calls himself Thomas Lewis here. I know him, but I can't say where he is right now or even if he's in the city. I'll put out word."

Laforque nodded and went away, satisfied with himself for knowing who to see in a matter like this.

Zekri was even more satisfied with himself. The Egyptian government wanted this American. So did Pritchett and the CIA. And along with Pritchett, a masked man who spoke Arabic with a Lebanese Christian accent. The Lebanese Christian spoke French. And now Laforque from government intelligence in Paris. Omar could not see anything that made sense there. Then there was Laforque's remark about nuclear technicians around the Citadel, although he did not mention Dr. Mustafa Bakkush by name. Omar decided quickly not to waste time trying to unravel the puzzle. He'd sell what he could about each one to the others and try to keep them all scrambling after one another while they improved his cash flow situation. He phoned Awad and Zaid.

They picked Omar up in their black van an hour later. To Omar's surprise, they did not balk at his demand for two hundred pounds. Zaid drove. Omar sat between them and told them about Pritchett and the masked Lebanese Christian, and about Laforque and France's interest in this American. Omar could sense that this came as a total surprise to them.

"Anything else?" Awad asked.

"That's it," Omar answered.

Awad grabbed him by the back of his jacket collar, yanked him off the bench seat, and threw him against the vehicle's firewall at his feet. Omar began to grovel and Awad's shoe descended on his neck.

Awad pressed the side of Omar's face down on the metal floor and held it there with his foot while Zaid bounced the van into potholes and over bumps as fast as he could go in the traffic.

No one said a word.

After a few minutes of this, Omar's hand raised up with the two hundred pounds they had given him. Awad took it and lifted his foot from Omar's neck.

"You whore's scum," Awad said, "we pay you every day by letting you live."

Awad slid back the side door and kicked Omar out of the slowly moving van onto the roadway in front of a small Renault, which screeched to a stop inches away from the man cowering on the asphalt.

Richard Dartley saw clearly that things were not going to work out for him if Ahmed Hasan simply continued to shuttle back and forth under armed guard between the presidential palace and the Citadel. Hasan took a dozen routes in random order, and Dartley never knew whether he would be in a Jaguar, in a crowded Range Rover or Jeep or invisible inside a military truck. The presidential palace was heavily guarded and the Citadel was literally a high-walled fortress. So long as the president kept to this way of life, he would be safe from Richard Dartley. But only so long as he kept doing what he was doing. Dartley could wait . . .

Dartley was sitting in a cafe after his morning walk, taking refuge from the crowds, leaking sewage pipes, traffic jams and construction sites. He was reading the daily English-language newspaper, *The Egyptian Gazette*, which was mostly a guide to movies, shows, fancy restaurants and late-night places, all of which Dartley was careful to avoid. One news item struck him forcibly. President Ahmed Hasan was about to pay a short state visit to King Hussein of Jordan. Hasan would spend the first day in the capital, Amman, and the second day at the Red Sea resort of Aqaba, from where he would fly back to Cairo that night. At last Ahmed Hasan might be where Dartley could get at him.

At first Dartley planned the hit for Cairo. The airport would be no good, because an airport is designed with no-go areas and security in mind and thus is easy to seal off. Even if Dartley infiltrated to make the hit, he would never get out alive. Hasan's armored cavalcade to and from the airport would only turn out to be a variant of the one he used every day, and he would be safe in that too, since Dartley could not tell which route he would take. Even if he could, laying a mine or radio-activated bomb or setting up an ambush would be extremely difficult to do unobserved in the teeming hordes of the city.

The president would travel by special plane. Perhaps Dartley could bring the aircraft down if the arms dealer Yahya Waheed could get him a Redeye or Stinger antiaircraft guided missile and launcher. Even if Waheed could supply him and even if Dartley was able to position himself by the fact that the aircraft would take off into the wind direction, he would still have to move around crowded Cairo with a four- or five-foot-long missile under his arm.

Jordan might be good, if Dartley could get there undetected. The Jordanians would have ultra-tight security, but at least they wouldn't be looking for someone of his description, like the Cairo secret police were. The capital city of Amman was not the place to go. Everything would be well organized there. Things might be looser in a resort town.

How could he get there? He could try disguise and go by commercial airliner from Cairo to Amman. An American doing this at any other time might not arouse suspicion. An American doing it now, to coincide with Ahmed Hasan's visit to Jordan, would be carefully checked out. An overland journey by bus or car had to clear military checkpoints in the Sinai and enter and leave the southern tip of Israel. He had almost settled on taking a bus to Suez and an Egyptian Navigation Company ship from there for a nine-hour voyage to Aqaba when he remembered Aaron Gottlieb. Surely the Israelis would be pleased to get rid of Hasan. He would level with Gottlieb and see what suggestions he came up with.

Dartley had assured Gottlieb at their last meeting that his mission was complete and that he was leaving Egypt right away. Gottlieb's response had been to give him a phone number to call if he needed further help. Perhaps Gottlieb had already returned to Israel.

It was while Dartley was telephoning that Omar Zekri spotted him. This hadn't taken Omar long to do. He had said to himself, where would a Westerner consider the best places to hide in the city? The man whom Omar knew as Thomas Lewis was tanned and he wore an Egyptian cotton suit. He certainly did not look like an Egyptian, but he no longer stuck out in a crowd as a newly arrived American. That was good—Omar was all for this man retaining his freedom while he sold his whereabouts to the interested parties.

First Omar would call Laforque, since he had paid the most money. He would give Laforque an hour and then phone Pritchett. Then he would speak to both these parties to see if they wished to make further investments in Thomas Lewis. If they did, good. If not, Omar would phone Awad and Zaid and they could dispose of him as they saw fit.

Dartley was having trouble with the phone. At last he got through but could hardly hear the person at the other end because of shouting and what sounded like plates crashing together.

"I want to speak to the boss's nephew," Dartley shouted in his rudimentary Arabic.

"Maalesh" came the agreed upon reply. "Don't bother."

The line went dead. Dartley was now to proceed

to a cafe in the New City and wait there, according to Gottlieb's instructions. He took his time getting there, and when he did he didn't sit in the cafe as arranged, but in one across the street which gave him a view of it without being observed. Aaron Gottlieb was already at a table here.

They laughed at how this coincidence in the way their minds worked had thrown them together, instead of achieving each one's intention of observing the other carefully before approaching him.

Omar Zekri phoned Jacques Laforque and told him to hurry.

Dartley—or Thomas Lewis, as he was known to Gottlieb—wasted no time in presenting his case. Would the Israelis help?

"Who the hell are you working for? Don't tell me CIA."

"A private foundation."

Gottlieb stared him in the eyes. "You'll have to do better than that."

"I can't. Tell your people whatever they want to hear. All I want is a plane into the place. A plane out would be nice also, but not essential. Get me in, that's my minimum demand."

"No problem if the people at home agree to it," Gottlieb said. "This will be top priority, so I will have an answer for you quickly. The only delay will be the coding and intermediary involved, since I can't send messages direct."

"Understood. Here then, tomorrow at noon?"

"Make it eleven tonight," Gottlieb said.

"You Israelis are very efficient at this game."

"We try harder."

* * *

Dartley waited five minutes after Gottlieb had gone, then paid for their coffees and stood up to go. Before he could leave, Omar Zekri came barreling into the cafe.

"Mr. Lewis, what a pleasant surprise. Sit down. You are my guest." He switched to Arabic to order more coffee from the waiter.

Dartley reluctantly resumed his seat. He was already familiar with the Egyptian people's wonderful sense of hospitality, and it would have almost amounted to an insult if he had refused Omar's offer. Not that Dartley minded insulting Omar, but he was curious to know if their meeting like this was merely a coincidence, which he found hard to believe. If it was not, he would never find out Omar's purpose by refusing his hospitality, and Omar had enough deviousness and knowledge of Cairo to make him a dangerous man to ignore.

It soon became obvious to Dartley that Omar was trying to keep him where he was with some purpose in mind.

"Sit closer to me," Dartley said to him.

Omar rolled his eyes. "Mr. Lewis, what a pleasure."

"Even closer," Dartley said. Omar shifted his chair again so that they were shoulder to shoulder at the little cafe table. Dartley said, "That's fine. I just need you this close to be sure of killing you first as soon as I see trouble walk in that door."

Omar tensed. "I don't say it's trouble, but I will tell you, just in case it is. A French gentleman wishes to speak with you. He paid me to find you."

"Name?"

"Laforque."

The idiot, Dartley thought. At one time Laforque wants to keep France's name out of this at all costs, then he gives his whole game away by contacting Cairo's best known information broker and stool pigeon.

"Stay where you are at this table," Dartley told Omar. "When Laforque comes in, tell him to sit at that table in the corner. You remain here after I join him and stay on here after I leave. If you move, send the waiter somewhere, or try to make a phone call, I will kill you. Do you understand?"

"Yes," Omar said. "There's no need for any of this—"

"I'll be watching."

Dartley left the cafe and stood looking in a store window where he could see Omar and Omar could see him. The Egyptian had set him up once before, on Zamalek Island, and he was not going to do it again.

In a short while Dartley saw Laforque walk along the opposite side of the street and try to peer into the interior of the cafe. Laforque passed by, then crossed the street and walked a couple of feet behind Dartley's back without noticing him until the very last moment.

They shook hands.

"Let's take a taxi," Dartley said, wishing to leave Omar and anything else the wily Egyptian might have plotted far behind him.

They left the cab and walked in the crowded streets without saying much until Dartley lost his patience.

"Is it off or on?" he asked.

"Everything's still go," Laforque said to the man he knew as Paul Savage. "My superiors grow nervous easily. They asked me to say hello to you. That's all."

"So you use Cairo's greatest gossipmonger to contact me."

Laforque shrugged. "A mistake perhaps. I had no other way."

"I'm thinking of an attempt on Hasan when he's in Aqaba."

Laforque thought about that for a moment. "Why not? It might work very well. How will you arrange things from here?"

"I hope the Israelis will help me fly in."

"The Israelis! Do they know about us French being involved in this?"

"Not unless Omar Zekri tells them," Dartley snapped back.

"The Israelis will fit in nicely, but don't let them get too close to your operation or you'll find them using you for their own ends. I can see why they might want to help you, because if you escape clear they're going to be blamed for Hasan's assassination anyway. They might as well have a hand in it. They would prefer to be involved, I think, so as to have some control over anything this big happening so close to home. They'd see Israeli involvement in this as a warning to other Arab states. No doubt the Arabs would too."

"Nothing is fixed yet," Dartley cautioned.

"What do you have on the ground at the other end?"

"Nothing."

"The Hotel Jarnac, on the beach at Aqaba, is

French-owned. Michelle Perret is manager there. I'll send word on. She will supply you with weapons and local information, whatever you need. But don't stay at the Jarnac. You can rely on Michelle more than you can on your Israeli friends."

Dartley wondered if he would have been offered French help if he had not raised the possibility of the Israelis offering theirs.

The Lear jet took off from Cairo airport. Gottlieb had arranged the charter of the plane from the Jordanian company Arab Wings, based in Amman, and it flew to Cairo to pick them up. Dartley had paid for the plane by phone through a Swiss bank account. They watched the fertile valley of the Nile slip away beneath them to be replaced by the sandy wastes between Cairo and the Gulf of Suez.

The British pilot was courteous, asked no questions and busied himself with his instruments and navigation.

"You'll see the Gulf of Suez beneath us very soon, gentlemen," the pilot told them. "After that we cross the Sinai desert in an east by east-southeasterly direction, then swing south to give Israel's southern extremity wide clearance—the plane has Jordanian registration numbers and since this is a jet, we would be forced down by fighters and held for hours if we strayed over their territory. So we'll swing south and cross the Gulf of Aqaba, north of the Sinai town of Nuweiba, enter Saudi air space and then swing north to Jordan. Cairo to Aqaba in a straight line is about two hundred fifty ground miles, a little over three hundred miles by our route. Sit back and relax, gentlemen. You'll be there in no time."

Dartley sat back, but he did not relax. He looked through his new U.S. passport and press pass in the name of Fairbairn Draper, correspondent with Associated Press. Gottlieb supplied the documents, after Dartley supplied him with a photo. Gottlieb, also with a new name and now a U.S. citizen born in Chicago according to his passport, was credited as a photographer. Naturally they were coming to Aqaba to cover Ahmed Hasan's trip to the beach. They had been given no trouble at Cairo airport—where Dartley had a few moments of bad doubt—and expected none at Aqaba.

The Lear jet swooped down over crystalline blue water, and they could see the waterside strip of luxury hotels that made up the Jordanian resort of Aqaba almost next to the similar strip of hotels that made up the Israeli resort of Eilat.

The pilot said in an amused way, "In all their Arab-Israeli wars, not a shot was fired down here, not a single window broken. You'll see King Hussein's villa—it's almost right next to the Israeli border. Damn expensive place, Aqaba."

The tall white buildings shone in the sun between the brown hills and blue water. Big ships were anchored off a port area at the eastern end of the resort, and beyond the port a dazzling white beach stretched away toward Saudi Arabia.

The Egyptian president was due in Amman the next day and in Aqaba the day after that. He would arrive in Aqaba early in the morning and leave before nightfall.

While their plane taxied to the terminal after landing, Dartley told the pilot, "You're free until the day after tomorrow. That day we may leave at any time—as soon as we get our story and photos. So be here early and have the plane fueled and ready to go. We'll head for either Athens or Rome."

Dartley figured that in a place like Aqaba an American would be less conspicuous in a luxury hotel than in a budget place back from the beach. A newsman on an expense account didn't bother to compare prices. He registered as Fairbairn Draper at the Aquamarina Hotel and Club, with its waterfront dining and water sports. The place swarmed with Arab tourists, obviously having a hell of a time away from the mullahs and the baked desert.

He had no idea where Gottlieb took himself off to. They had arranged to meet the next day at the beach, and the Israeli gave him an emergency phone number before he left. Dartley liked to work alone. If he could, he would cut Gottlieb out of the operation from now on and handle it himself.

The Hotel Jarnac was farther along the beach, a smaller place than the Aquamarina, with French cuisine and European haughtiness. Dartley ordered a Martell cognac at the bar and asked for the manager rather than for Michelle Perret by name. A wimpy Frenchman introduced himself as the assistant manager and said that the manager was off-duty. Dartley said he'd come back. He had another cognac and then drifted out into the blazing heat.

He had only walked down the steps in front of the hotel when a porter caught up with him and handed him a folded slip of paper. Dartley opened it and read: Room 202. No signature. He tipped the porter a dinar and retraced his steps inside the hotel.

Room 202 was opposite the elevator. He knocked on the door.

It was opened by a tall, pretty woman with green eyes and straight black hair to her shoulders. She had full breasts and she thrust one thigh forward provocatively beneath her pink silk peignoir. "Mr. Draper?"

"Right."

"Come in." She stood to one side to let him in the room. "What is your first name?"

"Fairbairn."

"Middle initial?"

"I don't believe I was given one."

"You weren't," she said. "And I don't know who the hell thought up 'Fairbairn.' I'm Michelle. What was it you were drinking? Martell, wasn't it?"

She was letting him know she knew her stuff, not to try to take advantage of her because she was a pretty woman. Dartley had been thinking it would be mighty pleasurable to have her around. She spoke colloquial English with a strong French accent.

They touched glasses. "Success," she toasted him. "What will you need?"

"I don't know yet. I won't until I get some idea of what itinerary is planned."

Michelle said, "Hasan is due in Amman tomorrow morning. His plane will land at a military airport outside the capital. He'll review an honor guard there and be given a big motorcade with soldiers of the Arab Legion. He'll water an olive tree from a silver urn on the Martyr's Monument and then have a private lunch with King Hussein and Queen Noor. After that, more speeches and visits. Tomorrow night there will be a big state dinner and Hasan will stay at the Inter-Continental Hotel in Amman. The day after tomorrow he comes here by air in the morning. He will have lunch with the king—who will arrive separately by air also—on the king's yacht. Other than the fact that President Hasan departs for Cairo before dark, no one seems to know what he will be doing here before or after the lunch."

"Do you think you could nudge someone into inviting Hasan to some kind of ceremony here in Aqaba or close by? Like throwing stones at the Israeli border, for instance."

"I'll see what I can do."

She fixed them another two cognacs and once again touched glasses with him, this time in a silent toast with smiling eyes.

"Will you let me help?" she asked.

"I work alone," Dartley said brusquely. Then he softened his tone. "It's best I do it that way in case things go wrong. The fewer involved, the more workable the operation. If I can do it solo, I will. If I can't, I'll call on you. Thanks for your offer."

"Let me know," she said.

"I assume there's going to be some kind of ceremony on land, either before he goes to the yacht or after he comes back. That's when I'll take him. Not at the ceremony itself—that will be too well guarded. No, I'll take him when he's leaving his hotel to go there. Although he's not spending a night here in Aqaba, he'll have a hotel suite in order to send and receive messages from Cairo, a place for him to go to the john. He's very vain. I'm sure he'll change his uniform several times during the day. I'll take him there. Find out which hotel he'll be using."

"You'll need a rifle then," she said.

"Two. One with a telescopic sight, one without, both automatic. And two semi-automatic pistols, .45 or 9 mm. Also some anti-tank missiles and a launcher."

"To assassinate someone outside a hotel?"

"Why not? I want to be sure not to miss him."

She laughed. "I don't think we'll have any problem in getting you the weapons."

"I'll need two cars, one to use and one as a backup. Not stolen cars. Hire them legitimately under a false name and make them regular cars, nothing unusual or eyecatching."

"All right."

"I'll need a driver."

She shook her head. "I can't give you personnel. Practically anything else, but not personnel."

"I'll get my own," Dartley said, not particularly upset.

"Who?" she asked with curiosity.

"I have these little elves and goblins who do things for me."

"Elves? Goblins?" She said the words in her French accent, searching for their meaning in her memory. "Ah, yes, I understand. Fairies, no?"

"I hope not," Dartley said.

They talked and joked for a while. Once, when Michelle was getting something, she brushed Dartley with her right breast. As she turned to face him, his eyes automatically looked at that part of her body.

She smiled at him for having drawn such an easy response from him, and he smiled back at her, eager now for her body and determined to enjoy it.

She picked up on his excitement and flirted with him, stirring the fires of lust in him. Her body undulated gracefully beneath the silk peignoir, which parted occasionally to reveal a lace-trimmed, short nightgown underneath. Her long, suntanned thighs were bared for a tantalizing instant to his view, then disappeared again beneath the slippery folds of silk.

Dartley took her in his arms, kissed her full on the lips, and pushed his tongue deep into her mouth while his hands ran over the contours of her hips and squeezed the cheeks of her shapely ass. She responded willingly to his touches. He felt her large breasts swell in his palms beneath the silky material of her peignoir.

Dartley peeled the garment off her and then stripped the nightgown from her inviting flesh. She sank naked and quivering to the thick carpet on the floor. Dartley swiftly climbed out of his clothes and joined her on the soft, heavy carpet. His powerful hands stroked her delicate body, and the smooth feel of her skin inflamed his senses.

He ran his lips and tongue over her whole body, driving her into a frenzy of desire, so that she twisted and turned in hot lust beneath his masterful and tender caresses. At last she couldn't take it anymore and yelled at him to penetrate her and ease her desperate hunger. He slowly entered her and heard her moan with pleasure.

She was small and tight. As he rammed home his

member in her moist, welcoming sex, he felt the waves of sensation rippling through her flesh.

He drove up hard and fast and deep inside her, in swelling energy and surging excitement—and forgot completely for a time why he was here in this chic Arab resort on the Red Sea.

Chapter
8

Richard Dartley woke early in his room at the
Aquamarina Hotel. He had a full day ahead of him in
which he had nothing to do. Ahmed Hasan would
arrive in Amman this morning and spend the rest of
the day and tonight there. After leaving Michelle
Perret the previous afternoon, he had contacted Aaron
Gottlieb by phone and met him at the Tourist Information Center, housed in what had once been a royal
palace. The Israeli agreed to drive for him and they
planned a timetable. Their meeting was short, like
any two tourists casually exchanging tips and information. Then Dartley hired a scuba diving outfit at
the Aquamarina Club and swam among the vividly
hued corals and tropical fish of the almost freshwater-
clear Red Sea. That night he ate the Jordanian
specialty called mensef—roast lamb stuffed with rice,
highly spiced with cinnamon, sprinkled with pine
nuts and almonds, and served with makheedh, which
was yogurt combined with mutton fat. Dartley was

beginning to feel like it might be a few years before he ordered lamb again after this mission. He discovered that in Cairo he had been drinking Turkish coffee, which was thick and bitter. The true Arabic coffee was quite different in taste—thin and heavily flavored with cardamom seed. He slept well and woke before the October sun had risen high enough to send the temperature into the eighties.

He swam in the sea opposite the hotel, preferring the natural seawater to the chlorinated liquid in the hotel pool. During breakfast at the hotel, he understood enough of the news on the radio to hear it confirmed that the president of Egypt was expected in the capital today and in Aqaba tomorrow. Dartley would be here with a personal welcome for him. Meanwhile, he intended to put Hasan to the back of his mind for today and enjoy himself.

Lawrence of Arabia was one of Dartley's heroes— not the Peter O'Toole version of the movie, but the real man, who besides being a great soldier was the author of *The Seven Pillars of Wisdom*. Back in his one-room apartment over the barn at his uncle's farm, Dartley had spent many hours reading the works of famed military men. Some couldn't write their way out of a paper bag and made themselves sound pompously foolish or else very ordinary. Lawrence was a military genius and wrote like a genius. His descriptions of desert warfare during World War I could make a reader feel that he was actually out on the sandy wastes, along with fierce nomadic tribesmen, riding to attack at dawn—on camels, naturally.

Aqaba had been the scene of one of T. E. Lawrence's

famous ventures. This region was part of the Turkish Ottoman Empire in World War I. The British sent Lawrence, then a young army officer, to stir the Arabs into revolt against the Turks, thus making it necessary for Turkey to send big numbers of troops—who might otherwise be fighting the British—to quell the rebellion.

Although Aqaba was no longer an important port since the opening of the Suez Canal, the Turks realized its strategic importance and stationed a strong garrison to guard the town. In July, 1917, Lawrence and Prince Feisal led a war party of desert tribesmen through the desolate, moonscapelike area of Wadi Rum. The Turks had not believed that any living thing could come that way and were wiped out in a surprise attack.

Aqaba became an important headquarters and supply base for the Arab forces in what came to be known as the Great Arab Revolt. The Arab forces harassed the Turks as they retreated northward and drove them into a British force on the Mediterranean coast. The Arabs and British cut the Turks into pieces and dealt a fatal blow to the Axis powers in the Middle East.

Aqaba had been a grimy little fishing village back then, and Dartley knew better than to expect to see what Lawrence saw in what was now an Arabic version of Miami Beach. But the Wadi Rum was still there, unchanged. He hired a car under the name of Fairbairn Draper and drove inland for an hour until he reached the fort of the Desert Camel Corps. This corps was the only remnant still extant of the Arab Legion organized by Lawrence.

The Desert Patrol was posing for photos when he arrived. The soldiers stood patiently next to their squatting camels as the tourists milled around. The soldiers wore full-length zabouns, crisscrossed by scarlet bandoliers and cartridge belts, into which were stuck ornate daggers and pistols. These Bedouins wore tribal red-and-white-checked kaffiyehs with a black cord. Their women wore long black dresses embroidered with bright designs. They all seemed to be enjoying the attention they were getting. They also looked like the kind of people who could be unpleasant if they became annoyed. The tourists kept respectful.

Dartley hired a camel and a guide. They headed out across the mudflats, away from the fort, the Bedouin tents, and ruined temple and the tourist buses and cars. Dartley was amused by his camel—it had the same bored indifference that he often saw in riding horses for hire, setting off at its own easy pace, regardless of what its rider was trying to get it to do. This one stayed at about four o'clock to the guide's camel, so that the guide had to shout back his information to Dartley in his extraordinarily rapid English and heavy local accent. Dartley would have understood him better if he had spoken Arabic slowly, but he said nothing, not wishing to cause offense. He just let the unintelligible babble of words flow over him, relaxed his body to the shifting motion of the camel's gait and looked around him.

The jagged massif of Jebel Rum stuck five thousand feet into the air. Other enormous slabs of rock thrust upward out of the desert floor. Sheer, towering cliffs of weathered sandstone rose out of the white and pink sands. Here and there battered ruins lay half submerged in the shifting dust. They passed through a gap in the cliffs and entered the vast, silent, seemingly endless interior of the Wadi Rum and other lesser wadis. This was the area known as the Valley of the Moon. The wadis, or river beds, had been dry for a million years, and their stones and sands were bleached by the sun nearly every day of every year for a countless span of time—certainly before mankind walked upon the earth.

Lawrence had not shied away from a place like this. He had persuaded the prince and his desert warriors to maneuver across this hostile terrain, scale the mountains behind Aqaba, and descend upon the overconfident Turks.

Just when Dartley had begun to feel he'd make a damn good desert warrior himself, out in the wastelands beneath the blazing sun, he noticed that the tip of his nose was bright red and starting to peel.

Dartley woke at first light the next morning. Michelle Perret had visited him in his hotel room late the previous night. After she rubbed Noxema on his nose, forehead and cheeks, they made love. The car he needed was in the hotel parking lot, the weapons in its trunk. A gray Peugeot. She gave him the keys. She told him the location of the backup car, a blue Honda. Its keys were in the dashboard ashtray.

"Have you got someone to drive you?" she asked.

"I'm doing it alone," he lied. "I don't need anyone."

She left alone, not wishing to be seen with him in case he was caught later.

"I came in the back way. No one saw me. I'll go

back that way." She kissed him hard on the mouth. "Be careful, please."

Dartley slept lightly, as he always did the night before a major challenge. But although his sleep was interrupted by periods of watchful consciousness, he felt rested and fresh early the next morning. No doubt making love to Michelle had helped drain the tension from his body.

He slipped out of the hotel and found the gray Peugeot in the car park. He wanted to check the weapons, but could not do so here unobserved.

He pulled on a pair of cotton gloves thin enough so he lost little sense of touch through them, and left another pair for Gottlieb on the seat beside him. They might never associate this car with the assassination and dust it for prints. Then again, they might. Dartley didn't believe in throwing evidence about the place when he could help it. The car handled well along the coast road, past the port and industrial area, and then out along the lonely stretches of beach toward the Saudi border. The gas tank was full. Things were beginning to check out. He felt a surge of excitement and his mind raced over all the details of what he expected to happen today. This was the feeling he most enjoyed about his line of work—not the killing itself, but the preparations, weighing the risks, the anticipation, the uncertainty, watching for the unexpected . . .

He pulled the car over at a deserted beach and hid it from the road behind a small dune. He switched the engine off, got out, and opened the trunk.

The weapons were inside. Two Colt M1911A1 pistols, two Galil rifles—one with a scope, three missiles stretching diagonally from corner to corner, and a cardboard container of ammo. The missiles were a big surprise. When Dartley asked Michelle for anti-tank missiles, all he expected to get were rockets. A rocket, launched from a container on the shoulder and propelled by the jet stream from a motor or from the combustion of an explosive, rarely had a flight time of more than a few seconds and therefore a limited range. In addition, once a rocket was fired, its trajectory was set—it could not be steered or maneuvered. Rockets were lighter and cheaper than missiles; he was amazed that the French had sprung for three guided missiles. But it certainly showed that Michelle had not bought his story about taking out Ahmed Hasan on the steps of his hotel.

He loaded the magazines and spares for the two pistols, then test-fired a few rounds from each. If they used these pistols, it would be for self-defense at close quarters—so he cared little for these guns' accuracy. So long as their mechanisms were cared for and smoothly operating, he was happy with them. The Colt M1911A1 was the old reliable .45 automatic that the U.S. Armed Forces had been depending on since the year in its model number—1911. The basic design of the gun had remained unchanged, and there were few complaints about it through two world wars, Korea, Vietnam and beyond. Protests began to be heard, however, when the Pentagon announced it was going to dump the .45 in favor of a 9 mm pistol, probably a Beretta, so that American forces would use the same ammo as the NATO allies.

He loaded magazines for the rifles and tested them. Like the pistols, they were in perfect condition. Both shot a few inches to the right and high, but he had no time to mess with that now—they would just have to shoot a few inches to the left and low. He played around with the adjustments on the telescopic sight until he was familiar with it. These Galils were basically Israeli ripoffs of the Soviet Kalashnikov assault rifle, with one important difference—they were better! The gun took 5.56 mm ammo in a thirty-five-round detachable box magazine, was gas operated and weighed about ten pounds loaded. Dartley knew the weapon well. It had only two drawbacks: the protective ring on the Valmet-type front sight, which could be sawed and filed off into wings if he had time—which he didn't—and the awkward carry handle, which always reminded him of a paint roller handle and which he removed from both guns.

He looked at the missiles, having left these for last. The three tubes had their warheads already fitted, each tapering to a fine point. Warhead and tube measured about four feet long, and the tube had four large fins along two-thirds of its length, sticking out about a foot.

Dartley knew what they were, though he had never used them before: the Messerschmitt Cobra 2000. He lifted one out of the spacious trunk, being careful not to damage it; it was not easy to lift because it was awkward to carry and weighed about twenty-five pounds. He set it down on the ground on two of its fins. The unusual thing about this missile was that it did not use a launcher. You just set it on its fins, making sure that the booster—placed between one pair of fins—was pointing toward the ground. You then wired the booster to the aiming unit, along with several other of these missiles. After firing a missile, you tracked the target with an optical sight on the aiming unit and sent commands to the receiver gyro assembly in the missile by means of a joystick. The messages were carried to the missile from the joystick through thin wires that the missile extruded as it traveled. The missile receiver-gyro interpreted these signals and activated spoilers on the fins to alter its path. A flare assembly at the rear of the missile acted as a visual flight monitor.

Dartley examined the warhead. It seemed to have an armor-piercing combined with shrapnel purpose, which would be ideal. This missile traveled at more than 150 mph and had a range of at least one mile. He couldn't have asked for better, and wondered again at the generosity of the French. He thought about test-firing one of the three missiles, but decided not to waste the projectile. He might need all three of the missiles since he would be shooting at a moving target which might have sophisticated defenses set up around it.

Dartley wasn't sure what could defend anything from a Cobra 2000, except maybe an eighteen-inch-thick steel plate. And the goddam Cobra warhead would probably bend that.

Richard Dartley and Aaron Gottlieb sat on a bench in a hotel beach garden. They sat back among the palms, bougainvillea, well-watered flowers and grass, as if basking in the sun and enjoying the view out to sea. Occasional hotel guests passing by hardly gave them a second glance. There was only one odd touch—they were listening to Arabic on a transistor radio.

An elderly couple, very British, came along the path.

"Glorious day," the man said to them.

It probably hadn't rained in Aqaba for six months.

Their dog, a white terrier, lingered behind them, nosing in the bushes.

"Skippy! Skippy!" the woman called. It was plain that she had heard how Arabs hate dogs and was not letting little Skippy out of her sight.

Dartley nudged Gottlieb.

Skippy was in a nearby bush, hind leg raised, urinating against the fins of a Cobra 2000 guided missile.

The woman came back to search for the dog. "Skippy! Here Skippy!"

Dartley's hand slid inside his jacket.

The terrier finished with the missile and trotted back onto the path to answer the old lady's calls.

Gottlieb eyed Dartley's hand easing its grip on the Colt .45 automatic inside his jacket. He asked, "Would you have shot them?"

"If they had seen something and then refused to sit beside us and keep still, of course I'd have shot them. Be a kindness to them both perhaps—sending them out together unexpectedly. Funny how something like a fucking little dog can easily cause a thing like that."

Gottlieb raised a hand for him to listen to the radio. After a while, the Israeli said, "You understood? The king has already gone aboard his yacht. He left on a navy launch from the port area an hour ago. No word on Ahmed Hasan."

"He won't keep the king waiting too long for lunch."

They looked at their watches—seven minutes to ten—and stirred on the bench under the increasingly intense rays of the sun.

Dartley was calm but tense. He had been up since dawn, and everything so far had gone smoothly. He had met Gottlieb at seven. They had set up the three missiles in the shrubs and bushes of the hotel garden after eight, when Dartley had gotten hard information from Michelle by phone that the Egyptian president's only onshore function was to be photographed taking a swim on Aqaba's beach.

He was doing this to promote tourism to Aqaba, it was announced. Dartley wondered who the hell would want to visit a beach because Ahmed Hasan had been there. These photos would be about as good an ad as if they'd invited Colonel Muammar al-Qaddifi or Fidel Castro. Maybe the ads would go down big in Iran.

Michelle said a navy launch would pick Hasan up on the beach in front of the Coral Beach Hotel to take him in his swimming trunks for lunch with the king aboard the royal yacht. Dartley and Gottlieb were down the beach a ways, beyond the ring of tight security forming around the Coral Beach Hotel.

Dartley left Gottlieb to babysit the three missiles at nine and drove to the airport in the Peugeot. The English pilot was with the Lear as promised. He was warming the engines up already and would be set to go in half an hour. On the way back to the bench in the hotel beach garden, Dartley checked the location of the backup car. It was where Michelle said it would be—two blocks from the beach, a blue Honda. Gottlieb had nothing to report when Dartley got back. Since then he had been sitting in the sun, and nothing more serious had disturbed the peace than Skippy the terrier.

The Peugeot was fifty yards behind them, parked on the side of the road. The two men each packed a Colt .45 automatic. The three guided missiles squatted on their fins in the bushes, their warheads pointing out to sea. All three were wired by separation cables to a junction box, which in turn was connected to the aiming unit, hidden directly behind Dartley's position on the bench in a small bush with waxy green leaves and pinkish cream flowers.

All they could do was wait.

At 10:30 a motorcade arrived outside the Coral Beach Hotel. Ten minutes later, there was a lot of fuss on the beach, with a helicopter hovering overhead. Then a big naval launch, with a heavy machine gun mounted on its foredeck, made its way across the water to the beach.

Gottlieb nodded to Dartley in a satisfied way.

"Looks like an old converted torpedo boat," Dartley said, staring out to sea at the launch. "She'll be fast, but too heavy to be maneuverable. Big enough to make a nice target, too."

"Hasan must be having his swim for the photographers." Gottlieb raised himself from the bench, casually stretched, and sat down again. He lit a Kent. "Everything looks quiet here. I'll head off anyone coming this way if I have to when the time comes."

The launch had beached at the crowded area and they could no longer see it.

"I'd better get my stuff together," Dartley said, reaching behind him and hauling out the aiming unit.

Two helicopters came over the water and joined the third one, still hovering over the beach. These choppers were gunships with rocket pods, forward cannons and a side door machine gunner. Then the two choppers moved offshore again a few hundred yards and waited. The launch left land and started out to sea toward an area where many big ships were anchored outside the port facilities.

"Shit, I wish I'd asked Michelle for binoculars," Dartley muttered, and peered over the dazzling waters at a figure standing at the stern of the launch, waving toward the beach.

"I'm farsighted," Gottlieb said. "That's Ahmed Hasan."

"I guess you're right."

The two choppers stayed over the launch as it went on its way. Sailboats and pleasure craft kept their distance.

Dartley peered through the optical sight on the control box. The battery power supply had been switched on. He would need to be fast since the range was only about a quarter of a mile. He launched the first missile and it streaked off the ground at a low angle and out over the sea toward the launch. He heard its sustainer motor in the rear section cut in and accelerate the missile on its journey.

Dartley tracked the launch as target through the optical sight on the control box, while he kept the missile in his line of sight and sent commands through its receiver gyro assembly by way of joystick control through the fine wire the missile payed out behind it as it flew. Except the missile was not obeying him! It was rising steadily into the air at a 20-degree angle, veering neither left nor right.

Dartley twisted the joystick violently around.

There was no response in the missile's trajectory.

"Must be a fault in the wire," Dartley hissed. "Or in the gyro. No knowing how much these fucking missiles have been bumped around before we got them. I'm switching to the next one."

Before Dartley got the second missile launched, the first one arced down, hit the seawater and sent a huge plume of spray skyward as it exploded at four or five times the distance of the launch.

They heard the thud of its hollow-charge warhead a few seconds later and saw figures on the launch run for cover. But not Ahmed Hasan, who maintained his position at the stern of the craft. He did quit waving to the shore.

"Thinks he's fucking de Gaulle," Dartley grumbled as he released the second missile, which tore into the air with a blast and screaming of air cut through by its fins.

This missile's sustainer motor cut in without a hitch and accelerated it on its path.

Dartley sighted on the launch and eased the joystick forward.

Nothing happened. Like the last one, the missile continued on its gently angled, upward flight out over the sea.

Dartley moved the joystick again. Still nothing. He

yanked the lever about on the control box, but he might as well have been pointing his finger to the missile for all the good it did.

"Goddam, I'm going to grab that rifle with the scope and see if I can use it to knock the bastard out of that boat." Dartley jumped to his feet and left the control box on the bench as he set out to run for the car in order to retrieve the rifle from its trunk.

Gottlieb seized the control box and searched for the target in its optical sight. He adjusted the joystick hopefully before launching the third missile.

Dartley had almost reached the road when he saw the chopper coming—not either of the two circling the launch, but the one that had remained hovering over the beach. It was now bearing down on them like a bat out of hell. Dartley saw the orange flashes from the guns in its nose.

"Get down! Chopper! Get down!" he yelled to Gottlieb.

The Israeli kind of stirred as he gazed through the optical sight, like someone indicating he didn't want to be disturbed while on the phone. Dartley saw the last missile shoot into the air—and he knew from its initial seconds of flight that, like the previous two, it was not responding to ground guidance.

The gunship caught the Israeli in the open, on the garden bench with the optical sight still to his eye and his right hand desperately flicking the joystick about. Dartley was yelling at him, and his voice was suddenly drowned by the roar of the chopper's engine.

Dartley felt the wind of the main rotor on his face. He saw Gottlieb crumple and the control box fall from his hands. He heard no gunfire over the sound of the engine, now almost directly over his head.

They had him too, if they wanted. They had seen him, standing there looking up at them. No point in his trying to hide now. No point in trying to help Gottlieb, either. He would be beyond that. Those large-caliber chopper guns would have seen to that.

The missile exploded far out at sea, and the helicopter veered away. Dartley started to walk. He hadn't far to go—no more than twenty yards to reach the gray Peugeot. The helicopter was still up there, hovering somewhere behind him—he did not look back.

He was proud that his hand never shook as he slipped the key in the ignition. He saw now what the helicopter had been doing—looking for a place to land in the garden. The pilot had found a spot where none of the trees and bushes were high enough to damage the rotors and he was easing the craft down. Time for Dartley to move! Even if they did not immediately associate him with the dead man on the bench who had fired the missiles, they would have questions for him about what he had seen. And that would probably end badly. . . .

The gray Peugeot went a couple of blocks inland, out of sight of the beach, and stopped behind a blue Honda. Dartley wanted to dump the Peugeot fast because the helicopter crew had seen him get in it and also in case there were immediate car searches after the unsuccessful attack on Ahmed Hasan. Two automatic rifles in the trunk was bad enough—but he had two Israeli rifles!

The door of the Honda was unlocked, as had been

agreed. The keys would be in the dashboard ashtray. Dartley pulled it out. No keys. He looked in the ignition. On the floor.

He did not waste time. He slammed the car door, headed back to the Peugeot and restarted it. He'd take his chances with it at the airport.

The British pilot was at the Lear, standing in the shade of one wing. Dartley could see him through the glass as he waited for the official to check his papers. They were handed back to him with a smile. Word of the missiles mustn't have reached the airport yet. It wouldn't be long now.

One of the ground crew helped them with the plane. Dartley sat in the cockpit and slipped headphones over his ears. He wanted to hear everything the control tower said to the pilot. His left arm brushed against the solid bulk of the Colt .45 automatic inside his jacket.

"Where to?" the pilot asked casually.

"Cairo."

The pilot gave the control tower their flight destination in English and was cleared for takeoff, also in English.

"Allah yisallmak," the air traffic controller said. May Allah keep you safe.

Over the Sinai, Dartley had the pilot change course for Alexandria, Egypt's second largest city, on the Mediterranean. He figured he might be subjected to less scrutiny there than at Cairo. People were gathered around those with transistors at Alexandria's airport to listen to the news about the attack on Ahmed Hasan at Aqaba when they arrived. The Egyptian president had already accused the Americans and Israelis of a joint conspiracy against him and pointed out that Allah had triumphed in saving him from these agents of evil. Hasan's subjects at the airport did not show any great joy at his escape from death. In Dartley's opinion, they showed a very healthy interest in the prospect of their president's destruction. No one at the airport's control tower or security or immigration apparently made any connection between this Lear jet arriving from Aqaba a couple of hours after the assassination attempt. It was an Arab jet, traveling from one Arab country to another with a foreign journalist as its passenger. All the same, Dartley was glad he had come here instead of Cairo, where controls would probably have been much tighter.

He hired a car from Hertz under the name of Fairbairn Draper and drove along the Corniche, where the luxury apartment houses and hotels fronted on the Mediterranean. He could have been on the French Riviera rather than in Egypt so far as these surroundings went. He followed the sweeping, crescent seafront, glancing out to sea from time to time at the cruise ships, fishing boats and naval frigates. He had had enough of boats for a while.

Why hadn't that control box worked for the guided missiles? Dartley knew enough about sophisticated armaments to accept that the more technologically advanced they were, the more things that went wrong with them. Probably some break in some damn microscopic wire in a microcircuit array less than the size of a fingernail. Someone might have dropped the control box. Or left it out in the sun too long. Hell, no, the Cobra was manufactured in Germany according to military specifications. Things didn't go wrong with something like that all that easily. If only he had tested the weapon when he had fired the rifles and pistols early in the morning—he had left the Colt .45 behind him in the Lear, hidden under his seat, not wanting to risk taking it through customs. But he knew he had made the correct decision early that morning. Either a guided missile works or it doesn't. It had to be taken on faith. He could not have endangered the whole mission by test-firing a weapon powerful enough to register on military surveillance equipment, let alone be seen exploding by ground observers ten miles away.

Such technical difficulties could have happened with any piece of sophisticated equipment. Dartley could even have believed that if it weren't for two other things that kept nagging at his mind. First, the helicopter gunship that bore down on them had been looking for one man only. Why not him also? He had been standing only thirty yards away from Gottlieb when the Israeli had been cut down by the chopper's guns. Any pilot would assume that Dartley too was involved—unless he had prior information that only one man was involved. Dartley had told Michelle Perret that he had not found a driver and did not need one now, he was going it alone.

The second thing that stayed in Dartley's mind was the fact that, although the Honda was where Michelle said it would be, its ignition key wasn't. That could have been deadly for him if he had abandoned the Peugeot and depended on the Honda to escape in.

As he saw it now, he had escaped only through Michelle's carelessness. He had never mentioned the Lear jet to her, and she had assumed he had come to Aqaba on a commercial flight, by boat, or by road from Amman. She hadn't bothered to check. As soon as Gottlieb was found not to be the American they were after, the roadblocks would go up and passenger scrutiny would become intense.

But they had Gottlieb's body and they thought it was his. The only person in Aqaba who could tell them otherwise was Michelle, and with typical Arab deference to the sensibilities of women, they probably did not like to ask her to view the riddled corpse. He still had maybe a few hours before they began hunting for him again.

As Dartley drove west out of Alexandria, along the coast of the palm-fringed Mediterranean, he wondered who Michelle Perret was working for. He felt no personal animosity toward her—she was a professional doing a job, same as him. And she had not fully bested him. True, she had saved Ahmed Hasan by supplying Dartley with faulty missiles. But he was still alive and still intent on killing Hasan, in spite of her efforts.

Were she and Jacques Laforque in on this together? Had Laforque intended that he be killed? Surely not before doing his job, which was killing Ahmed Hasan. That didn't make sense. Yet she was Laforque's contact. He had sent Dartley to her.

If she was working for someone behind Laforque's back, who was it? Only Laforque knew that Dartley was going to Aqaba. Unless he mentioned it to Omar Zekri. Would the Frenchman have been fool enough to do that? He had been fool enough to hire Omar to find Dartley. Now the Egyptian could guess that France was involved in whatever Dartley was up to. If Omar knew Dartley had gone to Aqaba, he could infer that France was behind the assassination attempt on Hasan. Laforque could be sloppy, but surely not that sloppy. Or could he?

Dartley felt himself unwind gradually as he drove alongside the miles of sunny surf and sand, interrupted only occasionally by a town or an oasis. After about seventy miles, he came to a little resort town which looked half deserted. The wind had picked up and blew sand off the desert along its streets. This was El Alamein.

This was the place where Montgomery's Eighth Army made their last stand against Rommel's Afrika Corps. Rommel had defeated the British at Tobruk, in Libya, and in other desert battles, and drove them before him as he swept eastward toward the Nile. In November, 1942, only Montgomery's forces stood between him and British HQ in Alexandria. Once Rommel took Alexandria at the mouth of the Nile, and Cairo farther up the river, nothing could stop him taking the Suez Canal. And after the Germans had taken the canal—thereby cutting off Britain's only short route to its empire in East Africa, India, Australia, New Zealand and Asia—they could overrun the Middle Eastern oilfields. Without Arab oil and easy access to men and supplies from its empire, Britain's war effort would collapse in a matter of weeks; Rommel and Montgomery were not simply fighting over who controlled the empty sands around the tiny Egyptian town of El Alamein.

A total of some eighty thousand men died in that conflict. But Montgomery held the line, and Rommel—Germany's greatest hero, who would later take poison on Hilter's orders for plotting against him—had his first sour taste of a major defeat.

The German and Italian memorials were farther west beyond the town, and they were hardly the place to mourn the loss of a Jewish comrade in arms. He went into the British War Cemetery on the eastern side of the town. The names of the Allied units that had fought here were listed on the walls of the entrance building.

Dartley walked among the more than seven thousand headstones in strict military rows, almost as if these men stood at attention forever in a parade ground in the memory of all free men. He was alone with all these dead heroes who had been sacrificed for the sake of freedom before he had been born. They were not the first. Already it was known they were not the last. Any reasonable guess would suggest there would be many more.

Dartley did not read the names on the stones. He just looked at them all as anonymous men, like every soldier was in combat, looked at the row after row after row of headstones, wreathed in purple flowers, stretching away into the desert sand.

It was here that Dartley chose to mourn the death of Aaron Gottlieb.

Chapter
9

Keegan picked up the off-green telephone connected to the KYX scrambler at this State Department office in Washington, D.C. He identified himself and listened. It was a long call, much longer than the usual briefings Langley chose to give him. Which meant only one thing—the CIA expected that shit was going to fly and that State was going to be hit by some or all of it.

The long and short of it, according to Langley's version, was that the Mossad had lent a man to the CIA in Cairo and that this was the man who had been killed while trying to assassinate the president of Egypt at a Jordanian resort.

Keegan felt the blood rush to his head, then leave it just as rapidly. He wanted to shout, but no sound came. He felt dizzy and gulped some cold coffee from a Styrofoam container on his desk. His hands were shaking.

"You—you're telling me you *borrowed* someone to kill President Hasan?"

"Hell, no, Keegan. Don't be stupid. The Mossad man went to help an American agent. When our man in Cairo verified that this American wasn't one of ours and didn't belong to the Pentagon or NSA, the Israelis figured he was with you. Or maybe the White House. He was doing what the Israelis wanted anyway—taking out Ahmed Hasan. So I don't suppose they gave a fuck if he was from Mars."

"You keep on saying 'this American.' What American?"

"That's what we'd like to know, Keegan. Poke around and see what you can find. There's no knowing if some half-cocked patriot didn't send someone over there—one of these dingbats on the fund raising side. Check into it."

"I will," John Keegan agreed. "You sure he's not a rogue?"

"We've covered everybody. We don't know who this fella is."

"I'll certainly inquire. Other than that, is there anything else we can do at State?"

"Sure." Keegan heard a harsh laugh at the other end of the line. "Keep your heads down when it starts to fly."

Omar Zekri shook hands with Pritchett when the American arrived at the hotel room. Pritchett always insisted on Omar getting a room someplace and then waiting for him there, sometimes for hours, when they had anything that would take time to discuss. Pritchett claimed that if he were seen in earnest conversation with Omar, it could endanger the Egyptian's safety. This was enough to convince Omar. He waited for the American to unwrap and open the bottle of Dewar's Scotch. Two empty glasses had been set on a table by Omar. He swallowed two mouthfuls of the amber liquid before he spoke.

Omar said, "The Israeli spy who was killed at Aqaba was here in Cairo before he went there."

Pritchett did not bat an eyelid, but then Omar decided that Pritchett had been expecting something anyway.

Omar went on. "When the newspaper said that this Israeli spy had entered Egypt as a Beirut Christian banker and spoke Arabic with a Lebanese accent, I recognized him in spite of his ski mask."

"So?" Pritchett asked noncommittally.

"He was with Thomas Lewis, the American wheat expert."

Omar smiled at Pritchett's visible discomfort.

"I think Mr. Lewis went to Aqaba also," Omar said softly. "To kill Ahmed Hasan."

"Do you really think Washington is that stupid, Omar, to send an American and an Israeli to an Arab town to kill the Egyptian president? Even your own newspapers are a bit suspicious of Hasan's claims of an American-Zionist plot against him. I tell you, this so-called wheat expert Thomas Lewis does not work for any branch of the American government. And I'd like you to pass that fact along to your Egyptian friends."

"Oh, they do not know that Lewis went to Aqaba. I have too much love for my American friends to tell the government here what I know about this thing."

Pritchett sighed in exasperation and got to his feet. "Listen to me, Omar. Do what you wish. Obviously, we'd be happier if no American was known to be directly involved in this affair. But I'm not protecting one if he is—because I don't know who the hell he is. We might be best served if Egyptian intelligence did put an end to him before he tries anything else."

"You wish me to pass that along?"

"No. All I'm trying to get you to understand is that this Thomas Lewis is not working for us. In any capacity, got that?"

"Oh, I know that, Mr. Pritchett. How do I know? Because I know who he is working for."

Pritchett sat down.

Omar took his time in refilling their glasses from the bottle of Dewar's. He sipped reflectively on his straight, warm whiskey. "I think five thousand dollars should just about cover my expenses on this particular aspect."

Pritchett grunted his assent. "Better be worth it."

"Jacques Laforque paid me to find Thomas Lewis for him on an emergency basis."

Pritchett's expression did not change.

Omar was not fazed by this. "You know how Laforque behaves so self-importantly when he's obeying orders. He was obeying orders. He was in a hurry. He represents the party behind the Aqaba failure."

Pritchett smiled. "Is Cairo into disinformation these days? Or does this come from someone else? Maybe Thomas Lewis himself? Perhaps he's hired you also."

It was beneath Omar's dignity to respond to such insults. He knew Pritchett was only playing for time as he sorted this new information in his brain.

"Is Laforque in Cairo now?" Pritchett asked.

"No."

"But you expect him back?"

Omar nodded. "And Thomas Lewis too."

When Richard Dartley returned to Cairo, he felt depressed by his failure on the Red Sea. Here he was back again at the starting point, with a few additional strokes against him. One of these additional strokes was the need for a new identification. When he dropped off the car he had hired in Alexandria with the Hertz depot in Cairo, he destroyed his papers in the name of Fairbairn Draper, along with those in the name of Thomas Lewis. Those were two gentlemen he had no wish to be associated with in future. He had a fake U.S. passport and Egyptian visa in the name of Paul Savage. But that name was a safety cushion and he intended to avoid using it if possible. It was just something to show the police if they stopped him in the street. His hair was now fairer—bleached by the sun—and longer, uncomfortably long for him since he was used to it clipped short. He was growing a mustache, wore aviator-style sunglasses, and bought French trendy styles in clothes. He was fairly sure he'd be hard to recognize from a week before. He sure as hell hoped so. There were some people here in Cairo he did not want to meet.

In his new role as a tourist, he spent the day walking around places he had avoided before. He climbed to the observation platform of the six hundred-foot-tall Cairo Tower on Zamalek Island. To the west, he could see the pyramids and the Sphinx, the desert stretching endlessly away beyond them. White-sailed feluccas dotted the Nile, with its ribbon of green vegetation on each bank and the luxury apartment buildings and highrise hotels—the Marriott, Sheraton, Meridien, Nile Hilton, Shepheard. North of the tower, on the island itself, were the grounds of the Gezira Sporting and Racing Club. Across the Tahrir Bridge was Tahrir Square, from which broad thoroughfares radiated out to all parts of the city. Away to the east, the medieval bulk of the Citadel loomed, with silver domes shining in the sun. Beyond the Citadel lay the Mokattam Hills.

With other tourists, he wandered among the bookstores, jewelry shops and boutiques on the elegant avenue of Kasr-el-Nil—not the kind of surrounding Dartley usually found himself in. He spent time in the bazaar of the Khan-El-Khalili and watched tourists bargain with craftsmen in the maze of twisting alleyways. Dartley was not wasting time. He knew exactly what he was doing. He was accustoming himself to his new role as a tourist. Even when he did understand what was said to him in Arabic, he pretended not to. His previous line of attack in Cairo had not worked—which was why he had gone to Aqaba—and now that he was back, he would have to try something new. He was not sure what as yet.

He was almost surprised to find himself enjoying what had first appalled him about the city—the noise, anarchy of the traffic, the construction sites everywhere, the crowds, the fumes, the heat. He got a chance to see the beautiful old mosques and walk down wide boulevards lined by parks and vivid flowers. When he was fully satisfied with himself as a tourist, he went to find Omar Zekri.

To Dartley's satisfaction, Omar did not recognize him. He even tried to sell him a small stone statue of a cat which he claimed had been found in a tomb dating back to King Tut's time.

"Where can I find Laforque?"

This question stopped Omar in mid-sentence. He tried to peer around the sunglasses to see the eyes. "Mr. Lewis? What a pleasant surprise." The stone cat was slipped into a side pocket. "I don't think Monsieur Laforque is in town at present. I will inquire. Where can I contact you?"

Dartley smiled a cold smile and poked the Egyptian hard with his fingertips in the solar plexus. "You little shit! I ought to kill you!"

It hadn't been much of a blow, but it winded the plump Egyptian.

"Thing you better never forget, Omar, is you're sitting out here, an easy target any time I take a violent dislike to you. Now I got the notion you've been crossing me up. So how long do you think I'm going to put up with that? Come on, tell me. You're a good judge of character, Omar. How long would you say I'm going to put up with crap from you?"

"Mr. Lewis, please understand, I have never done anything to—"

"I asked you a question, Omar. Answer it."

"No more crap, Mr. Lewis."

"That's better. When do you expect Laforque to come back?"

"I don't know," Omar said truthfully. "He stays at the Hotel des Roses when he comes, under his name."

"Does Pritchett at the American Embassy know about Laforque looking for me?"

Omar hesitated a moment. "Yes."

Dartley laughed. He had come to see that intrigue was an essential part of life in Cairo, and that for this reason, no one could hope to operate unnoticed by professional observers in spite of the huge size of the city. Instead of hiding, from now on Dartley intended to use people. If Laforque's stupidity gave away France's secret involvement to U.S. intelligence, all the better!

"Come with me, Omar. I want you to hire a car for me under an Egyptian name. There'll be some cash in it for you."

Omar Zekri watched the American drive off in the hired car. Omar was frightened. He was used to threats, he was even used to occasional beatings, but he normally knew how far he could go and expect to survive. He survived because people needed him. At some moments they might want very badly to kill him for something he had done, but his future use to them outweighed the immediate satisfaction they would gain from killing him right away. Omar knew Awad and Zaid would not kill him—he feared torture and maiming from them. Pritchett and Laforque didn't even dare push him around; they needed him more than he needed them. But this American called Lewis was a different matter. That one would kill him and not think twice about it. Like throwing a cigarette away.

Why hadn't he asked Omar more questions? Tried to catch him in lies? This American did not even

IAN BARCLAY

bother to play the game of pretending that they could deal straightforwardly with each other. With him, it was do this or you're dead. It was only a matter of time before he decided—rightly or wrongly—that Omar was responsible for something he didn't like and killed him for it. As the American had openly said, Omar was an easy target. Omar couldn't change that. The nature of his business dictated that he be easy to find, and he made himself available by following regular rounds every day without fail. Those who knew him were aware he would be in a certain place at a certain time of day. An easy target.

But Omar hadn't lived this long by standing passively around and letting things happen to him. Omar believed in preventive action—not by himself directly, of course. It was always easy to find muscle.

Pritchett's attitude decided him. The CIA man had definitely not suggested that this American called Lewis be liquidated, but he definitely had said it was no concern to the embassy what happened to him. This Thomas Lewis would be no loss to anybody.

Omar was also a little worried about the fact that he had been contacted by Laforque, Lewis and the Israeli spy who got killed at Aqaba. An outsider might reasonably make the mistake that Omar too was involved in the assassination attempt on Ahmed Hasan. After all, he had met all three participants. It would be hard to believe he did not know what they had in mind—especially since he had said nothing about them to his Egyptian intelligence contacts. Who would believe he had thought them after atom secrets and that it had never occurred to him they were out to kill Ahmed Hasan? No one would be-

198

lieve it. Omar's involvement with any of this must never become known to Egyptian intelligence.

He toyed around with telling the Cairo authorities about Laforque, but decided not to for the same reason he had not done so before—his own position in the affair would not be believed by them and he would be worse off than if he had kept his mouth shut.

Now this Thomas Lewis was back in Cairo, threatening him and forcing him to hire a car for him. While this man Lewis was in the city, things were not going to stay quiet, die down, fade away, evaporate . . . Things were going to get much worse. And Lewis was already involving him.

Omar stopped at a public phone. He had to try three times before he got through, losing his coins each time, but he persisted until he succeeded.

Zaid answered at the other end of the line.

John Keegan's superior at the State Department, F. Conrad Bigglesley, told his secretary he was not taking any calls and closed his office door.

"John," he said, "we've been reviewing your report of possible French involvement in the Aqaba incident. I've passed your memo to me to various other levels. To tell the truth, reactions vary. But a few very similar comments came back from nearly everyone. I'll summarize them for you. The French would never work with the Israelis on something like this—their mutual distrust would make it highly unlikely. The second thing that struck nearly everyone forcibly was the suggestion to you that this American might be associated in some way with the

Department of State or even the White House. That strikes most of us as grasping desperately at straws. It makes us almost certain he's tied to Central Intelligence or Military Intelligence or the NSA. He may not be a salaried employee. He might be one of these dreadful freelance people they favor doing business with. I like your suggestion that he could be some kind of rogue employee, and I think your Langley contact was a little too quick to deny this possibility. In other words, we all think Langley is trying to pull the wool over our eyes."

John Keegan had expected this. "I think that's a very sensible set of reactions, Conrad, based on past experience. The only thing we have to be wary of, then, is whether we're putting too much reliance on past experience, and by doing so, possibly missing a new development. And, I should add, a new development our friends at the Agency will be able to justifiably say they gave us timely warning about and were ignored."

"Are you telling me that you believe the French government is involved in trying to assassinate the Egyptian president?" Bigglesley asked with an edge in his voice.

"I don't see why we must be put in a position in State where we have to believe or not believe. I'd like to keep an open mind on this."

"That's fine, John," Bigglesley snapped, "just as long as you keep your open mind to yourself."

"If you say so."

"I do."

Keegan tried another angle. "Surely the Agency contacted the White House staff independently on this. What does the National Security Adviser have to say?"

"He disagrees with the Secretary of State."

Keegan laughed. "Nothing new there."

Bigglesley assumed a paternal air. "That's what I'm warning you about, John. You tend to throw your opinions around without testing the air. That can easily be misinterpreted. You could find yourself trapped in alliances that would do your career no good."

"So what do I do?" Keegan asked with resignation. "Tell Langley they're full of horsefeathers?"

"Absolutely not. Pretend to go along with them, as if we believe every word they're feeding us."

"Very well."

"Good." Bigglesley was pleased. "I must say Alice looked delightful at the Paraguayan Embassy cocktail party."

Yes, and you couldn't keep your goddam paws off my wife, Keegan felt like saying.

But he didn't.

Ahmed Hasan was back to his old ways, tearing back and forth between the presidential palace and the Citadel, always surrounded by his armed body-guards. The speed, suddenness, and chaos of these moves were what protected Hasan most effectively. Dartley watched from his parked car at four points for two of Hasan's trips, coming and going. It began to look like he would have to wait for Hasan to break his routine again.

Time was beginning to work against him now. Sooner or later the government agents would get lucky and pin him down. His only hope was in the recklessness of Ahmed Hasan himself. Hasan had stood erect on the stern of the launch while everyone else on board had sought cover. On his return to Cairo, there seemed to be no extra security precautions in place. Plainly Hasan liked to live on the edge . . . play with fire. He might even taunt a would-be assassin with his seeming accessibility. Certainly he was not running away or hiding himself more than he had done before.

The newspapers and TV and radio broadcasts were strident with accusations against Washington and Tel Aviv. But there was nothing much that was new there—it was more a matter of increased quantity than any change in quality. Yet American tourists wandered the suqs and visited mosques, unable to understand the Arabic vituperation beamed about their homeland from transistors everywhere, which seemed only to amuse the Egyptians. They rarely showed dislike of these corrupting foreign agents of the Devil with their dollars and their interest in what they liked to call Egypt's majestic and mysterious past.

Zaid had no idea where Awad had taken himself off to and did not know when he would be back. He put the description of the hired car out in a bulletin, with instructions that the vehicle or its driver was not to be approached, only their whereabouts reported and surveillance to be maintained. Zaid himself was ready to move, before any clumsiness on someone's part alerted the American to the fact he was being watched. The men would receive instructions to withdraw after Zaid himself arrived, and he would take it from there.

Zaid's wolfish face broke into a grin. He'd show that fat slob Awad what he could do without him. Still and all, if Awad showed up before the call came in that the American's car had been located, Zaid would be glad to have him along. But Zaid wasn't waiting. And he wasn't going to take some other agent along, someone he wasn't used to working with. He'd feel safer on his own than working with someone he didn't know well enough to trust. The fact was, the only one he could depend on was Awad.

He would go on his own.

If the call came in. If. Zaid had no illusions about that. However, the bulletin was coded as a government request, and that might frighten some of them into bothering to read registration plates. When the government wanted something, there was always the chance that it was Ahmed Hasan himself who was making the request. That possibility was enough to frighten a lot of people, especially the more intelligent ones who had been hearing things.

No sign of Awad. He took off like this at times, without a word to anyone, in a black mood. At times he would be gone for hours, at times for days. Then he would be back, and no one dared ask for an explanation. There were whispers that he took secret assignments. Zaid knew better. Awad spent these times in a cheap hotel room sleeping off his depression. Sometimes he would have hashish or liquor, but mostly he just slept. Zaid knew him well enough to see the really bad spells coming on.

If Zaid went out and took this American, dead or

alive, by himself, Awad would be so infuriated he'd grumble about it for a year.

From time to time, Zaid raised hell because there was still no response to the bulletin—just letting them know that results were expected so that they in turn could put pressure on men in the street. He checked on the men he had placed at the Beta depot on Mahmoud Bassionni Street, where the car had been rented. These men's instructions differed from those of others. If the car was returned, they were to kill the driver if he was a foreigner and take him alive only if he looked Egyptian.

The call came in. The car was parked near the Citadel, with the driver sitting in it. Zaid rushed to the black van. He drove recklessly across Cairo until he neared the area. Then he eased along until he saw the green Renault. He checked the plate numbers to be sure as he pulled into a space some distance behind the car. The driver was behind the wheel.

In a few minutes he noticed a black Citroen with two men pull away from the opposite side of the street. Those would be the ones who had spotted the car—probably regular police. They had done a good job. He had no complaints. Zaid settled himself down to wait.

Sitting quietly in a car was one of the most effective forms of surveillance. A man sitting in a car went unseen because he was below the visual level of most people. He was not exposed, so that particulars about him as an individual did not arouse the curiosity of others. Nor was he loitering or obviously trying to hide. He could keep in radio contact with others, take photographs, record sound and keep quite large weapons ready next to him. The American could be doing any or all of these things, but the first question Zaid had to answer was, why here?

Zaid wondered what the American was watching. Nothing seemed unusual to him, but maybe that was because he was Egyptian and took something for granted which the American considered important. Zaid told himself he must try to see his native city through this foreigner's eyes. Much as he tried, he still saw nothing of interest to an American spy. He was mystified.

The American might be waiting for someone who was late in turning up. But why wait in a car in hot sunshine, next to the fumes of traffic? He was sure the little Renault did not have air-conditioning, to which Americans were so devoted. Something was keeping him here.

Three Range Rovers charged by at top speed, bristling with guns and crowded by people in camouflage fatigues. Zaid recognized the presidential party leaving the Citadel for the presidential palace. So that was it! No matter how often the president varied his route, he would pass by this spot close to the Citadel maybe ninety percent of the time. This was what the American was watching.

Zaid started the van's engine and waited. The American would give the president's group a few minutes and then leave. No doubt he was selecting a similar spot that had to be passed most of the time near the presidential palace. Then he would compare the advantages of one with the other before choosing his ambush point.

The green Renault pulled out and drove away. Zaid followed at a distance. The car was headed toward the presidential palace when it made a sudden turn. Zaid slowed and followed cautiously. The Renault was up ahead. It made another turn. Zaid speeded up so he would not lose sight of it. He followed the little French car through heavy traffic right across Cairo to the east bank of the Nile, caring little anymore whether he was seen as a tail because of the difficulty in following.

Several times it occurred to Zaid to radio for assistance. But that would have been a triumph for Awad. With Awad along, he had never had to radio for assistance. Awad would laugh and claim Zaid could not handle anything alone! Zaid compromised by deciding to phone, next opportunity he got, to see if Awad had returned. He would not radio for help.

The Renault found a gap in the traffic and speeded onto the 6 October Bridge. Zaid followed as best he could, and saw the car exit onto Zamalek Island. He wondered if the American, through some twisted sense of humor, was luring him back to the same residential street where they had tried to trap him before and lost four men. But no, he had not gone that way. For one bad moment, Zaid thought he had lost him—then he saw the green Renault pulled up near the Marriott Hotel. He checked the rear plate. It was the one. But there was no sign of the American!

He couldn't have gone far. Zaid pulled his black van into a space two rows back and turned off the engine. No one was about, although it was early evening and the day's heat was gone. He sat for a minute, hoping to see something.

Had the American had time to enter the hotel? Hardly. But Zaid couldn't be sure. Perhaps he was staying there. The Marriott had more than twelve hundred rooms, in two highrise blocks, one at each end of a royal palace facing the water. There were gardens, swimming pools, tennis courts—and lots of foreigners. Zaid knew that the foreigners stayed here so they could live in the finery of corrupt kings, drink alcohol, fornicate, and escape the vengeance of Islam in the heart of an Arab country! It was an insult to Allah. Zaid would radio for a search team to scour the place while he waited here.

But first he would do something. Zaid slid open the door and climbed down from the van with a smile on his face. He drew a revolver and advanced quietly on the Renault. It was a simple trick—to park quick and duck down out of sight so the car looked empty.

Zaid had a strong feeling that this American had not gone far—that he was still in that Renault, crouched down out of sight, waiting for Zaid to chase into the hotel after him. He crept alongside the car, crouched down below window level, then stood suddenly and pointed the revolver at the side window. The car was empty, front and back.

After a quick look in some nearby bushes, gun at the ready, Zaid decided that the American had gone into the hotel after all. He would call in a search team.

He strode quickly back to the van, reholstering his revolver, and slipped through the open door into the driver's seat. He reached for the radio transmitter.

As he did so, something dropped in front of his

face and tightened with the speed of a serpent around his neck. He felt it bite into his throat and raised both hands to pluck it from his neck.

But this was not a long, thin snake which had attacked him. He tried to force his fingers between his neck and the scalding plastic line, but the electric flex had bitten too deep into the muscles of his scrawny neck.

It burned like fire! He tried to suck in air. Nothing came. He could not cry out. Blood was throbbing in his neck. His face was twisted. He could not close his eyes.

Again he tried to tear the line from around his neck. He tried to twist his body about to face the attacker behind him, but his head was yanked savagely back against the headrest and held pinioned there by the wire around his throat.

Enough! He'd had enough! Zaid signals with his hands. His lungs were bursting! He had to breathe! He could not see! Everything was red before his eyes.

Air! Air! He needed air.

Please.

In sha 'allah.

Chapter
10

Omar Zekri carefully stapled the papers to the top of a small rug, dirty and with ragged ends. When all the papers were secured by their corners, he rolled the rug up tightly and bound it with string. Then he put the rolled rug under one arm, left his apartment and strolled jauntily through the streets. He was on his way to sell this rug to an undersecretary from the American Embassy for six thousand American dollars, five for the information on Laforque plus one for other services. The rug itself wasn't worth a dime.

Pritchett was not coming today, and Omar avoided handing papers to other Americans when he could. Nobody thought anything of an Egyptian selling any kind of garbage to tourists, but if an Egyptian national was seen passing papers to a foreigner—immediately everyone thought espionage! In his case they would happen to be correct. Which was all the more reason for him not to be seen doing anything suspicious. Those at high levels knew about him, of course.

What Omar feared was being caught in the act by an ordinary policeman and being kicked to death by an enraged mob in the street or cellmates in a jail before he could be rescued. But if he lost his cover to that extent, would they bother rescuing him? The answer was no.

While Omar had a carefree look and a confident walk, his mind always seethed with anxiety. He had seen too much, done too many treacherous things to ever have peace of mind. Now he did what he could to keep the dragons at bay. He knew that one day, at the appointed hour, he would not be able to wriggle away. He kept a wary lookout for anything or anyone that looked as if they might be part of that fateful hour.

The American wheat expert Thomas Lewis had been such a one. Omar instinctively sensed it. He was glad he had phoned Zaid about him the previous day. It also showed Zaid and Awad that he was cooperating with them, being a loyal Egyptian and supporting the Islamic revolution—in his own way, of course.

As the English liked to put it, think of the devil and the devil appears. He had just been congratulating himself for having delivered Thomas Lewis to Zaid the day before when who should he see waiting for him at his usual cafe for this time of day but this same American who should be dead by now or chained in a dungeon in the depths of the Citadel at the very least. Omar turned away from the cafe and continued along the crowded sidewalk, hoping to have slipped away unseen.

Even if he had not escaped unseen, what could the

American do to him on this crowded sidewalk? His fellow countrymen would never stand by and let a foreigner—an American!—attack an Egyptian on a Cairo street. Omar glanced over his shoulder. The American was there.

No use running. Do not show guilt. The American had no proof he was the one who sent Zaid. Maybe Zaid could not trace the car. Of course! Why hadn't he thought of that? He would act friendly and find out where the American was going, then call Zaid and Awad again. Maybe this time they would get it right.

"My friend," Omar greeted Dartley. "Mr. Lewis, are you enjoying yourself? You had a pleasant drive in the car yesterday?" Omar cursed himself silently for even mentioning it. But what could the American do here, even if he had guessed the worst? "You were waiting for me, I suppose. It is always a pleasure to do your bidding, or nearly always. You see, today I am in a hurry. Maybe in three hours time? We will meet then, yes? You tell me where to come or you find me yourself at my usual places. I will be free. Goodbye."

As Omar talked, he tried to move away from the American, but the big foreigner rudely bumped people aside and walked very close to Omar, towering over him. He had something in his hand. Not a weapon. Something small. Omar wanted badly to hurry away, but his curiosity overcame him.

It was a small glass bottle with a yellow Bayer aspirin label. There was no cap on the bottle and it was filled to half an inch from the top with a clear liquid. Omar noticed how carefully the American held this bottle as he walked, taking care that not a drop should spill.

The American walked on his left side while he carried the rolled rug under his right arm, so it was easy for the foreigner to hold the bottle suddenly next to his belly. Omar looked down and saw the top of the clear liquid tilt back and forth inside the bottle, catching the light and winking at him like an eye.

"By the time they find an alkaline antidote," the American said in an eerily calm voice, "this acid will have eaten a hole through your belly large enough to show everyone your guts inside." As a kind of pleasant afterthought, he added, "If you try falling down or running away, I will throw it over your head. You might prefer that."

It was good that the American had mentioned falling down because Omar had been just about to genuinely faint with fear. He dreaded this calm, evil foreigner and needed no astrologer to warn him to avoid this danger.

"Whatever you want! Anything!" Omar heard with contempt the fear in his own gasping voice. "My knees! My legs! I will have to sit down. But don't pour acid on my face."

"On your eyes," the American said in a friendly voice. "On your lips."

Omar looked desperately up the street. "There is a little park. You see the trees? There are seats."

The Egyptian hurried, and Dartley withdrew the bottle, so as not to hamper him. The last thing he needed was this little rat to pass out on him. He saw

the grayness in Omar's puffy cheeks and the beads of
sweat rolling down the unhealthy looking skin, drops
of pure terror, cowardice distilled.

This made Dartley want to kill. He felt the urge
rise up in him. Just as fleeing prey stirs a predator's
ferocity, Dartley felt the urge to strike out and smash
a man who cowered before him.

But Richard Dartley had put in long hours training
himself, learning to control his impulses—not in
repressing them but learning to channel his wildness
to fit his purposes. This was his blend of spirit and
mind and physique which made his enemies tremble
the instant before they died.

Omar just about made it to the park seat. He had
the shakes so bad he nearly tore a cigarette pack to
pieces trying to get one out. He was beyond pre-
tense. If he tried to lie and bargain, he guessed the
foreigner might haggle too by using drops of that
clear liquid.

"What do you think it would feel like, Omar? Cold
or hot? I think acid would feel like an invisible cat
scratching you, refusing to stop, scratching harder
and harder."

Omar just sat there, puffing on the cigarette, in
fear and misery.

Dartley held the bottle up to the light for a
moment and then quickly turned to Omar. "Do you
think I would be able to force you to drink it? I bet I
could." He smiled as if he were issuing some silly
challenge. "The acid would eat away your tongue.
Everyone would be amused with the justice of that.
They'd all say, whoever it was who took care of Omar,

he had a sense of humor, you'll have to grant him that."

Omar began to look groggy and dazed.

Dartley spoke urgently. "What have you for me to buy back your life? Quickly. I am willing to sell your life back to you. Undamaged. A one-time offer you can't afford to overlook. What will you pay?"

This was the kind of talk Omar understood. His glazed eyes lit once more with the fire of hope. He feverishly began to untie the string around the rug.

"I have the very thing for you here," Omar said with the zeal of an Arab merchant showing a gullible tourist expensive trinkets in a bazaar. "What I am about to show you is worth two, three times the value of my life."

"A pack of cigarettes is worth that."

Omar paused, alarmed again. "Now you are joking, Mr. Lewis. To Omar Zekri the life of Omar Zekri is worth pearls and diamonds and barrels of fine old whiskey. Yet Omar Zekri admits that the value of his own precious life is exceeded by two of the objects which he is about to show you."

Omar unrolled the rug and held it up by two corners for Dartley to see the papers stapled to it. His fear had made him forget his earlier caution. Before he left his apartment he had been afraid to be seen slipping papers to an American. Now he was holding up a dirty rug with papers stapled to it—an odd enough sight to attract the interest of anyone who happened to be in the little public park.

The Egyptian gently removed two of the papers, snapping away each corner so that the staple pulled through the paper and left only a tiny tear.

Dartley gestured to the other papers.

"They are of minor interest," Omar assured him. "These two are the gems of the collection."

Dartly muttered threateningly, "If they turn out to be no good..."

"They will turn out to be so good that the next time you see me you will press bundles of dollars in my hands and tell me I am your lifelong friend."

Dartley grinned. "I have a hard time imagining that." He folded the two papers, glancing at them before he put them in his pocket. They seemed to be diagrams of clusters of buildings, labeled in Arabic handwriting. "What are you going to do to replace them?"

"I have Xeroxes," Omar said brightly.

Dartley left him on the park seat, rerolling the rug. He walked quickly, pausing suddenly at store windows and crossing streets unexpectedly, reconnoitering for a tail.

He had snapped on the plastic cap and flipped the aspirin bottle of water in a garbage can.

Dartley phoned the number Aaron Gottlieb had given him. Again he heard the shouting and crashing of crockery. It might be the kitchen of a busy restaurant or a factory in which they made something that clattered like plates under chaotic conditions. He raised his voice so the man at the other end of the line could hear him.

"I want to speak to the boss's nephew." He spoke in simple colloquial Arabic.

"Maalesh." The code reply. Meaning don't bother. The man hung up.

Dartley headed for the cafe in the New City. He wondered whether he should sit in the cafe this time since he would not recognize the person he was meeting, or whether he should do what he had done before—sit out of sight in the cafe across the street and observe what went on. Maybe the Israelis were furious with him for having caused the loss of their agent. His opening line over the phone about wanting to speak to the boss's nephew presumably identified him, each contact being given a different code. Instead of coming to talk this time, the Israelis might send a couple of heavies to spray the cafe with Uzis. A seat out of sight across the street was definitely indicated.

Or maybe not. Gottlieb would have reported that this was where he met him rather than at the agreed upon rendezvous. To hide across the street was what they would expect him to do, and any professional assassin with a yen to survive did not do what people expected him to do.

He could not properly size up the situation by walking past the cafe periodically because it would mean he would not have the cafe in sight all the time. So he hired a taxi, bought a magazine for the driver and told him he might have to wait an hour. The man was willing, drove to the appointed place and parked the taxi where Dartley had a view of the two cafes on opposite sides of the street.

From the moment he first saw her, Dartley figured she was his contact. She was tall, with jet black hair piled on her head in loose waves, and had a narrow face and pointed chin. He could not tell much more from the distance at which he sat inside the cab. He hung back a while and watched her select a table and order a coffee from the waiter in the cafe in which they were supposed to meet, not in the one across the street where he and Gottlieb had run into one another.

Why had they sent a pretty woman? It was not unusual in Cairo to see a woman enter a cafe by herself. The mullahs had not managed yet to deprive Egyptian women of their relative independence, although their publicly announced goal was to install every grown female in a shapeless black chador. This woman was dressed in a pantsuit which modestly concealed whatever bodily charms she possessed.

Dartley paid off the driver and approached her. He had no prearranged signal to exchange with her and so tried his telephone code again.

"I want to speak to the boss's nephew."

"Maalesh." She gestured to a seat at her table.

Dartley ordered a Turkish coffee from the waiter. They observed each other wordlessly until after it was served. This lady was tough. She wasn't yielding an inch. And she had an amused look in her big brown eyes, almost as if she half expected him to ask her if she came here often.

Dartley placed his folded copy of the *Egyptian Gazette* on the table. "There's a handwritten account here of what happened to Aaron Gottlieb. I'm sorry about how it ended."

"We understand."

He had given them all the details, including his suspicions of Michelle Perret's treachery. Let her explain things to some mean Israelis. She could tell them how she wanted him killed, not the Mossad agent.

"There are two documents—maps—of what seem to be nuclear facilities. I got them from what I think is a reliable source, Omar Zekri is his name, but he's off to paddle them around town. If you want to make use of them on an exclusive basis, you're going to have to act fast."

"I'll see that they get top priority," she said coolly.

"There's also a photo of me. I need an American passport."

"No problem."

"That's it then," Dartley said. He had made sure that the photo, like the previous one he had given Aaron Gottlieb, was of poor quality and showed him with an uncharacteristic expression on his face, a photo that was definitely of him when compared to his living face by some official, but one of little use in a file for future identification purposes.

"Tonight, about midnight, at the bar of the Marriott." She gave him a quick smile, picked up the newspaper, and was gone.

Mustafa Bakkush returned from the airstrip to the flat-roofed military hut in which he, his wife, two daughters and son lived. The hut was in an abandoned air force base in the middle of the Western Desert, halfway between the Nile and the Libyan border, distant from all Bedouin camel routes. He kept Aziza and the children with him in the wilderness for their own safety, although her well-to-do family at Aswan had pleaded that they stay with them until Mustafa's project was finished. Mustafa could not tell them his project would never be finished, because he would not let it be finished, regardless of the consequences to him. But that still lay in the future and while he could he wanted to have his family near him so he could protect them and enjoy their company. Aziza naturally resented his frequent trips to Cairo while she remained confined on a military base in the hot, dry, endless desert, but the memory of her and the children's abduction from London in crates was still fresh enough in her mind to make her see the sense of her husband's course of action. What he did not tell her was that he would find a way out of Egypt for her and his children before he did whatever he had to do to prevent Ahmed Hasan from possessing an atom bomb.

It had been a long, hot day, and his family sat in camp chairs in the shade of the hut, sipping tea. Mustafa had brought a plastic bag of ice cubes which the children squabbled over, spilling some of the precious objects onto the sand at their feet.

Mustafa chatted with them as they watched the sun sink in blazing red and gold over the empty wastes of sand. But though he smiled and joined in the children's games and told his wife the latest gossip from the capital, he felt weighted down by a slow burning rage. This was not merely a resentment at his present lot in life or an unfocused bitterness. It was a strong personal hatred of Ahmed Hasan that grew mightily every day, so that it was almost a living, moving part of him, real, like his blood except that it was poisoning his mind rather than sustaining him. Would he go mad? Maybe. But first he had to get his family out.

He looked toward the airstrip in the setting sun. Some cargo planes and a few fighters were on the concrete expanse before the terminal building and control tower. Scientists, technicians and pilots lived in other huts, but most were empty. As few personnel as possible were stationed at this base.

Someone who didn't know the place could easily have dismissed, even at close range, the sandy swelling in the ground among the huts as a desert dune. Most of the vast concrete dome was underground. Sand had been bulldozed as a fortification around much of the dome that protruded aboveground. From the air, not even the swelling of the land surface was visible.

Beneath the huge, brown, dusty concrete dome, a nuclear reactor processed its uranium fuel into plutonium and other products. Next to it a chemical extraction unit separated the plutonium from the other products. In a lead-lined concrete cistern sunk deep in the sand, the deadly fruit of this harvest was gathered and stored.

This had been one of Ahmed Hasan's nasty surprises for Mustafa Bakkush. The physicist had expected to work with Egypt's known nuclear reactors which were subject to international inspection. Whatever cheating that might have gone on at these reactors would have been on a reasonably modest scale and at a fairly slow rate, because of the necessity of accounting for fuel and interruptions for inspections. This secret reactor changed all that. Here everything went toward producing plutonium. In addition, the other reactors were doing their share as had been planned for them. It would not be so long after all until Ahmed Hasan had the radioactive material for his bomb.

Mustafa saw he could not interfere easily with this stage of the process. He would strike at Hasan later. For example, a faulty bomb design would use up time, parts, and fuel. . . .

The children heard them first. They saw nothing until the planes were almost on top of them because the aircraft flew with the setting sun behind them. First one aircraft swooped low. Antiaircraft guns followed it. Seconds later, eight more planes swooped in, dropping long cylinders, almost a third of each plane's length, onto the concrete dome.

Mustafa understood what he was seeing. The pilots carefully aimed their bombs at the dome so they would not bounce the bombs off the concrete. The first bombs had delayed explosive impact so that they sank into the concrete through their falling weight before exploding.

The first bombs, dropped by four planes, lifted great chunks of thick concrete out of the dome. The second four planes swept in out of the setting sun and dropped their bombs through the holes made by the first! Mustafa had seen and read of many bombing techniques, but he had never thought such precision and accuracy possible.

The explosions were now deep beneath the dome, destroying everything the giant shell had been built to protect. Great orange billows of flame shot out of the ruptures and cracks in the fiery egg.

The green-brown camouflaged jets had disappeared, streaking low across the desert.

"There may be fallout," Mustafa warned and

shepherded his family inside the hut. He sealed the doors and windows.

His five-year-old son cheered and clapped his hands at the raging inferno visible through the shattered concrete dome.

He asked, "Can we go home now?"

Three hours later, Dr. Mustafa Bakkush was at the Citadel. They had come to the hut for him with a protective suit and flown him in a high-speed jet fighter to Cairo. A military car rushed him from the airport to the courtyard within the Citadel where not so long ago he had seen men executed and saved the life of a rebellious engineer. Maybe this time Ahmed Hasan wanted his head.

The scientist passed beneath the stony stares of soldiers who looked as if they might know something he did not. Mustafa pulled himself together. For better or worse, he would defend himself against all accusations. If there was slaughter, he was not going to be led to it as a silent lamb.

A high-placed civil servant whom Mustafa recognized stood outside a pair of large double doors inside a building in the Citadel. Mustafa knew what lay beyond them. In there was the hearing room in which he had tried to explain nuclear weapons to the contemptuous Light of Islam mullahs.

The civil servant nodded to Mustafa's military escort and they marched back along the corridor.

The government man paused before he turned the handle of one door and murmured, "Be careful."

Mustafa nodded gratefully and went in.

To his relief, he was not facing a row of fierce,

bearded mullahs. Only a few were present. Ahmed Hasan sat at the opposite side of the long table. A number of uniformed military men stood in a row in front of him, with several paces between each of them, as if they were each trying to disassociate themselves from the others.

Mustafa joined them, making sure not to get too close to them, but deriving a certain comfort, all the same, in not being out there all by himself in front of Ahmed Hasan.

The president did not acknowledge Bakkush's presence. He went on shouting at one of the military men.

"Tell me how—*how*—nine Zionist planes, one F-15 and eight F-16s, could reach that location deep in our air space without alerting our air defenses?"

"They fooled the radar, sir, by flying in tight formation so they looked like a large commercial airliner on the screens. When challenged, one pilot identified himself as a Saudi Arabian Airlines Boeing 747 en route from Riyadh to New York. The radar image was on the correct flight path and moving at the right speed, and the call numbers and identification data checked out. There was no air or ground visual contact reported to contradict what seemed to the radar operators to be a routine flight. I can't fault them. They followed procedure. We have a weakness in our system."

"All I hear are damn fool excuses and explanations!" Ahmed shouted. "I don't want excuses and explanations! You don't have to explain things that work! You don't excuse yourself when you win! No more excuses and explanations!"

He glared at all of them for a moment. Then his feverish eyes settled on another military man and he began to shout again.

"You told me that concrete dome could not be seen from the air and that, even if it was, the reactor beneath it would escape undamaged in a hit-and-run raid like the one today."

"We all believed that, honorable president," the officer replied. "We did not think it possible for jets to drop bombs through holes in the structure. Nor would it have been possible for them to do what they did today were it not that they somehow received the plans for the dome and calculated the weakest points."

Another officer put in, "They would also have had to make many practice runs in order to develop such a precise technique in placing their bombs. In other words, sir, they knew the structural plans of the dome for some time. What they may not have known until very recently was its exact geographical location." The officer added dryly, "Since they came in on the attack in a single pass, they were obviously supplied with accurate details on that also."

"Spies! Traitors! We're surrounded by them!" Hasan crashed his fist on the table and ground his teeth. Then his eyes settled on Mustafa Bakkush, who looked vulnerable with his poor posture next to the row of uniformed officers. "You! Are you a spy? Tell me! A lot of you scientists are Jews and Zionists! Do you write to them? Do you telephone overseas?"

"I have contacted no one outside Egypt since my return," Mustafa said in a loud voice.

"No one?" Ahmed echoed unbelievingly. "What

about your colleagues in England? I bet some of those were Jews."

"Some were, but not necessarily Zionists. I did not discuss politics with them there. I receive scientific journals from overseas and also letters. But no phone calls. And I have not responded to any letters. Your own security people could probably tell you that—if they knew their job."

Ahmed was visibly stung by the scientist's touch of sarcasm, and several of the officers looked sideways at Bakkush in puzzled admiration. They knew scientists were crazy, but this crazy?

Ahmed's mood changed. He spoke now in a soft, cold whisper. "How do I know that you did not call in these Zionist planes on our reactor?"

"Because I was there with my wife and children, only a few hundred yards from where the bombs fell. Do you think I would call in an air strike on my wife and children?"

Ahmed smiled. "I do not, Mustafa Bakkush. Indeed I do not. My doubts about you are cleared. You must help us. How soon can things be repaired?"

Mustafa shook his head. "I have not seen the damage and it may be months before anyone will be able to. My guess is that the facility will be unrepairable because of contamination. We will be able to salvage whatever plutonium and uranium that is not destroyed by fire. But all the equipment and the structure itself are a total loss."

"We must begin again?"

"I think so. At another location. The construction won't be a problem. I think getting another reactor might be."

"Why?" Ahmed was playing dumb.

"Well, because of Egypt's ... ah, political gestures toward certain Western countries."

"You mean America?"

"Yes, I do," Mustafa said. "All you'll get from Russia is outdated junk. You can't hope at this stage that America will be willing to supply you directly. However, if relations were better between Cairo and Washington, they might not scream too loudly if we bought another reactor from France or Italy. As things stand, I think Washington will prevent such a sale."

"Good, good. Dr. Bakkush, at last I'm hearing plain sense instead of empty explanations and lame excuses."

As Ahmed made some more complimentary remarks about him, all Mustafa could think about was doors opening to the outside world through which he and his family could escape. He would be the most knowledgeable one to send for a hurried purchase and he would not go without his wife and children. But Ahmed would never trust him that far. . . .

The president was now talking to the mullahs, requesting them to restrain the other Light of Islam clergymen in their attacks on the United States. They seemed agreeable to his request.

Ahmed Hasan turned back to the military men. "We must make friendly gestures. How? Where can we begin?"

An officer said, "There's a tour of American amateur archeologists in Cairo at the moment, sir. I've had to give them clearance to enter several military zones to see the temples there. It seems many of them are very important men in America and are very happy with how they have been treated here. Perhaps a presidential palace reception and a few words from you—"

"Excellent!" Hasan beamed at them. "Tomorrow night. I want you all to be there." His wild eyes included Mustafa in the invitation.

Mustafa groaned inwardly, knowing that the madman would notice if he did not show up. He would take no risks. Ahmed Hasan's sudden upswing of mood after today's disaster was certain to be followed by an equally sudden downswing that might cause heads to roll.

Richard Dartley was making his way on foot across Cairo toward the Nile, along the cool night streets, when he heard men shouting on a side street. He was about to hurry on to avoid becoming accidentally involved in a fracas when he heard a woman scream and a Southern good ol' boy's voice rasp: "Dang it, Emily, you keep out of this!"

Dartley decided to take a look. Without thinking about it too much, he usually went to the help of fellow Americans when they were in trouble abroad.

Beneath a streetlight, a youth of about twenty in a white djellaba was waving a knife with an angled bend in its long blade at a red-faced, overweight American about sixty. The red-faced man's wife was of a generous girth also, accentuated by a bright floral pattern on her dress. She was swinging her purse by its straps and seemed anxious to take on the knife-wielding Arab herself.

In that instant in which a fresh observer takes in

all the details of a scene and puts them together in his mind to make sense of them, Dartley guessed that the Arab was furious enough to attack, but was confused—perhaps because the woman had attacked him. This would come as such a surprise to a young traditional Arab male, he might be temporarily at a loss what to do. On the other hand, both Americans seemed drunk and belligerent, the woman saying to her husband, "Don't give him a dime, Harry."

None of the three saw Dartley approach in the dimness outside the streetlamp's yellow pool of light.

Harry held out an unopened pack of Marlboros to the Arab, clutching the bottom of the pack with his fingers and pushing it into the Arab's face so he could see what the peace offering was.

With a flick of his right hand, the Egyptian sliced the Marlboro pack in two. The razor-sharp blade left the bottom half of the pack still in the American's hand.

Dartley was impressed by this bladework, realizing that the Arab could have just as easily run the blade across the American's throat if he had chosen to do so. This was maybe beginning to dawn on Harry too, and he quieted down real fast. But Emily was having none of it. She took a wild swing with her purse at the Arab's head.

"Ungrateful little foreigner!" she yelled. "You ain't going to get our cash! Harry, you kick that boy's ass right now, y'hear?"

Harry was kind of thinking things over. The Arab was looking at the swearing, purse-swinging woman as if she had two heads and a tail.

"Inta malak?" Dartley asked the Egyptian in a calm voice. What's wrong with you?

His answer was to turn his anger from his confusing previous pair of adversaries and focus his rage on this newcomer, an infidel who dared question him in Arabic. He charged Dartley with his knife.

That was his mistake. He would have been hard to handle if he had weaved and sparred. Dartley had seen more than one martial arts expert go under to a skilled knife fighter. But the Egyptian's rage clouded his mind and he thrust himself headlong at what he saw as a new and hated American challenge.

The Arab came at Dartley with the knife held close to his right hip. Dartley checked the arm of his knife hand with a left-handed reverse grip, thumb down. At the same time he delivered a right vertical flatfist to his attacker's deltoid muscle joint. Still holding onto the Arab's arm, Dartley brought his right arm across the back of his opponent's neck, pushed his head down and brought his right knee up into his face.

He forced the Egyptian's right arm up behind his back and applied a reverse hammer lock with his left arm. Dartley had to rip the Arab's little finger from the knife handle to loosen the grip on the weapon.

Dartley dispatched him with a blow to the base of his skull and let him sag unconscious at his feet.

"He'll be all right," Dartley reassured the Americans. "When he wakes up he'll have a bit of a headache."

Emily squawked. "Son-of-a-bitch is going to have a pain in his gut, too." She drove the pointed toe of her highheeled shoe into the prone man's belly. "Damn mugger!"

"I don't think he was trying to rob you," Dartley said, pushing them both firmly before him out of the side street and into the main thoroughfare. "There's very little street crime here. He was behaving as if you'd insulted him."

"He didn't speak English, we don't speak his lingo," Emily reasoned. "How the hell could we insult him?"

Harry wasn't saying anything.

Dartley gave him a hard look.

"Well, back there a ways I had to take a leak," Harry offered. "Happened it was against one of their churches."

"Who ever heard of anyone getting threatened with a knife for relieving himself against a church?" Emily wanted to know.

"A foreigner urinating against a mosque is the sort of thing some of the Light of Islam fanatics imagine in their nightmares," Dartley explained, now walking along between the two of them. "Don't you know how things are here?"

Emily said, "I'm a Baptist from Alabama and it still don't seem reasonable to me."

Dartley laughed. "I'd feel sorry for any Arab you caught relieving himself against your Baptist church down in Alabama."

Harry guffawed. "She'd cut his pecker off with one swing of that purse of hers."

"I'm a lady," Emily protested, "and I won't tolerate that dirty talk. Though I could use a drink."

Dartley considered that a drink was the last thing

either of them needed. Yet they would provide good cover for him at the bar of the Marriott Hotel. He glanced at his watch. Twenty to twelve. He would take a cab.

"Where are you staying?" Dartley asked.

"The Sheraton."

"That's not far from the Marriott, which has the best bar of all the hotels. Let's grab a taxi and I'll buy you a drink."

It was in the taxi that Emily dropped the bombshell.

"You're a nice man," she said to Dartley. He had told her his name was John and she had forgotten it. "You saved our lives from that mugger and we haven't even said thank you. Where's your manners, Harry?"

"Cab and drinks are on me," Harry said, and punched Dartley in the arm.

"My invitation," Dartley claimed.

Then Emily's bombshell: "Very well. But you come with us tomorrow night to meet the prez at his palace."

"The who?"

"The president," she said. "What's his name, Harry?"

Harry couldn't recall. "I seen him on TV back home though, mouthing off like they all do. We're all sitting out in the garden late this afternoon, having a little drink or two, when the clown and a bunch of juvenile delinquents with automatic rifles nearly run us down with a truck first of all, then rush around with phony grins while they shake our hands, and next thing we know they're going to send limos for us tomorrow to come to a reception at the presidential palace. He even made a joke about no booze being served there and so to make sure we've had a few before we go."

"Ahmed Hasan said that?" Dartley asked.

"Sure," Harry confirmed. "You ask me, he's loony as they come."

There was no sign in the Marriott Hotel bar of the pretty woman who had met him that afternoon in the cafe. Dartley found himself disappointed. He had assumed, with no good reason he now realized, that she would be the one to meet him.

He stayed with Emily and Harry at a table for twenty minutes or so, until they got to chatting with other Americans and he was able to slip away to the bar. He would phone them at the Sheraton tomorrow to go with them to see the prez, as they called him. Harry was an auctioneer in Birmingham and had collected pre-Columbian artifacts for years. Now that supply was tightening up and so he was checking out Egypt. They both referred to themselves as amateur archeologists. Dartley privately considered they were being a little kind to themselves. In better times, he might have put Harry together with Omar Zekri. They could have done business with each other.

A small, seedy looking man who blinked his eyes a lot stood down the bar. Finally he said to Dartley, "Terence Hunter?"

"'Fraid not."

"Yes, you are. If you follow my meaning."

Dartley nodded. "I was expecting someone else."

"She's in room 422."

"Are you coming too?"

He shook his head.

"Then I'll ask you now. Can you get me a floor plan of the presidential palace by tomorrow morning?"

"Will noon be all right?" the man asked, blinking his eyes.

"Sure. You want to make it here?"

The little man nodded and faded away into the crowd at the bar.

The nameless lady from the cafe was in room 422. Dartley, as always, refused a drink.

"That much I have in common with the mullahs," he joked.

She handed him an American passport. Terence Hunter. Schoolteacher, Huntington, Long Island.

"Hi, I'm Terry," he said.

"Nina."

This woman did not waste words.

"Your friend downstairs is bringing me some floor plans tomorrow at noon."

She sipped on a vodka straight. "So you might as well stay here."

"That's kind of you."

"Not at all. My superior told me to make very sure you paid for this room."

Dartley laughed.

She pouted. "Israel is a poor country. Only Americans can afford to stay in these luxury hotels."

"And some Arabs."

Nina was dressed in the same modest pantsuit she had worn in the afternoon. When she saw him watching her, she put down her drink and eased the tunic off. Then her pants. She seemed to have no shyness in disrobing opposite him. Next she slipped out of her blouse. All she wore now was bra and panties and highheels. She pranced up and down, sipping her vodka, eagerly displaying her body before his eyes. Finally, the bra and panties came off, but she kept the shoes.

She stood still while he ran his hands over her body in soft little caresses and strokes that sent sensual shivers through her flesh. Dartley lavished attention on her statuesque, naked form with his tongue. The tip of his tongue traced arcs and patterns across her flawless, smooth skin.

She grew crazy with excitement, clasped his head in both her hands, pressed his face and tongue where she felt most sensitive—then stood before him with her legs wide apart and let his tongue stroke and slip inside the opening of her inner joy.

He carried her to the bed, pulled off his clothes, and took pleasure in the warm silky feel of her body against his. He stroked and fondled her until she no longer knew who or where she was, until she felt she was just a mass of melting sensations crying out to him to ease her heat.

She lay on her back, heaving with passion, legs parted submissively. He drove his member deep within her, withdrew to the very tip and then thrust its full length forward again into her parting, quivering tissues, enjoying fiercely the duty of his manhood, filling her needful want with the mastery of his cock.

Chapter
11

The two men's camels followed their Bedouin guide's camel through the cold desert night. All they could hear were their own breathing and the sand-muffled thumps of the camels' feet. Sometimes the Bedouin muttered in Arabic, or one of the two men he was guiding said something in French—careful of what he said since the Bedouin also spoke that language. From time to time, vast black masses of rock loomed up close to them out of the darkness, and they veered away from them like small boats at sea avoiding fog-shrouded cliffs. It was clear to the two men that the Bedouin was using these occasional rock outcrops as landmarks on their nocturnal voyage, yet how he managed to navigate on the long tracts between the rocks remained a mystery to them. When one of the two men suggested in French that maybe the camels themselves knew the way, the Bedouin did not laugh. They were heading due south, and so they saw the dawn begin to break off to their left. The camels

plodded onward at their unvarying pace as bars of
gray light appeared gradually.

"This shitty animal is crawling with ticks," one
complained. "I've been bitten at least a dozen times."

The other answered, "I'm so goddam seasick or
whatever from sitting up here swaying around all
these hours, I probably haven't noticed them biting
me. Not to mention freezing my ass off. I've forgotten why the desert gets so cold at night. You're the
scientist here. Why does it happen?"

"Why not ask our guide what his explanation is?"

"He'll probably say Allah did it to keep us infidels
in our hotels at night."

This time the Bedouin did laugh.

The sky lightened by the minute, yet they could
see nothing close up to them. The camels seemed to
be walking over vast empty sands. It was another
twenty minutes before the pink rays of the as yet
unrisen sun poked up from behind hills to the east.
Then they saw the scoured, eaten rock formations,
pinkish brown, towering around them on all sides.
One remarked that he felt they and their guide, even
though mounted on tall camels, were like three ants
on an early morning boulevard. The scale of the
high, bare crags and level, windblown sands made
them feel miniaturized. Their guide told them how
Lawrence and an Arab prince had come this way, as
they were doing, to descend on Aqaba in secret. The
two men deliberately refrained from exchanging a
glance, and the Bedouin smiled at them with glittering
eyes and asked no questions. When they neared
another of the monolithic structures he pointed out
script carved in the rock thousands of years ago,

script older than Arabic or Hebrew, perhaps telling ancient travelers where to find water. There was water here then, he informed them. There was none now. The sun had just barely cleared the rocks to the east when the Bedouin signaled his camel to bend its four legs and drop on its belly to the sand. The two other camels followed suit without their riders' bidding. The three men dismounted. The Bedouin pointed south into the reddish-purple mountains and the two men nodded. Each shook hands with the guide, then heaved a knapsack on his back and began to climb the steep incline. The Bedouin secured their two camels on a line behind his own, remounted and struck north. Neither he nor they glanced behind them again.

Alain Mendes and Luc Jacob were sweating and exhausted when they tramped down from the mountains into the town of Aqaba. They consulted a map and found their bearings for the Hotel Jarnac. The French waiter looked at them with an unwelcoming stare as they trooped dustily into the hotel breakfasting area, but he mellowed when he heard their Parisian accents. It had been six years since the waiter had been home and he was soon plying the two men with coffee, croissants, and cognac while they told him the latest from the French capital and gave him a current copy of *Paris-Match* and some newspapers. This early morning chatter about life in Paris soon brought Michelle Perret to their table. As they talked, she looked the young men over and they both flirted with her. Luc was fair-haired, with blue eyes beneath his tinted aviator glasses, with sun-reddened skin, tall. Alain was more her type—he was gentler, softer, with dark brown hair, olive skin, understanding brown eyes, and had less to say than Luc, but she could tell that he was more intuitively understanding of a woman. They told her they would love to stay at the Hotel Jarnac, but could not afford to do so.

Michelle could hardly believe it when she heard herself saying, "I know the room prices here are probably higher than you intended to pay, being students at the Ecole Polytechnique, and I can't give you a reduced rate. I do have a small servant's room empty on the top floor that I could let you have for nothing, but it would only fit one of you. Maybe Luc could stay there. Alain, I suppose you could sleep on the couch in my room."

"Great," Alain said.

She was flattered at his enthusiasm.

"We could stay on for a few days," Luc suggested.

"Certainly," she agreed. "It will be wonderful having you both here. You can see how much excitement you've caused already among us poor exiles in our lonely isolation when you arrived here out of the blue with your talk and atmosphere of Paris." She sniffed Alain appreciatively. "I can practically smell the Metro off you."

He grinned. "I haven't had a shower in a couple of days. I didn't know I smelled that bad."

"The Metro smells wonderful," she protested, "especially after all this horrible fresh sea air. I want to smell Gitanes and wine and fresh-baked bread! You want to shower now, Alain? Use the one in my room. Luc, you have no shower. You come down later from your room." She touched Alain's forearm. "Shall we go up?"

Michelle sat on the bed and watched Alain through the open door of the bathroom as he squirted shaving cream on his hand from an aerosol can and looked critically at his grizzled face in the mirror. After he had finished shaving, he took off his clothes and stepped into the shower stall. He thought she might join him, but she didn't and he didn't ask her. Leaving the water running, he stepped quietly from the stall and peeped into the room through the crack between the door hinges. Michelle was hurriedly going through the contents of his knapsack. Alain smiled and slipped back in the shower. Finally, he turned off the water, came unhurriedly out of the stall, didn't bother to dry himself, only wrapping a towel around his middle. He took the shaving cream can from the top of the handbasin and carried it into the room.

Michelle was sitting on the side of the bed, as if she had never moved. She looked at the shaving cream can in his right hand. "Are you kinky?"

He laughed. "You've been away from Paris too long. Look, I'll show you." He twisted the head of the can and then depressed the top, holding the nozzle close to her face. Instead of shaving cream, gas escaped. "Breathe deeply," he urged.

She inhaled the gas. "God, it's so long since I've been high—I never smoke." She inhaled again. "I like this. What is it?"

"Nitrous oxide. Laughing gas. What the dentist gives you. It's harmless."

She said, "I remember once, at a party, in the Marais, we passed around a balloon of this for everyone to sniff, then we all took our clothes off, but were too zonked to do anything." She inhaled again and again. "Oh, I feel dizzy and numb, and my fingers and toes tingle." She giggled.

Alain asked her questions and gave her more nitrous oxide to sniff every few minutes to maintain her high. And she was high! She never noticed he was taking none of the gas himself. He could not have stopped her talking if he had wanted to, which of course he didn't. His only difficulties were to keep her mind from wandering away from what he wanted to hear about and to keep from incidentally inhaling too much of the gas himself. He wanted to hear who had ordered Aaron Gottlieb's death in Aqaba, and she wanted to talk about her lack of a full emotional life in this desert resort. She told him how she had not even known an Israeli agent was involved, how she had assumed along with everyone else that the body was that of a CIA agent, an American who had come from Cairo. She gave him the names of her French intelligence contacts in Amman, described her doings as a French agent in London and Madrid, mixing in just about everything she knew about French intelligence, which in his opinion was not very much. Alain Mendes gave her an extra strong whiff of gas—enough to put her out for a few minutes— and left her smiling dreamily on the bed. He dressed, took the room key, and climbed the back stairs hurriedly to Luc Jacob's room.

"I got everything she knows, all on a minor level," Alain told him. "She didn't know an Israeli agent was involved. She thought he was an American. I don't think we should kill her—she won't remember what it is she's told me and she didn't deliberately order the death of a Mossad operative."

Luc shook his head grimly. "Nabel said over the phone that Gottlieb was a friend of his. Nabel used to go to his kibbutz and plant lettuce with him or something. Nabel said she was to die. You want me—"

Alain said sharply, "Wait a few minutes and then come down."

He left the tiny room, went down the back stairs and used Michelle's key to unlock her door. She was sitting up on the bed, wiping her eyes and shaking her head sleepily. "Oh, there you are." She was still smiling.

He put her out again with more nitrous oxide. Then he went to the bathroom, dropped the aerosol can in his shaving kit on the handbasin, and removed from it a hypodermic syringe and an unlabeled bottle of clear liquid. He pulled the plastic protective cap off the hypodermic needle, pushed the plunger all the way home, and pressed the needle through the rubber top of the bottle. He inverted the bottle and, keeping the needle tip below the liquid level, pulled the plunger slowly out, filling the syringe with the clear liquid. He drew out the needle from the rubber cap, replaced the bottle in the kit, walked back to the bed, and held Michelle's bare right arm immediately below the elbow with his left hand. The inside of her arm faced him, and he squeezed with his thumb across it to block the flow and make the blood vessels stand out. He glanced at her face. Her eyes were half closed and she still had a goofy smile. He picked a long blue vein running just beneath the skin in the middle of her arm and he eased the needle into it. He released his grip beneath her elbow and pulled back a tiny bit on the plunger until he saw a spurt of blood enter the clear liquid inside the syringe, showing that the needle was properly inserted in the vein. He looked once more at her face, then slowly drove the plunger home, saying softly, "I won't hurt a bit. It's Nembutal. I once had to do this with my mother's dog."

The smile never left her face.

When a gentle rap sounded on the door and a voice said, "It's Luc," he let him in. Alain went to pack his shaving kit in his knapsack.

Luc closed the door behind him and dropped his own knapsack on the floor. "Ready to go?"

"Sure."

"You got laid?"

Alain shook his head.

"I thought you might have because of the smile she has on her face. At least you got a shower out of it." Luc walked over to Michelle's body on the bed and raised one of her eyelids with his thumb. The pupil did not contract from the light.

"Are you checking up on me?" Alain asked.

Luc didn't answer, just let the eyelid drop back in place and gazed coolly at Alain from his own calm blue eyes behind his tinted spectacles.

They shouldered their knapsacks, went down the back stairs, and out into the town. No one paid attention to the two foreign hikers crazy enough to walk places in the morning sun. They climbed back into the hills behind the town. At a lonely stretch of empty desert, they plodded through hot stones and baked mud to cross over the invisible border into Israel.

In the morning, Richard Dartley hired a felucca on the Nile. He and Nina went out on the water as the sun's heat grew, after they had visited a suq in the cooler early morning. Nina was curious about Dartley's purchase at the suq, but she said nothing. The boatman was a wiry, shriveled man with leathery skin, and Nina had bargained with him intensely before they got into the craft, south of the Kasr-el-Nil Bridge on the East Bank. There was a lively river breeze upstream and they sailed with it past Roda Island, which had at its southern tip the Nilometer, a marked column which was once used to measure the height of the river at certain times in order to forecast how well crops would do, since all agriculture depended on plentiful Nile water.

The pyramids were to their right as they sailed upriver, relaxing in the roomy felucca with its large, more or less triangular sail which the boatman handled effortlessly. When they came to a reach of the eastern bank which was empty of people, Dartley announced that he wanted to go ashore.

The boatman waited in the craft after he had beached it on the riverbank, while Nina and Dartley walked hand in hand—boatmen were used to such ungodly intimacies in public on the part of tourists—along the bank until they were hidden from his sight by bushes.

Nina laughed and said, "He probably thinks you got horny and we stopped for a quick fuck." She looked him in the eyes, hopefully. "Did we?"

Dartley smiled and unwrapped his purchase from the suq. "First things first." He produced a dozen cheap metal tableforks of various design and size. He said, "I need to practice."

He threw a fork hard at a mudbank about fifteen feet away. The kitchen utensil turned end over end and buried its tines into the mud with a loud splat.

"Very good," Nina said in a patronizing voice. "This must make quite a change from a Browning Hi-Power."

"You just try bringing a Browning into the presidential palace."

"Don't you think they'll ask why you're bringing in a dozen forks?"

"Stop giving me a hard time, Nina."

He buried four forks, tines first, into the mudbank in quick succession, followed by a fifth which hit sideways and fell to the ground.

Nina giggled. "I was just thinking, if that happens with Ahmed Hasan, he'll probably never guess you're trying to kill. He'll think you're mad because you don't like his food."

Dartley tried to keep a straight face and buried the remainder of the forks with deadly accuracy and force into the mudbank.

"How do you know Ahmed Hasan is going to feed these Americans at his reception?" Nina asked.

"Because he's already told them he's not giving them booze. He has to lay something out for them."

"Maybe he'll expect them to eat with their fingers," she suggested.

"Then I'll strangle him."

She watched him practice with the differently

sized and shaped forks. His speed in handling them increased, and the force with which they now hit the mudbank buried them halfway up their handles into the soft river muck. Nina tried her hand at throwing some, claiming before she did so that it was easy. She never managed to stick a single fork.

"One more question," she said in a while, "and this is a serious one. I know this is not a suicide mission, but I don't see how you can do this at a crowded reception and expect to escape unseen. How?"

Dartley paused with six or seven of the forks in his hands, and he half turned to her and looked in her direction as the forks shot from his right hand, one after another. They buried themselves in the target area of the mudbank while Dartley himself was facing nearly in the opposite direction.

"I'm beginning to get the idea," Nina said, impressed.

"Maybe it'll work," Dartley said. "It's worth a try. Meanwhile we don't want to disappoint our boatman. How about that quick fuck?"

The American amateur archeologists were sitting in the well-tended gardens of the Sheraton when Richard Dartley arrived. Dartley registered many of them as dotty, harmless types, along with some earnest academics. A few looked like lost souls who might have come on the wrong tour. And then there was Emily and Harry, who kind of stuck out from the others because of their wheeler-dealer attitude. Also, they were drunk again.

"Hey"—Harry couldn't remember the name Dartley had given the previous night—"good to see you."

"Terry," Dartley said shaking Harry's hand. "Hi, Emily." He pecked her on the cheek.

This was all Emily needed to launch into an account of how Terry had saved them from the "mugger." Her current version of the happenings did not include Harry's pissing against the mosque, and Harry didn't interrupt to volunteer anything about this himself. It was a clear case now of robbery being the motive.

Dartley had other things on his mind than discussing this story, but he went out of his way to be charming to several old dears who might come in handy later when he might need to chat with them if they happened to be standing near Ahmed Hasan. The floor plan had not been of much use to him, except to get a general idea of the layout of the palace. No one had any idea in what part of the presidential palace the reception would be held or even whether it would be held indoors or outdoors. In fact, there was no advance information that the reception would definitely take place at the presidential palace. Dartley no longer cared where they held the damn thing so long as it took place, so long as there was food, and so long as they were not expected to eat with their fingers.

Emily was launched into an account of Isis and Osiris, and it seemed from her version of their lives, the mullahs would not have approved of them. Osiris, as the eldest brother, became ruler. He chose his sister Isis as queen, which seemed to cause problems in the rest of the family. Another sister, married to another brother, got Osiris drunk so they could hit the sack together. This other brother, Set, persuaded Osiris at a banquet—he must have been drunk again—to lie down in a box. Set nailed the lid shut, dumped the box in the Nile and became ruler himself. When the box was washed up, the widow Isis recovered the body—but Set seized it and cut it in fourteen pieces, which he widely scattered. Isis found all these pieces, except for the phallus, which was eaten by a Nile river crab (Harry supplied this information). She joined the body together and managed to conceive a son with it—Dartley didn't ask Emily the obvious question about the piece of property the crab had run off with. Anyway, this son set out to avenge his father's murder by Set, and when his mother Isis tried to stop him, he cut off her head which she replaced with the head of a cow, and so on. . . .

After Harry and Emily had consumed about another pint of alcohol each, three air-conditioned charter buses arrived to pick the guests up. No invitations had been handed out and now no identities were checked, which suited Dartley fine. As Harry put it, they were off to the palace to meet the prez.

The thing Harry didn't know was that Dartley hoped to make it an unforgettable occasion.

Dartley spotted the metal detectors as they were ushered through a long hallway in the presidential palace. Everyone had to pass through in succession, but they were artfully concealed as decorative arches. Their courteous operators, posing as welcomers, greeted people with smiles, but at the same time blocked enough of the passageway so that the newcomers had to pass through each detector in single file. There were more than a hundred Americans in all.

The detectors did not sound any alarms while those with Dartley went through. Dartley admired the smooth, ultra-professional way the palace security men had set up this electronic search—probably most of the amateur archeologists were unaware they had passed through one metal detector, let alone three. Dartley hoped that the rest of the palace security was a bit looser. If not, he was in trouble.

Like the old central part of the Marriott Hotel, the presidential palace looked like it had once been a royal residence. They trooped through enormous chambers and past ornate staircases and balconies. Dartley reflected on the fact that once rebels seized power in the name of the people, the first thing they always did was move into the luxury quarters of the tyrants they had deposed. The Bolsheviks did it in Moscow and St. Petersburg. When the French mob stormed the Bastille prison, they knew enough to totally destroy it—so that the Place de la Bastille today was just a big space with little cars whirring about it at high speed. However, Mitterand, the present left-wing socialist premier of France, lives like a king under a blaze of chandeliers.

Ahmed Hasan had found the tools of repression in place—even if not in use—when he seized power. It just came naturally to him to put the dungeons of the thick-walled medieval fortress of the Citadel back to work, and to live in splendor like a great potentate in this palace himself. He probably felt it was the least his grateful countrymen could do for him.

Only after Dartley had been abroad many times had he come to appreciate the lack of palaces and so forth in America. In America, so long as men were free to bear arms, they need never bow to some upstart autocrat. And as Dartley's uncle liked to say, the day Soviet paratroopers hit American soil, they'd be cut to pieces by the members of the National Rifle Association before the army could get to them.

They entered a big ceremonial hall and milled about for a while. Dartley slipped away from Emily and Harry because they were loud and attracting attention, which was the last thing Dartley wanted to bring on himself.

In order to remain inconspicuous, he got into conversation with a little old lady, a retired pharmacist from Cincinnati, and was genuinely interested in her talk of how the ancient Egyptians held certain animals sacred, among them the crocodile. She told him that crocodile cemeteries had been discovered in which the reptiles were mummified and buried with their newly hatched or even with their eggs. She said that when Egypt became part of the Roman Empire, one particular crocodile god at a place called Crocodilopolis—she swore she was not putting him on—became a big attraction for Roman tourists. Each worshipper brought an offering of meat, bread and wine. The big old croc sunned himself on the bank of his private lake, with gold rings in his ears (Dartley was fairly sure crocodiles didn't have earlobes, but he wasn't about to spoil her story by mentioning that) and gold bracelets on his forelegs. One priest held open his jaws and another threw the meat and bread and poured the wine into his maw.

While the little old lady from Cincinnati was telling Dartley about crocodiles, he was searching the room with his eyes for signs of dangerous human reptiles. Apart from a few low-level Egyptian functionaries, there was no one apart from Americans in the big hall. Why had Hasan brought them here? Dartley had no answer to that, and he would not have been surprised at that moment to see soldiers at one end of the hall mounting machine guns on tripods. . . .

A group of Egyptians arrived—uniformed military officers and men in pinstripe suits who Dartley could tell from their smooth smiles and polished manner were career diplomats. Coffee and tea were served and the chatter started up afresh. No sign of Ahmed Hasan yet. No doubt he would make a grand entrance later.

Dartley felt eyes on him. Yet when he turned around, no one in particular struck him as a threat. But he knew he was being watched. His sixth sense. Someone.

Then Dartley caught sight of him. The small, thin physicist he had trapped in the cafe near the Citadel, who had told him that Ahmed was using plutonium for his bomb. Bakkush. Yes, Dr. Mustafa Bakkush.

The Egyptian looked furtively at him and sidled away into the crowd.

Dartley went after him but couldn't find him in the mob of archeologists, civil servants, military officers and waiters rushing everywhere with trays of tea and coffee. Had he gone to sound the alarm? Probably not. Dartley knew Bakkush had been watching him for a while. If he was going to turn him in, he wouldn't have waited around to be discovered. Dartley cursed himself for his own carelessness in not spotting Bakkush sooner. He had been on the watch for palace security men and for Ahmed's bodyguards, not inoffensive, pint-sized scientists. And judging by the scared look on Bakkush's face, he had not expected to come across Dartley here either!

Without bringing attention to himself by moving too fast among the throng, Dartley floated about with a vague, benevolent smile on his face while he scanned every inch of the place for Bakkush. Dartley remembered how this man's family had been brought to Cairo in crates, forcing his return. He intended telling the Egyptian that if he opened his mouth against him at this reception, his children—Dartley couldn't remember how many the man had—would die lingering painful deaths, aware that their father's words had brought this suffering upon them.

Dartley was the kind of man who could put a lot of feeling and authenticity in a message like that, because mostly he meant exactly what he said. People looked into his cold, steady eyes and they believed what he was telling them.

He found Bakkush hiding behind three tall men. Before the Egyptian had a chance to disappear again, Dartley strode down on him with a killer smile and grasped his right hand in a firm handshake. Dartley squeezed until he felt the hand bones crackle in his grip and the Egyptian uttered a small, high-pitched yelp. He released the scientist's hand, but before he could describe how the man's children would have boiling water poured on them and be skinned alive,

Bakkush whispered fiercely to him, clutching his damaged hand, "You're wasting your time! Leave things to me!"

Dartley shook his head slowly.

"Very well. I think I know what you will try to do here. I will help in any way I can. Again, I no longer think it necessary in the short term." He spoke quickly and precisely—a man with a disciplined mind but a little bewildered at the prospect of immediate action. "There is no urgency for you because of the destroyed reactor. For me, yes. Ahmed has to go. What do you want me to do?"

Dartley was alarmed by the physicist's behavior now, for the opposite reason that he had been minutes ago. Before he had been worried that the man would turn him in. Now he was apprehensive about the Egyptian's enthusiasm to get rid of Ahmed Hasan! A gung-ho amateur's self-confidence could be more deadly to his partner than their adversary's best weapons.

"Do nothing," Dartley told him firmly, "unless I tell you to. Stay fairly close to me if you can, close enough to follow the action and so I can find you. But remember, I'm the one who will do the job."

"In sha 'allah."

"God willing," Dartley confirmed.

Dartley eased away from a group discussing Heket, a frog-headed goddess who, as a midwife, assisted every morning in the birth of the sun. He figured he had enough things on his mind already without confusing himself further with this kind of talk. He avoided the groups talking with Egyptians, in case some word or look might arouse their suspicions. And he kept away from Emily and Harry, who were creating a ruckus about something at the other end of the big hall. He was relieved to find two guys with paunches and bloodshot eyes talking about the Forty-Niners and the Rams. They hadn't heard any game scores since they'd arrived in Egypt and it was killing them. Mustafa trailed him at a distance and set about charming some sprightly matrons.

A short time later, the president made his entrance with fifteen or so armed teenage bodyguards who ran before and after him like hounds around the foxhunt whip. The military men snapped to attention and saluted. The diplomats bowed and scraped. The American gaped. Ahmed Hasan, in a freshly pressed khaki uniform with lots of ribbons and medals and a cap heavy with brass, clasped the right hand of random, startled archeologists in fervent handshakes.

He gestured to his bodyguards, and they slunk off in twos and threes to lean against walls and leer at the guests. Dartley guessed they reminded many of the Americans of urban punks back home, except these carried automatic rifles. Anyway, the initial fright apparently felt by some of the guests soon evaporated and they were flocking around the smiling, talking president to hear what he had to say.

Dartley kept his distance. He checked out the bodyguards. They should prove no problem—at the beginning, anyway—since it was clear by their attitude that they had sunk into bored apathy at the sight of all these harmless old farts. Five of the bodyguards were girls, all very pretty, with full bodies. They had tailored their combat fatigues to fit their bodies tightly, especially over the ass and legs, and the tops of their breasts showed in their open-necked shirts. Each wore a bush hat, set at her personal choice of angle, on a cloud of black hair. Obviously the mullahs didn't mess with these babies.

One sultry beauty saw Dartley eyeing her, thrust out a hip and parted her lips. Dartley had to admit that if he was president, he too would make her his bodyguard. . . .

Ahmed Hasan clapped his hands like a sultan, and immediately long tables displaying plates of all kinds of foods were wheeled into the hall by white-tuniced waiters. Dartley's eyes may have been the only ones in the place which did not go to the food; he searched for forks. They were there—heavy, silverplate, of old-fashioned design, ideal for his purpose. Dartley felt the blood pump faster in his veins.

He lined up with others to get a plate, napkin, and fork, then to pass along the table and select what he wished. Mustafa Bakkush was ahead of him in the line. He passed Dartley a piece of folded paper and said, "In case you need to hide . . ." Dartley nodded, hoping it would not come to that. He picked up his plate and napkin, put one fork on the plate and slipped another into his left hand out of sight beneath the plate. He would need only two forks—one to throw, the other to have on his plate to show he hadn't thrown it. He would get only one throw, only one chance to bury the fork deep in Ahmed Hasan's throat, rupturing the blood vessels there and ending the tyrant's life. He had already selected his escape route with the aid of the memorized floor plan of the palace.

All he needed now were one or more small groups
between him and Hasan, a fairly crowded location to
block the bodyguards' view, a lightning flick of the
wrist, and it would be all over. He would walk away
before anyone fully realized what had happened.

He maneuvered closer to Hasan. Finally, he
positioned himself in a suitable place. The president
was less than fifteen feet from him, where Dartley
stood eating lamb kebab and rice from his plate. He
put down his fork in the food and reached under the
plate for the second fork. A woman moved out of the
way, giving him a clear view of Hasan, directly facing
him and talking animatedly to several people. Dartley
readied the fork...

A loud shout caused everyone to look down the
hall. Some of the bodyguards were running and
yelling at those nearer the president to protect him.
Dartley looked at Hasan. There were three or four
people in the way now. Seconds later, the bodyguards surrounded their leader and ran him from the
hall in their midst, their automatic rifles pointed at
the stunned Americans.

Dartley put down his plate on the table and headed for a door. He saw Mustafa Bakkush on the way
and gave him a dirty look. Had the scientist had a
last-moment change of heart and raised the alarm?
Bakkush saw his look of anger, quickly approached,
and caught him by the arm.

"I saw who raised the alarm," he whispered. "Quick.
Out this door."

Dartley suspected a trap for a moment, until he
reasoned that Bukkush needn't do this to entrap him.
All the Egyptian had to do was yell.

A long corridor ran parallel to the hall on the other side of the door.

"Stop," Bakkush said. "He's standing in the next doorway up that way. He can't see us here. Wait until he moves and you will see his face. I saw him look at you and then warn Hasan's guards."

Dartley saw a tall figure in a business suit partially concealed as he stood in the doorway along the corridor. The man turned to move into the corridor, away from the hall. Dartley shrank back, lingering only for a glimpse of his face. It was Jacques Laforque. The same man who had hired him to kill Ahmed Hasan had now saved the president from him!

Dartley squeezed Mustafa's arm, exited from the opposite corner of the hall, descended a staircase, opened French windows into a garden and walked beneath a row of chestnut trees. He nodded to the two armed soldiers at the barred gate which led to the street and disappeared into the city crowds.

One thing only was on his mind.

He had failed again.

Chapter
12

Richard Dartley sat on a tombstone in the City of the Dead and watched the dawn break. He ran his hand over the bristles on his chin and cheeks, smoothed the moustache he had recently grown and wondered whether he should now grow a beard. Having a beard would help him blend in more, but he would never pass as an Egyptian. Time was running out. He had failed twice to assassinate Ahmed Hasan. Dartley now had a feeling that this whole matter was going to be settled one way or the other long before his beard got a chance to grow.

He could only hope to keep out of the clutches of government agents a short while more, if that. He could not easily hide out other than as a tourist or foreign businessman, unless he buried himself here on the outskirts of Cairo in this shantytown grown up around and within the vast graveyard.

After he slipped away from the presidential palace the previous day, Dartley considered returning to his hotel, but thought better of it. Presumably Laforque would have provided a description of him, so that agents could comb every hotel in the city overnight to find someone who answered this description. Maybe not, but Dartley could not take the chance. Had the alert at the palace been dismissed as a false alarm? No, Hasan would take Laforque's word that an American assassin was present there, if Laforque told him that the American was an assassin. Laforque might not have said that, since it could implicate his own government. He might have simply said that a foreign spy or agent was present. Yet this would hardly have resulted in the bodyguards hustling the president to safety. No, Laforque had said a threat was present. Even if the radio last night said nothing about it, Hasan himself knew he had survived another attempt on his life and his men would be hunting down the would-be assassin.

Dartley had looked at the slip of paper Dr. Mustafa Bakkush had given him at the reception. It was an address farther along the street on which he walked. He found a tailor's shop, and the tailor told him to stay out of sight at the back of the shop until it was nearly dusk. Then they took a taxi to Salah Al Din Square, southeast of the Citadel. From the square they walked south past the Manshiya Prison to Sharia Al Imam Al Shaf'i. They entered Al Khalifa, or the Southern Cemetery, the older of the two Mameluke cemeteries, so vast they were known as the Cities of the Dead.

The Mamelukes were originally slaves brought to Egypt from the tenth century on. They became a soldier caste and were so fierce at their job, they took over the country in the thirteenth century. For the next two hundred fifty years they ruled Egypt as savage autocrats. They held onto a lot of their power after the Turkish conquest of Egypt in 1517 and fought Napoleon in 1798. Dartley had read much about them and their military exploits, and he knew that the Southern Cemetery held mostly twelfth to fourteenth century Mameluke tombs. What he hadn't known was how much this City of the Dead had become one of the living.

As he and the tailor walked in the gathering dusk along the edge of the huge cemetery, which had its own streets, boulevards and squares with fancy stonework mausoleums, cenotaphs and walled enclosures, he saw how Cairo's poor had moved in among the marble tombs, often using a grave marker as part of the construction of their homes. Clothes dried on lines strung between two memorials, and a pair of dignified sculptures served as goalposts for a boys' soccer game. Children swarmed everywhere, and the smoke of cooking fires blackened tomb walls next to crowded shanties. Women bustled about their work. Men sat smoking on tombs and they gave Dartley and the tailor curious looks. Dartley reckoned they didn't see too many foreigners around here with night approaching.

The tailor departed hurriedly after he had introduced Dartley as Terry Hunter to a hollow-eyed, starved looking man called Abdel Ibrahim. The Ibrahim clan seemed to control all the surrounding area of cemetery, and Dartley met a rapid succession of brothers, cousins, uncles and nephews, but not one woman, although they came to peep at him from a distance and whispered among themselves. He ate rice and beans with the men, was treated courteously, asked no questions, and was shown a bed of clean, dry rushes beneath a plywood tent. Depressed by his failures rather than physically tired, Dartley excused himself and crept into his bed of dry rushes early. He escaped into a deep, soothing sleep.

At dawn he was up, sitting on a tombstone, scratching the bristles on his cheeks and chin, thinking. Time was running out on him.

Abdel Ibrahim appeared from one of the shacks, stretched, rubbed his eyes, then suddenly noticed Dartley and immediately became a gracious Arab host. He inquired how his guest had slept, whether he had been comfortable, if he had any immediate needs. Dartley praised Ibrahim's hospitality and continued the polite formal exchanges which he knew were essential in opening a conversation with an Arab.

"Terry, I must tell you this: I love Egypt." Dartley grew uneasy as the man went on describing how much he cared for his country—it began to sound like an elaborate apology for turning Dartley in to the authorities. Then Ibrahim's train of thought took a sudden turn. "Why then, you might ask me, am I willing to help you if I am a patriot? Yes, I am willing to help you—to hide you like a deadly asp in the breast of the mother country. Who are you? What have you come here to do?"

"To kill Ahmed Hasan," Dartley interrupted in a casual tone.

The Arab stopped and looked at him. He had not expected his rhetorical question to be answered. His gaunt, starved face cracked in a huge smile. "That is what I hoped you had come to do. You are a foreign infidel, yet it is the duty of devout Muslims and loyal Egyptians to aid you in ridding us of Ahmed Hasan. He uses Egypt and Egyptians like a child plays with flies. Two of my brothers were arrested, jailed in the Citadel. They have never been heard of again. I know they are dead." He waved his hand. "Their widows and orphans live here with us, and no day passes in which we do not mourn their loss. No day passes when my family does not look to me to seek vengeance in their name. I have spoken to men I trust about this. Now Allah has delivered you to us!"

This was the first time Dartley had ever heard himself described as a godsend and he was not sure how to react. It was clear that Ibrahim was demanding a role for himself in whatever was to happen, that personal revenge and shoring up his position as family head were his motivations in wanting to help rid Egypt of Hasan. But Dartley was a lone wolf. He worked alone.

Already on this job, he had sacrificed this principle and it had cost an Israeli agent his life. Dartley blamed himself for Aaron Gottlieb's death, since Dartley's mode of operation was to set up situations that were high-risk to no one but himself.

"I'm not sure about Allah sending me to you," Dartley said with a smile. "I don't think you should depend on that. Fact is, I like to work on my own. But I need help, I don't deny that. Any members of your family who work with me must be told they are putting their lives in danger."

"Agreed."

Dartley saw that the Egyptian was maneuvering him into making conditions, to all of which Ibrahim would agree, so that Dartley, before he knew what was happening, would find himself with a not entirely welcome new set of partners in the Ibrahim clan.

"Before we agree to anything," Dartley said, "I have some questions I must ask."

"Terry, you are my friend. No question is too intimate for me."

"How come you speak such good English?"

The Egyptian beamed, complimented. "I am fifty-eight years old. When I was young, the Union Jack flew over Egypt. The teachers in my school came mostly from England. Some of them had spent fifteen years here without learning more than fifteen words of Arabic. They thought they were civilizing us—I think they genuinely believed that—and of course the first step to civilization in their eyes was to speak English. My family were simple fellahin, as we still are, as nearly everyone in Egypt is." He waved his hand at the shacks and tombstones. "But now we are fellahin without land. My father toiled from sunrise to sunset on his small plot, and for him English words were almost magic talismans. He spoke Arabic, but for everything we were too poor to own, he used its English name. He sent all his children to an English-language school and was proud that we spoke English well. He thought that we would have all those things he could never afford to buy, all those things he called by their English names."

"Things didn't work out that way?"

Abdel Ibrahim gestured elaborately. "We—my brothers and sisters and I—all had government jobs when

President Mubarak was overthrown. We were not rich, but we owned our own houses. My oldest brother was accused of helping some of the president's aides escape to the American Embassy. When they tried to arrest him, he resisted with the help of another brother. So they took them both away. That was the last we ever saw or heard of them. When I demanded to know what had happened to them, I lost my government job. Then anyone who was a family member was expelled from government-subsidized housing and their jobs."

"Do you know anyone on the American staff?"

"We get money to keep us alive."

"Who gives it to you?"

"I cannot remember his name," Abdel said with a polite shrug.

"Pritchett?"

"It is a name very like that."

"I know Pritchett," Dartley said. "Don't tell him or anyone else at the embassy that I am here."

"Agreed."

Back to conditions, Dartley saw. "What about this place? Won't someone inform the police that an American is with you here?"

"Hasan's friends around here have all died or moved away."

Dartley was impressed with the sinister tone in Ibrahim's voice.

Abdel went on, "When you come and go, take different routes. There are many tourists here and the devout pass through on their way to various tombs."

Dartley was aware of the Arabic custom of picnicking at the family burial ground, and he knew that pilgrims flocked to the mausoleum of Al Imam Al Shaf'i not far away. Some of the mausoleums even charged tourists admission, so he would not be out of place as an American during daylight hours in the City of the Dead.

"Do you know Omar Zekri?" Dartley asked.

Ibrahim scowled and spat on the ground.

"Find out what he is doing," Dartley said.

Omar Zekri sat beside Awad in a battered, brown Saab. They paused outside the huge doors of the Citadel. Awad displayed his pass, the guard signaled and a door swung inward to admit the car. Awad was cleared by two more separate sets of soldiers before they were allowed to enter a building after leaving the Saab in a courtyard.

Omar was terrified. He had always been convinced that if he ever entered the Citadel, he would not leave it alive. They walked down a long hallway and into a large, bare, high-ceilinged room with no windows, badly lit by a single naked bulb suspended on a wire at the center of the room. Awad just stood there, letting his big belly relax and hang out over his belt. Omar moved restlessly about, fretting, worrying. Awad seemed to have forgotten him.

"I already explained that you can't blame me for what happened to Zaid," he whined. "I only telephoned information, like both of you told me to. Zaid knew that man was dangerous. You can't blame me because he went alone and got himself killed."

"No one is blaming you, Omar," Awad said soothingly.

"Then why am I in the Citadel?"

"Maybe I just want to torture you." Awad laughed at his own little joke.

Omar was reassured. This was the predictable Awad that he knew. He did not dare ask any more questions, knowing anyway that he would receive no straight answers until Awad felt like telling him why they were here.

Awad never did. They spent more than an hour in the empty room, Awad just standing in one place and hardly moving, Omar pacing up and down and from time to time starting up conversations that took him nowhere.

Ahmed Hasan strode into the room with his bodyguards. Awad bowed. Omar saw this and bowed even lower, pale now and starting to sweat.

"Honored president," Awad said, "this is the one man who can positively identify the American dog who drags his filthy carcass over the pure world of Islam."

Ahmed Hasan looked at the nervous, sweating Omar critically. "The Frenchman Jacques Laforque recognized him when it mattered. Why do I have to depend on a foreigner to alert me? Where has this Egyptian been until now?"

"He has been working with me," Awad said, "and with my partner, who as you know sacrificed his life for your excellency."

Hasan bowed his head in respect for the dead. "He will not be forgotten."

Everyone there knew Hasan could not remember Zaid's name.

Awad pointed proudly to Omar. "This man is not a

foreigner. He is an Arab. An Egyptian. A Sunni Moslem. A patriot and a believer you can depend on, not some whore from Paris like Laforque."

Ahmed Hasan looked from Awad to Omar and back again with an amused look. He said to Omar, "I have heard of your activities. You should be careful not to disappoint Awad, now that he has placed his trust in you. Like me, Awad is a hard taskmaster. He does not tolerate failure. How many days have you given him, Awad?"

"I had not presumed," Awad answered with uncharacteristic meekness.

"Two days," Hasan announced with finality.

"For what?" Omar asked, alarmed.

"To find the American dog," Awad told him. "I will be with you every hour and every minute of your search. We will not sleep until we find him."

"Two days," the president repeated.

"You will have to try very hard, Omar," Awad rasped. "Everyone here knows you for a cock-sucking asshole who does not deserve to live! We will let you fly to Beirut, Omar, and take your money with you if you give us this American. Before everybody here, you have my word on that."

"You will have my protection and thanks," Ahmed confirmed.

"But you only have two days," Awad cautioned the terrified Omar. "You heard his excellency give you two days. He is being very generous to a known spy such as yourself, Omar."

The only sound the sweating, trembling Omar was able to make was a small wheeze of protest.

"Spies!" Ahmed shouted, making Omar jump. "They

infest Egypt! They must be rooted out!" He rushed to the door. "Guard! Guard!" A dozen armed soldiers gathered before him. "Bring me a spy."

A sergeant stepped forward. "Who, sir?"

"What does it matter, soldier?" Ahmed shouted. "All spies are enemies of Egypt and Islam. Bring me a spy!"

They came back with a frightened, soft looking, middle-aged man who might once have been a prosperous businessman. The sergeant trussed the man's thumbs behind his back, pushed him into the room and shouted after him, "Kneel before our glorious president, defender of the Light of Islam."

The prisoner staggered to Hasan, dropped to his knees, and bowed his head.

Ahmed Hasan turned to Omar Zekri. "You see? That was not low enough. Kick him."

"Me?" Omar asked.

Awad shoved him. "Your president has ordered you, stupid dog."

Omar waddled over to the kneeling prisoner, who was now bowing desperately so that his forehead touched the floorboards. Omar kicked him gently on the thigh.

"Not gently!" Ahmed Hasan bellowed. "Hard! Like this!" He kicked the cringing Omar on the leg, and the chubby man squealed and nearly lost his balance.

But Omar got the message. He hauled off with a good boot into the bowing prisoner's side, which made the man crumple into a gasping knot of pain.

"Again!" Ahmed yelled. "Harder!"

Omar stood still and looked at him in mute appeal. When Hasan took a step toward him, Omar rushed to comply. He balanced on his left foot, drew back his right foot and kicked the prisoner with a mighty thump. Omar hopped about, holding his right ankle, which the kick had strained.

Ahmed smiled at this performance, walked over and kicked Omar on the rump. He pointed to the prisoner, now agonizedly trying to crawl away. Omar kicked him on the side of the head, which flipped the man on his back. Omar kicked the man again and he became unconscious.

"So you defy me?" Ahmed asked in an interested voice. "You try to cheat this spy from feeling his deserved punishment? Well, remember this, my friend: I will not let you slip away into unconsciousness to escape me if you don't hand over this American to me." He strode to the spread-eagled prisoner, contemptuously turned him over with one foot, then brought his heel down on the back of his neck and loudly snapped his backbone. He turned to Awad and pointed to Omar. "He has two days. No more."

As the president made for the door with long strides, his bodyguards clustered around him.

Awad gave Omar a pitying look and sneered, "You keep this up, Omar, you're doing just fine."

Richard Dartley and Abdel Ibrahim walked out of the Southern Cemetery and kept going until they came to a cafe with a public phone. Dartley got through to the Hotel des Roses after the usual difficulties with a Cairo phone and asked for Jacques Laforque. The Frenchman's voice came over the line a few minutes later.

"Monsieur?"

"Meet me in two hours where we met before," Dartley said without identifying himself.

"D'accord."

They took a taxi to the Hertz depot and Dartley gave Ibrahim money to hire a car. Ibrahim drove to a suq on Dartley's instructions. There Dartley bought the carcass of a lamb and a sack of rice, which they loaded in the trunk. Nothing was said—it was simply understood that Dartley would not insult Ibrahim by offering him cash at this stage. The Egyptian was free to change his mind later when he came to understand that this was business with Dartley, not revenge or heroics.

They were an hour early for his meeting with Laforque, and they sat in the car parked a distance down the street. Dartley expected the worst. The Frenchman had betrayed him at the palace. Presumably, he would try again if given the opportunity. Laforque did not know Dartley had seen him at the palace reception. There had been no mention of the incident on the TV, radio or newspapers. A meeting like this would be an ideal way for Laforque to hand him on a plate to the authorities. Yet Laforque was a professional and so he would know that Dartley could not be easily lured into such a trap. Anyway, Dartley had no choice but to meet his "employer" to find out what was happening.

They saw Laforque arrive and enter the cafe. Dartley left the car and Ibrahim drove past the cafe, turned about and stopped outside the cafe on the way back. He beckoned to Laforque, who stood immediately and joined him in the front seat of the gray Opel. As Ibrahim returned to where Dartley stood, there were no suspicious movements of other cars or people that he could detect. When the Opel stopped, Dartley climbed into the backseat. He said nothing to Laforque and kept busy looking for patterns in the traffic behind them, such as one car turning off and being replaced by another. The chaos of Cairo traffic would have made any sophisticated tailing operation very difficult. When Dartley was sure they were not being followed, he told Ibrahim to drop them off at a crowded intersection.

When Laforque had gotten out, Dartley set up a meeting place with Ibrahim in two hours. He recalled the Egyptian's often sketchy notion of time and tapped the man's digital wristwatch. "Be there."

"What do I do now?"

"You might take the lamb home before it starts to stink up the car during the hot part of the day."

Laforque seemed content to walk.

"Anything new?" Dartley asked.

"Yes. Very important. We want to cancel your contract. Keep the money. Go home right away."

Normally, Dartley would have shrugged and headed for the airport. He found himself saying, "Why?"

"High-level decision," Laforque said.

"Just like that."

Laforque shrugged. "No reflection on your abilities."

"Although I failed twice to achieve my goal?"

"Twice? Whatever you say. We're very pleased things turned out this way."

"I lost a man at Aqaba."

"You recruited him, not me," Laforque said. "That was bad luck. You don't throw good luck after bad to try to even things out. You get to keep your money without completing the job. Don't complain."

"Michelle Perret, your contact at Aqaba, set me up. Why?"

"She works for the same people I do. It's possible they gave her different orders behind my back. She doesn't report to me."

Dartley had to admire Laforque's cool dismissal of his implied charges. They both knew that Laforque was low-level and could be just as much a victim of his Paris superiors as Dartley was meant to be.

"Why did you give the alert when you saw me at the presidential palace?"

"Me?"

"You told the bodyguards, then stood in a doorway."

Laforque laughed. "I was certain you hadn't seen me. Very well, I'll tell you. As you know from all the screaming on the television and radio, the Israelis bombed Hasan's nuclear reactor and set his program back by a couple of years. Now Hasan needs a new reactor worth a hundred million American dollars or so. France is about to sell it to him. I was at the palace to deliver some negotiation details from Paris before going out to search for you, when to my horror I saw you, no more than fifteen feet away from France's suddenly most valuable customer, about to pull some lunatic ninja stunt. If Hasan goes, so does our contract. I did what I had to do to stop you."

"And now?" Dartley inquired.

"I've been searching for you everywhere to tell you to go home. I could have put the bodyguards onto you at the palace, but I didn't."

"It's also possible you guessed that I was within

271

seconds of striking down Hasan, knew they couldn't find me in time among all those Americans, and thought I'd never escape from the palace anyway."

Laforque laughed scornfully. "If I sat down with you, we could theorize all sorts of explanations together. It's always easy to do *after* the event, but when something is happening you never get a chance to think. You just act. Maybe I could have done things better. But look at how things are: Hasan is alive and will give France the contract. You're alive and richer by a million dollars. Forget all this. Go home and spend it."

Dartley grinned. "When you put it that way, it makes sense."

Omar Zekri did not want Awad to find out about the Ibrahims. They were too valuable to Omar to lose. He funneled money from Pritchett at the American Embassy to them, keeping a hefty chunk of it for himself. The Ibrahim women and children picked up many of the information packets from his informants and could be trusted to pay them the agreed amounts—such honesty in Omar's eyes being proof of their insane dedication to revenge. Where else would he ever find ragged urchins or fellahin women upon whom he could totally depend? He used their menfolk on missions which involved physical danger. And for all this, they charged him not one piastre, assuming that the money sent by Mubarak's aides inside the American Embassy should be answered by their efforts.

Omar had taken a strong liking to one of the family's teenage boys and talked with him and gave him cigarettes whenever he could. Omar had managed to rid himself for a few hours of Awad's almost constant presence and used this time to contact the Ibrahims. The boy had let it slip. They had an American staying with them. An American living in a cabin in the City of the Dead! The Egyptian poor would not permit a hippie foreigner to do this. It had to be the one Omar still thought of as Thomas Lewis, the wheat expert.

If Awad knew this, he would have the Ibrahims detained and Omar would lose their valuable services. He had to find a way to feed the American to Awad without involving the Ibrahim clan. He could think of only one way. Having taken a notebook from his pocket and torn out a page, he printed a message in block letters: URGENT. SEE ME TODAY. OMAR Z.

He folded the paper and gave it to the Ibrahim boy along with a ten-pound note so he could buy himself cigarettes.

Then he rushed off to find Awad.

Abdel Ibrahim struck the youth with his fist on the mouth, splitting his lip. The teenager's hangdog expression did not change, and he made no attempt to defend himself, either physically or verbally.

Abdel and Dartley walked away as Abdel said, "That one is no good. He is not my boy—I would beat him unconscious if he were. He's my oldest brother's son. He means no harm, but he is weak. The others will watch him while you are with us."

"Let's find Omar and see what this is all about," Dartley said. Privately he thought it was some other change of mind which Laforque had to transmit to him, and the Frenchman had hired Omar to find him again.

Abdel knew Omar's daily route even better than Dartley did. At this time of day he would be in Garden City, not far south of the American Embassy. The British had developed this part of the city as living quarters for themselves in the 1930s, and Garden City remained today as one of Cairo's most pleasant areas.

Omar was standing by himself on a street corner. The intersection was broad, and Dartley motioned Abdel to pull in the car on the opposite side.

"Have him cross the street to us," Dartley ordered, slipping beneath the steering wheel himself as Abdel got out.

Dartley watched Abdel wait for a break in the traffic, then hurriedly cross the street to Omar, who didn't spot him until then. Abdel shook hands with Omar and tried to lead him by the arm back across the street. Omar balked. They argued.

It was then that Dartley grew nervous. He threw the car in gear and let it slide forward slowly along the street while he watched developments on the far side. Only after the car had moved more than twenty feet did he see a fat man with an open sports shirt hanging over his pants. The man stood back against the building wall, out of Ibrahim's sight as he talked with Omar. Dartley would have bet the farm that the fat man had a pistol tucked somewhere in his straining waistband beneath the loose shirt. And Dartley had a damn good idea who the fat man was waiting for to approach Omar. Himself.

Ibrahim was going too far. The hungry looking

man, who was just skin and bone, was punching the fat cowering Omar and forcing him to cross the street. Dartley cursed. This wasn't what he wanted. He had no need to speak with Omar now. Omar had no message for him.

Abdel had forced Omar out into the traffic when the fat man pulled a pistol from beneath his shirt and went after them. Dartley accelerated the Opel at right angles across the traffic moving in both directions. The Cairo drivers, used to such unpredictable behavior, honked their horns, but didn't slow down much as they swerved around him. Dartley stopped the car two-thirds of the way across the broad intersection. He leaped out, then reached behind the driver's seat to Ibrahim's shotgun on the floor.

Dartley's maneuver with the car had distracted the fat man from shooting Abdel, but now he was lining up the gun barrel on Dartley's head. Dartley pumped a shell into the chamber and loosed off a shot at the gunman, which did more damage to the vinyl on the roof of a passing car than it did to its intended target.

A bullet whistled past Dartley's ear like a crazed hornet as he pumped another shell into the chamber. He snapped off the shot without taking aim. The fat gunman was peppered with birdshot, but it had spread out too much to cause him serious damage. All the same, the stinging impact of a dozen pieces of shot got across the message to him that his pistol was no match for a pump-action shotgun. The fat man turned and ran.

Dartley reloaded the chamber of the gun and aimed from the hip at Omar. Abdel Ibrahim's eyes widened in alarm and he backed off fast to one side.

Dartley's voice was easy, raised only loud enough to be heard above the honking horns of the traffic which the shooting had backed up. "Omar, I guess you never heard the good advice to never be the bait in your own trap."

He loosed off a blast from the gun which caught Omar in the chest, knocking him over like a soda bottle. He sat up in the roadway, an unrecognizable pulp of blood, hair and gristle. Dartley sent a second load of shot into his half-butchered carcass.

This time the bloodied torso fell back and lay still.

People were screaming, shouting and running from the shots between the cars.

Dartley gestured to Ibrahim with the smoking barrel of the gun. "You drive."

Chapter
13

The elevator was not working in the Adli Street apartment building, which although new was already run down. Richard Dartley and Abdel Ibrahim climbed a staircase to the seventh floor, where the Pensione Cornwall was located. Other people in the stairwell gave them no more than a passing glance.

Inside the pensione, which seemed clean and well cared for, there was no one at the reception desk. Dartley hammered on the formica top with his knuckles.

An Egyptian in shirtsleeves, about thirty, came out and looked over the unshaven American and his emaciated sidekick from the City of the Dead. "Sorry, we have no rooms left."

Dartley held out his half of the $100 bill the arms dealer had ripped in a jagged tear across the middle.

The man in shirtsleeves showed no surprise. He took the bill and disappeared back into the pensione. While he was gone, Dartley slowly lifted the phone receiver on the reception desk. There was a dial tone. He put it back.

"He might have another line," Dartley suggested. Ibrahim shook his head.

In a minute the man returned with the two leather suitcases Dartley had last seen in the trunk of the arms dealer's green Mercedes in the underground garage. He decided not to check the contents. Even if everything was gone, replaced by bricks or rocks, he did not want a confrontation on the seventh floor of an apartment building with no working elevator in the New City.

He was reaching for the bags and planning a quick exit down the stairs when the man behind the desk spoke in an unexpected tone in Arabic that Dartley understood.

"Have courage, Abdel Ibrahim."

"You know me?" Abdel asked, not pleased.

"Our cause is just. Allah will assist us."

"Mutta shakker," Dartley thanked him, then hustled Ibrahim out the door in front of him, carrying the lighter suitcase. When they were out of earshot in the staircase, he asked, "Who was that? Another of our cousins?"

"No," Abdel replied, not seeing the joke, "I do not know him. Yet he seemed anxious to let us know he was one of us."

"Too anxious," Dartley snapped.

"You judge him too quickly. He is a patriot, Terry. He heard about my brothers and recognized me. Can't you feel it? The people here have had enough. They are getting ready to rise up against their oppressors."

"Until the mullahs tell them to sit down again," Dartley said sarcastically.

"You are mistaken there. We are Egyptians first, Arabs second. We are not like other Arab countries, where what you say might be true."

They stopped talking when they heard others climbing the staircase. They passed them by, went out to the street and put the two suitcases in the Ford hired from Bita. They had turned in the Hertz Opel after the shotgun incident in heavy traffic. Fortunately, Ibrahim had hired it under a false name, as he did this Ford. Dartley was aware of how adroit Abdel could be behind his humble appearance.

"Take us out into the Western Desert so we can test-fire these guns," Dartley said, determined not to be caught a second time with faulty weapons.

As they crossed the Nile, Dartley returned to their previous conversation. He wanted to make one point clear to Ibrahim. "You were saying that man in the pensione wanted to let us know he was one of us. Who's us? Don't tie me into any of your patriotic games."

Ibrahim silently concentrated on his driving.

Dartley went on. "I'm here to do a job for pay. If this job happens to help the Egyptians, that's great, but it's a side issue with me. I'm using you. You're using me. But we don't have any purpose in common. Is that clear to you? I'm doing this for greenbacks. If you want to work for me, that's your concern. I'm willing to pay. Generously. Like I get paid. Only I don't want to hear any shit about me or you dying for the sake of Egypt. Or even getting scratched for Egypt, you hear?"

Ibrahim continued to gaze ahead out the windshield with a confident smile on his face. "It's too late for you now, Terry. You cannot back out."

Anger flashed in Dartley's eyes. "Like hell I can't! The guy who hired me thinks I've already quit and gone home."

"You told him you would?"

"Sure."

"You meant it?" Ibrahim asked with interest.

"Since I got to keep the money, it made sense. Though it kind of bugged me to leave that shithead Ahmed Hasan trailing slime above the ground. I was going to take time to think about it."

"So it was Omar and Awad who decided you?"

"Maybe. Is Awad the fat one with the pistol who ran away?"

"Yes. I heard that you killed his partner Zaid." Ibrahim made a cord of two fingers around his throat and stuck out his tongue. "I think Awad must be losing his nerve—which is not good when you are a policeman on special assignment to Ahmed Hasan. Do you think Hasan will let you leave Egypt after you have garroted one of his most feared strong-arm men and publicly humiliated another, just because you have changed your mind about assassinating him?"

"It's not as if I'm trapped in a box," Dartley protested.

"Do you think the person who hired you to kill Hasan believes you will not do so now—after the way you killed Omar Zekri?"

"He can't be sure that was me."

Ibrahim laughed. "Terry, who else is there in Cairo

who would try a shootout in the middle of the street? You heard what they called you on the TV news— Jesse James."

Dartley grunted. This thing was getting way out of hand.

Abdel Ibrahim's mouth dropped open as Dartley swung in a tight half-circle and chipped pieces from the tops of rocks with short bursts from the silenced Heckler & Koch MP5 submachine gun. Dartley emptied about twenty of the thirty shots in the magazine and showed Ibrahim how to fire off the rest. The gun worked faultlessly.

Dartley had expected to work alone, and as a result he had only one submachine gun. He liked to use a Browning Hi-Power semiautomatic pistol as his backup piece. In fact, he liked the big Browning so much he often carried two of them on a close-combat mission, one as the primary weapon instead of a submachine gun, and the other as the backup. He had four in the suitcase and he wanted to test-fire them all. From now on, he and Ibrahim would keep one concealed on them at all times. Dartley was getting on a war footing. He wanted to wrap this damn thing.

The reliability and simplicity, plus the thirteen-shot magazine, made this 9 mm Browning pistol the handgun of choice for hostage rescue units and counterterrorist units all over the world. The FBI National HRU used them. So did Britain's SAS and Mexico's Brigada Especial. The Hi-Power was J. M. Browning's last pistol design. First introduced in

1935, it incorporated what Browning had learned since designing the classic Colt 1911 .45 pistol.

The Browning had no recoil spring plug, and in it the barrel link was replaced by a strong block. The Hi-Power's slide stop was placed farther back than the 1911's, and this helped speed up changing magazines. Dartley didn't like the Browning's barleycorn foresight and U-notch rearsight, but he didn't expect to be doing any target shooting this time out.

These four pistols were made by FN in Belgium, and accordingly were labeled GP for Grande Puissance instead of HP for Hi-Power. But they were the same goods, and they had an awful lot of stopping power out to more than fifty yards.

After Ibrahim had emptied several magazines, there was a fighting glint in his hollow eyes. Dartley could see he was going to be hard to control.

Ahmed Hasan looked up from his desk and said to his aide, "Tell him I won't see him, that he should be ashamed to show his face here. You can say to Awad that I wanted to put him to death, but that you and some others persuaded me that I should let him live because he was the only one who knew this American by sight. Say that you even persuaded me to believe that his pistol jammed and that this was the only reason he ran away."

The aide nodded. "Of course, if Awad kills this American, you will reward him well."

"I will. And I mean that sincerely. Awad was a man I could trust. I need men like that. But he must prove himself first."

The aide left the presidential office. The president

nodded and two intelligence agents were shown in. They warned Hasan that the renegade American's reputation was spreading among underground armed resistance groups, which had been quiet for some time in the capital.

"Now they see things happening they had believed impossible because of our security net," one agent said. "If we can't catch this foreign interloper very soon, we must expect others to imitate his terrorist atrocities."

Ahmed nodded his agreement. "You make a good point there. We must make an example of this infidel assassin. Yet we must not seem to be worried by him. Our attitude must always be that he is merely a flea, a minor irritant, on the great hide of the state. I will not change my routine. Don't let your extra efforts be too visible—that will panic our supporters and give hope to our enemies. Watch the American Embassy."

"We have been, sir. But I think he keeps well away from Maglis el-Sha'ab Street."

"Laforque, the French special attaché, warned me that this American was on loan from the Mossad to the CIA," Hasan said. "He won't be working through normal channels."

After the two intelligence officers left the office, one said to the other, "He's so damn calm today. He's weird when he gets like that."

His companion laughed. "Yes, I feel safer too when Ahmed is shouting and waving his arms."

Awad heard the radio call and raced to the scene. The dead foreigner still lay on the roadway next to a

Volkswagen van with German plates. A woman with long blond hair wept and argued with plainclothesmen standing sheepishly about, passing papers to one another.

When one of them saw Awad, he rushed forward to explain. "We ordered the van to stop and we fired only when the driver laughed at us and kept on going. . . ."

Awad brushed him aside, reached down and pulled back the blanket that covered the body. The subject had a mustache and a few days' growth of beard, the hair was right, and the general build and height—but it was not the American.

Awad let the blanket fall to re-cover the body on the street. He shook his head and turned to leave.

Jacques Laforque was in a grim mood as he left the Hotel des Roses. Out of pride, he had turned down Ahmed's offer to him to ride with Egyptian government agents in search of the American. Ahmed placed great value of Laforque's eyeball identification of the American at the presidential palace reception, but so far seemed to have no suspicion that the Frenchman and the American had any connection with each other. Would the American talk if they took him alive? Of course. They all did. That might cost Paris the contract for the new reactor.

"Baksheesh! Baksheesh!"

Laforque ignored the urchins running alongside his long strides. If a foreigner gave something to one, the others would pester him nonstop until they too got something, while meantime others gathered from nowhere like vultures around carrion.

Paris was taking the situation seriously. In their last message to the French Embassy in Cairo, they had included a mild rebuke to him for informing them that the American assassin was withdrawing from Egypt. Why hadn't he just gone home? Why had he killed Omar? There was no doubt it was the same man—a hundred people had seen him gun down Omar in the street. Jesse James, they called him now. Paris was concerned, so the undersecretary had said when they shook hands at their embassy. Laforque noticed from the cable that no one was asking for his analysis of the situation now. They were sending down two men from the Gendarmerie Nationale counterterrorist unit, the GIGN, where he had once been the top assault man. The message was clear—all he had to do was find the American and the two GIGN men would do the dirty work. It was plain they no longer considered him capable of doing it himself.

The begging children stayed with him, shouting and looking up into his face as he walked along. He knew they would give up once they realized that they could not harass him into giving them money. He hadn't seen street kids as persistent as these in years. A sign of the times...

Laforque had no idea where he was going, though out of habit he paced forward very purposefully. The only approach he could think of was to look up as many of the shady characters who trafficked in miscellaneous things around the suqs and bazaars and offer to buy information from them. They would all, of course, have previously been pressured by government agents and the secret police. However, the promise of hard cash sometimes turned up things faster than threats from the authorities. He would be open about it, say that France was helping Hasan against his enemies.

He finally began to pay attention to the tallest of the urchins pestering him. He noticed that she spoke good English.

"Sir, take a taxi to the Al Azhar Mosque. Your American friend will meet you there."

He offered the children an Egyptian pound, which they refused before walking away in their rags with a dignified air.

As he sat back in the taxi, Laforque surreptitiously checked his French army pistol. It was the larger, fifteen-round version of the 9 mm MAB. Unusual for a pistol, it operated on the delayed blowback principle. The barrel was prevented from recoiling relative to the receiver, and in addition, initially locked the slide. The initial gas pressure rotated a barrel lug in a cam slot and released the slide to complete the mechanical cycle when the pressure was at a safe level.

It would be a patriotic act for him to use this French pistol to fire a French 9 mm parabellum at this paid American assassin who was no longer of use to France. Apart from that, his taking care of the unruly Yank on his own would show Paris he was still a first-class field operative. Also, it would show his old pals at GIGN that he could manage without their help, *merci beaucoup*.

There was no sign of the American outside the Al Azhar Mosque. Was he inside? Surely not.

Two teenaged boys approached. They wore Western clothes, but looked poor and malnourished.

"Mr. Laforque? I will take you to your American friend." He turned to his companion. "Telephone them now."

The other boy ran off and the one with him told him to hail a taxi. They climbed in and the boy spoke to the driver in such fast, colloquial Arabic that Laforque could not catch what address he had given. He wasn't much worried, not with the secure dead-weight of the big MAB in his shoulder holster.

He tried to talk to the boy further in English, but could not extract another word from him. Laforque was struck by the fact that the boy had spoken in the same excellent English as the little girl he had thought a beggar outside his hotel. They could even be brother and sister—they had the same strange, hollow eyes and starved look.

When they left the cab at a cafe near the southern edge of the city, Laforque was met by still another teenager with the family likeness.

"Your American friend will be here in a few minutes."

Laforque nodded, left them behind and went into the cafe. He sat at a table with his back to the wall where he could see the door. He slid the MAB from its holster and, keeping it under his jacket, he released the safety catch and eased a shell in the chamber. Then he slid the pistol back into the holster, repositioning the gun so it was loose and easy to draw. He sat back and tried to relax.

Dartley did not keep him waiting long. From a parked car, Abdel Ibrahim had been watching the Frenchman through high-power binoculars and guessed what he had been adjusting beneath his jacket at the cafe table. Dartley set up his Browning for instant fire, dropped it back in his shoulder holster, winked at Ibrahim and got out of the car. He threaded his way through the traffic to the cafe across the street.

"Bonjour," Laforque greeted him politely and stood to shake hands with him. Dartley was reminded of how the handshake evolved in the first place, as a way for meeting swordsmen to keep everyone's right hand in view.

Dartley ordered coffee and Laforque remarked casually that he thought Dartley would have left for home by now.

"Just a few minor complications in the travel arrangements," Dartley remarked. "Like I think I'd have to seize the airport before they let me on a plane."

Laforque dutifully smiled at this little display of humor. "Too bad."

"Looking back on a lot of recent difficulties I've had, I think now I have you to thank for them."

"If you're talking about that woman in Aqaba—"

"And other things," Dartley went on calmly. "For instance, I thought when you hired Omar Zekri to find me, it was a dumb move on your part since it exposed France's involvement in the affair to a paid gossip. But you saw that the Egyptian government agents would not take Omar's word for that. What Omar would do was tip off the government to my presence. You had no way of knowing that Omar already knew about me."

"He was harmless," Laforque said. "Why did you kill him?"

"Because he was very good at finding me."

"That was enough to make you kill him?"

"Of course," Dartley smiled glacially. "I never allow anyone to get in my way."

"Is France in your way?" Laforque asked in an amused tone.

"I don't think in such big terms. I think in terms of you, Laforque. And if I want to send France a message, I'll do it in terms of you, Laforque."

The Frenchman's humor suddenly evaporated. He grew tense. "There was never anything personal intended in my handling of your case. I see no need to get personal now."

Dartley spat out the words angrily. "Up till now, you've been behaving like the servant of someone so important it gave you immunity, too. You thought you were so big you could fuck me over, and even if I did survive it, I could do nothing about it. You wanted me, as an American, to make an attack on Ahmed Hasan and, of course, fail. But you wanted me to get caught or killed and have the CIA blamed. You would have found a way to make France look good, a Western nation coming to aid its Arab friends. Nukes in exchange for oil. I was never meant to get Hasan—you saw to that, first at Aqaba and then at the presidential palace. I was only meant to try and fail. Laforque, you set me up as a sacrifice."

"So what?" Laforque shrugged. "I can arrange safe passage out for you now. Why not go? Why keep after Hasan?"

"When there is some genuine change in my sponsor's plans, usually I'm pleased to oblige," Dartley said. "But when I find out I was never meant to do what I was hired to do because someone thought I couldn't do it, I get tempted to prove him wrong. I'm not out to kill Hasan because he's an asshole despot. I'm going to kill him to show your people in Paris not to fuck with me."

"I've never heard of anyone with an ego as big as that," Laforque said goadingly.

"When an American tells you not to tread on him, he's not just pulling some kind of personality trip on you. You're in my way, Laforque. I'm going to send you as my first message to Paris. Hasan will be the second. Draw!"

"Pardon?"

Dartley laughed harshly. "Let me explain it to you. In a few seconds I'm going to reach for the gun in my shoulder holster. I know you're carrying one too." Dartley tried not to let his eyes follow Laforque's right hand as it glided off the table and began to move across his body. "Doing the gentlemanly thing, I'm giving you notice of my intentions and a split-second advantage to get started. You ready? Now, draw!"

Laforque couldn't believe what was happening to him, but he had been around long enough to know when a man was serious. He went for the big 9 mm MAB in his shoulder holster, his right hand already more than halfway there.

Darkley yanked his 9 mm Browning out of his holster, hoping not to set the trigger off accidentally. He got his hand nicely around the grip and snaked his trigger finger forward as he brought the barrel up to bear on the Frenchman sitting opposite him at the small cafe table.

Laforque was more careful, more precise, slower.

Dartley squeezed the trigger when the Browning was pointing somewhere in the middle of Laforque's chest.

The bullet snapped off the top of the MAB and buried itself in Laforque's neck.

Dartley's trigger finger was already sending a second shot home, and this slug hit Laforque in the solar plexus with a dull whop. The bullet ripped through his innards and embedded itself in his backbone, severing the spinal cord.

The first shot lifted the Frenchman up out of his chair and the second sent him crashing backward into other tables and chairs.

Yet the last threshing movements of Laforque's body, as life leaked out of it, caused less damage to cafe property than the stampede of other customers to safety. They jumped over and kicked aside the tables and chairs, sending cups and saucers and other customers flying.

They were still trying to untangle themselves and escape when Dartley placed a $100 bill on the counter, holstered his smoking gun and headed out into the street.

While he made his way through the traffic toward the car waiting on the opposite side of the street, he heard some kids behind him shouting, "Jesse James! Jesse James!"

When Ahmed Hasan heard how Jacques Laforque died, he lost his aura of calm.

"This is an open invitation to the lawless, godless elements to riot!" he screamed. "Where were the police when this shootout was going on? How can this man conduct gunfights in crowded streets in Cairo and nothing happens to him? Awad ran away! He is making the state security forces look like fools. The lawless ones will think we are weak. We do not respond. One man can challenge us successfully right here in the capital city. I can see them now! The rebels are digging up their guns and oiling them! The spies are watching! They are like wolves. When they scent weakness, they attack." He paused in his rapid pacing up and down the presidential office and stared at the assembled military and security officers. "We need a diversion. Yes! Exactly! Get a mob to storm the American Embassy and we'll hang Mubarak and the others."

"President Reagan has told us loud and clear," one general pointed out, "that if the embassy is attacked, either by us directly or if we let a mob do it, the American Air Force will lay waste—"

"I know all that!" Hasan shouted, but he cooled down a bit. "Then let's get your soldiers on the move. Have them do something."

"Right now, sir, they might do more harm than good," the general spoke up again. "We have a bit of a morale problem. There's no telling which side they might end up fighting on if we let them mix with the city mobs."

They watched Ahmed carefully and saw him register this advice. He was raving, but his brain was still taking things in, even if they were not what he wanted to hear.

"What about the police forces then?" he asked in a much more reasonable tone of voice.

"We're already doing our best, sir," another man said.

"And it is not good enough," Hasan judged. He looked at them all in silence for a full minute with a crooked grin on his face. Finally he said, "I know some of you think I am mad. Talented but unpredictable and very dangerous, isn't that what you say behind my back to foreigners at cocktail parties? Very well. Listen to this. It will confirm your fears. I want you to put the whole city on a riot alert. Cancel all leaves. Bring every possible man on duty, both police and army. I want you to do this as secretly as possible, so that this does not become a self-fulfilling prophecy. Tell them we think Israeli paratroopers may attack. They'll curse and groan, but they will all show up. Keep the assault squads restricted to barracks and be ready to move out. Any questions?"

There were none, apart from a few raised eyebrows.

"Dismissed."

Pritchett entered the mosque. He was curious. It wasn't often that anyone from the American Embassy got an invitation from the mullahs in Cairo. This time these Light of Islam people had specifically asked for him. Pritchett waited in the entranceway for someone to approach him.

A young mullah with a sparse beard came up to him and said something in Arabic.

Pritchett gestured that he did not understand.

The mullah pointed to a door at the end of a long corridor at the left of the mosque entrance. Pritchett walked down to the door, banged on it with his fist—but the wood was so heavy his knock would not be heard on the other side of the door—then pressed down its latch and pushed it inward.

The big room on the other side was dimly lit by small windows high in its walls. Two mullahs sat on carpets scattered about the floor. A third man with them was no more than twenty-five and he wore jeans and a burgundy T-shirt with a white Harvard University insignia on it. As his eyes grew accustomed to the light, Pritchett recognized the mullahs— both leaders of the so-called moderate wing of the Light of Islam. One had a huge white beard and the other a sharp, black, pointed one and black fierce eyes.

Pritchett had been through this shit before and he wasn't about to let them intimidate him with their silence and their stares in their mosque.

"Hi," he said, left his shoes at the door and lowered himself onto the carpets next to them. "You a Harvard boy?"

"Yes," the young man said, evidently a little surprised by this American's approach.

"I went to Boston University myself," Pritchett lied.

"Oh." The young man had nothing to say to that.

"You the interpreter?"

"Yes."

"What do they want?" Pritchett asked, like he was in a hurry and these people were taking up his valuable time.

"I don't know."

"Ask them."

The usual elaborate formal greetings followed, which Pritchett returned patiently; then a short denunciation of the United States, which made Pritchett yawn. Then the mullahs got down to business. A popular uprising was about to take place—within hours—against Ahmed Hasan and the more fanatical Light of Islam zealots. The two mullahs were aware that the CIA had several arms dumps hidden at strategic points around the city. Would the CIA release these arms to the rebels?

"Because of the rising popular unrest of the last few days," Pritchett told them, "I have already discussed this subject with my superiors. While I cannot speak for the CIA, since I am not a member of that organization, and while the CIA denies the existence of such arms dumps in Cairo or anywhere in the sovereign territory of the Arab Republic of Egypt, I can tell you the following: The State Department in Washington, D.C., strongly supports President Ahmed Hasan and will not permit any American intervention that might destabilize his administration."

The translation of this statement was met with hard looks from the mullahs. Their reply was polite and forceful. "We will pursue the course which Allah has pointed out for us, even without the help of potential friends. And we have long memories."

"If Ahmed Hasan were . . . somehow removed from the presidency," Pritchett suggested, "I can't see how the State Department could object to our support of the more moderate faction in the ensuing chaos. Especially if that faction agreed to reinstate ex-President Mubarak."

The two mullahs chewed this over between themselves for a while before replying. "We will move against our oppressors without your assistance."

"I know of a cache of Kalashnikov rifles and Makarov pistols," Pritchett volunteered. "I don't suppose it would do any harm for us to give you these. But I can't give you American weapons while Hasan is still in power. I'll send someone here in an hour to show your people where to find these Soviet arms."

Pritchett left. He was not the one who made decisions, he just followed orders. He smiled to think of the furious faces of State Department guys at the embassy when they heard about the mob with Russian guns. There was no way they could trace these to the Agency.

The fighting broke out in the huge courtyard of the Mosque of Ibn Tulun in southern Islamic Cairo. Bullets ricocheted off the intricate lacework of decorations and gouged out pieces of carved stonework and stucco. The fighting then spilled eastward into Saliba Street and on to Salah Al-Din Square, near the western gate of the Citadel. Government reinforcements did not have far to go.

The fellahin fought the police and soldiers with modern shotguns and hunting rifles, with antique weapons that had gold or silver inlays and filigrees, with a mysterious but small supply of Soviet rifles and pistols, with World War II British Enfield rifles and Webley revolvers, with Molotov cocktails and cobblestones.

The soldiers and police started out with tear gas, stun grenades and rubber bullets. In minutes they were using live ammunition from their Rashid and

Hakim rifles, Carl Gustav submachine guns and Beretta pistols. The bodies started piling up in the suddenly deserted streets.

The same thing happened at five other points in the city. Before the fighting could spread and a mob build beyond the point where it could be controlled, crack units descended on the undisciplined rebels. The highly trained police and military units took out the leaders of each group in a quick assault, then let the others escape into the crowd so long as they dropped their weapons and ammo.

Although these government tactics resulted in few arrests, they served to quell the disturbances quickly, since the leaderless rebels lost the will to fight to the death when they saw an opportunity to run now and come back another day. In sha 'allah.

Chapter
14

When Abdel Ibrahim told Richard Dartley that Dr. Mustafa Bakkush wanted to meet him, Dartley was enthusiastic. In his stay at the City of the Dead, Dartley had learned that Ibrahim had wide contacts in the rebel underground against Hasan and many of the Light of Islam zealots. He was even regarded as being a major leader of this leaderless, disorganized, hard-core mass of dissenters. Dartley remembered how the man at the reception desk of the Pensione Cornwell had recognized Ibrahim when they came to pick up the weapons.

Most of the rebel factions disagreed with one another in their attitude to the Light of Islam mullahs, but they were all united in their hatred of Ahmed Hasan. So far as Dartley could tell, Ibrahim had emerged as the pro-Mubarak strongman in the movement. Both of his brothers had died in serving the ex-president, who with his family and some associates had taken refuge in the American Embassy after the overthrow of his government by Islamic fundamentalists.

Certainly Abdel Ibrahim was a lot more than a half-starved occupant of a shack in an ancient graveyard. He had stayed out of the unsuccessful uprising against Hasan. Dartley did not know that this was because he had been advised to do so by a message from Pritchett at the embassy. On his part, Pritchett would have been enraged at Ibrahim if he had known he was sheltering the American madman who was causing everyone so much trouble—particularly Pritchett himself, who was still shamefacedly reporting to Langley, Virginia, that he had no notion who the man was.

Mustafa Bakkush had sent Dartley, via the tailor, to Ibrahim. Dartley hadn't seen or heard of Bakkush since then, and looked forward to talking with this world-renowned scientist. He found it a little peculiar that the scientist had arranged to meet him in a mosque. Although Dartley expected that Bakkush's request to speak with him would have some hidden motive attached, he was amazed to find two mullahs waiting with him whose faces Dartley recognized from the Cairo TV news. He did not know their names or exactly what they stood for, except that they were Light of Islam and he wanted none of them.

Dartley headed back toward the door where he had left his shoes, with his hand on the butt of the Browning in his shoulder holster. He stopped only when both Ibrahim and Bakkush pleaded with him to come back.

"I've seen these two on TV, cussing out the U.S.,"

Dartley said. "The one with the white beard called us the devil's spawn, and the one with the little pointed beard, who, if you ask me, looks like the devil himself, called us something else. I'm not going to sit down with them, no matter what. As I see it, they ain't good enough to kiss Ronald Reagan's ass."

"Things have changed," Bakkush said. The little scientist looked out of place next to the two crazy looking mullahs and the fellahin rebel from the City of the Dead.

"Things always change when someone wants something from someone," Dartley said. "You go ahead and translate what I said about them, and say slowly so I can understand your Arabic enough to make sure you get it all in. And you can add that if they start ranting about the evils of the West, this particular devil is going to hightail it out of here."

So far as Dartley could follow, Bakkush told the two mullahs everything he had said. The one with the white beard even laughed and said politics are politics and must not come between men of good will.

They must want something from him real bad, Dartley decided.

Bakkush spoke hurriedly now, before the American and the two Light of Islam mullahs could tangle any further. "I was brought back to Egypt under duress. It is common knowledge that I preferred to live abroad. Now I am here to stay—I will remain even after I am free to go. Abdel Ibrahim loves this country too, even though it has cost the lives of two brothers. The mullahs here are harder for you to understand. I suppose we Muslims like our religion strongly spiced, so we get what we deserve. These two religious leaders are perhaps like some of your fierce Southern Baptists in the United States, which makes them moderates here. The most important thing for us about them is that they think their power should center around the mosque. They do not believe they should take over the government and rule the people, as many of the other Light of Islam mullahs do. Thus they are on the same side as Abdel Ibrahim and I."

"Good for you," Dartley said warily.

"We want to tell you only two things," Bakkush resumed, "two very important things. The first is that we cannot get arms released until the tyrant Hasan is ousted. Nor will the people join an uprising until they truly believe he is gone. That much is evident from what has already happened. You are going to kill Ahmed Hasan. We need to know when."

"Forget it," Dartley said.

"We must know for our planning," Mustafa Bakkush protested.

"I'll get Ibrahim to tell you when we decide," Dartley said, privately vowing that Ibrahim would know nothing until the latest possible time. Dartley was damned if he was sharing his schedule with Light of Islam mullahs, no matter how friendly they pretended to be.

"The second matter is just as important," Bakkush continued. "The government agent known as Awad— no one knows his real name—is the one whose partner, Zaid, they say you garroted in his van and is the one who ran from you when you shotgunned Omar Zekri. This Awad is at the moment combing the city not only for you, as he has been doing for days, but for members of the underground movements. He will torture them and some of them may have heard rumors of where you are to be found."

Ibrahim nodded. "You know how people talk loosely. And Awad is a skilled torturer. I think there is a great danger. You must go with Mustafa. The mullahs will hide you both."

"Hold on," Dartley said. "Why do you mention only Awad? Aren't there other government agents?"

"That is how Ahmed Hasan works," Abdel said. "He assigns a task to one man and holds him alone responsible for it. Awad's task is to find you. Besides his fear of Ahmed Hasan, Awad must kill you because you made him run like a cowardly dog and because you killed his partner Zaid. None of the others will search for you like he is doing."

"So let's go find Awad," Dartley said to Ibrahim while climbing to his feet. "Mustafa, you and I have got to talk sometime." He nodded to the mullahs. "Pleasure meeting you gentlemen."

"The hunter often forgets he can be hunted too," Dartley remarked as he and Ibrahim watched the secret police patrol from the front of their car.

They had found Awad where they heard he would be, near the intersection of the Sharia Al-Azhar and the Sharia El Muizz. They had watched three secret police patrols searching the buildings in this crowded, noisy sector before they found the one Awad was with. He directed them all by a hand-held radio, which meant the other patrols were not far away and might number more than Dartley and Ibrahim saw.

"You drive and concentrate on that," Dartley cautioned. "Try to give me a back door if things go wrong."

Dartley would take care of Awad himself. He felt no personal challenge in this, as he often did in putting himself against someone else who knew he was a marked man. Awad was only a bully. Now that he had others with him, he would know no fear. It would not even occur to the fool, as he terrorized people in his search for rebels, that he too was being stalked at that very moment.

"Follow them till they go in the next apartment building," he told Ibrahim, "then hang back here till they start coming out. As soon as you see Awad emerge, put your foot on the gas and move up fast."

Dartley took his jacket off as they watched Awad and the five other plainclothesmen pass five doorways and enter the sixth. Dartley draped the jacket over his left arm, picked up the Heckler & Koch MP5 submachine gun from the floor at his feet and concealed it as best he could beneath the jacket.

He opened the car door and said to Ibrahim before he got out, "Hang back here. I can take care of myself. Don't come till Awad shows unless I wave to you." He grinned. "It's really going to freak them out when they see me walking right at them."

Dartley stopped at a store window next to the house the secret police were searching. He looked like a hot, perspiring, foreign tourist examining curios in the window. The two secret policemen who came together out of the building didn't even notice him. They walked up the street, lighting cigarettes and talking to each other. The next man down spotted Dartley. He dived for his shoulder holster, but Dartley knocked off a pair of shots from the MP5, which placed two red splotches on the front of the man's shirt. His legs gave way beneath him and he hit the sidewalk.

Even if the traffic had not been so hellishly noisy, the first two policemen would not have heard the two dry coughs which the MP5's silencer made. It was like an invalid clearing his throat.

Awad walked out the door of the building with another man. He stopped, transfixed, and looked at the crumpled body in front of the door. He looked up the street at the backs of the other two cops, still talking and smoking. Then he looked in Dartley's direction.

Dartley had waited for that. He wanted to see recognition dawn on this bastard's face before he quenched the life in his sick brain.

The MP5 gave three bronchial rasps and Awad rolled on the pavement. Dartley took out the other man with a couple of shots. Then he put another two slugs into Awad's still moving, fat pig carcass.

Passersby were taking shelter behind parked cars and in doorways. The street traffic tore heedlessly by.

Ibrahim braked the car beside him, Dartley got in and they passed the two secret policemen farther up the street, who were still smoking and talking.

The seven ragged fellahin carried rusty picks and battered shovels. They plodded wearily and unseeingly through the city streets until they came to an intersection. Here they dumped their picks and shovels in the middle of the intersecting streets. Teams of ragged urchins ran to them, carrying portable traffic barriers which they had obviously scavenged from other sites. The men erected these barriers in a square around themselves and their equipment.

They began to break into the road surface with their picks, levering up the paving stones with crowbars and stacking the stones in small piles banked by shoveled earth. The traffic flowed around them as they worked. The urchins continued to arrive with more barricades.

As the work spread, the traffic slowed as it navigated around the excavated part of the intersecting streets.

Drivers cursed. A policeman directed traffic for a while and then left. The seven workmen, all still in their teens, had sunken eyes and thin faces—all had an amazing resemblance to one another, as if they were close cousins. But no one noticed, since no one pays attention to workmen in a street.

No one asked who had sent them or what they were doing there.

Ahmed Hasan and his bodyguards were nearing the Citadel in three Range Rovers. The president had received word of Awad's death and thought about declaring a state of emergency. It would be a sign of weakness on his part, Ahmed decided, if one man or at most a small group could force him to do this. Any panic on his part, any backing down, any display of fear would only further lower the morale of the army. He felt he could depend on the police forces—the army he had doubts about. The officers plotted against him among themselves, and the enlisted men were ignorant and easily roused.

So far the Light of Islam mullahs had controlled the Cairo mob, but Ahmed could see that their grip was slipping. The mullahs themselves were now split by dissent. This in one way was a benefit to him. If the mullahs had been united, they might have turned on him and pacified the people by blaming all the wrongs on him. That would not happen. They had chosen him and would have to stick by him now that the dissenting liberal mullahs were denouncing him.

The three Range Rovers were slowed by the traffic as they neared the Citadel. The drivers went up on the pavement at times and people scattered out of their way. Roadwork at an intersection was causing most of the mess. The drivers nosed their Range Rovers into the slowly moving cars again, keeping their 1, 2, 3 pattern and staying close together. They were almost at the Citadel now.

One of the bodyguards in the leading vehicle shouted that the roadworkers looked more like they were building fortifications than replacing cables or pipes. The vehicle's driver saw it too and radioed back an alarm to the two Range Rovers behind them.

But all three were stuck in the slowly moving traffic and had no room to maneuver.

One roadworker rolled a grenade beneath the first vehicle and all seven ducked down behind their fortifications. The grenade blew and flipped the Range Rover onto its side.

Another grenade rolled beneath the second vehicle, and two beneath the third. The second Range Rover was flipped on its side by the explosion, lik the first. The third was lifted ten feet high by the simultaneous explosion of the two grenades beneath it. The military vehicle crashed down squarely on all four wheels, shattering its axles.

Black smoke billowed everywhere. The second Range Rover was on fire and its occupants desperately struggled out of its upward-facing door.

None of the bodyguards noticed the seven road-workers slip away through the stalled cars and hysterical drivers at the crossing. The force of the blasts had shattered windshields and side windows of cars, but no innocent passengers, drivers or passersby seemed injured. They just added to the chaos by shouting and running in all directions.

Richard Dartley and Abdel Ibrahim stood inside a dark store looking on at the scene through its window. Sacks of coffee beans were piled everywhere, and gleaming brass scales stood on the counter where the merchant weighed his customers' purchases. The merchant and two women assistants—one or both perhaps his wives—stood at the back of the store and wrung their hands. The two armed men had been in the store an hour, had locked the door and put a sign on it saying CLOSED. The foreign one had promised to kill them with his silenced submachine gun if they annoyed him in any way. They shrank back into the shadows when he came near them.

"No sign of the fucker yet," Dartley grated, as he calmly watched the cut, bruised, bleeding bodyguards help each other out of the first two vehicles. Two seemed to have broken arms, and most of the others looked battered and had lost their weapons.

No one stirred from the third vehicle, sitting squat on its chassis on the street.

"Damn, they're waiting for reinforcements before they come out," Dartley said. "We've got to flush Hasan out if he's in there."

Ibrahim gestured wildly at a youth outside the store window. He nodded and walked quickly away. Ibrahim unlocked the door and opened it a few inches. Then they saw the youth again, walking fast toward the third Range Rover with a two-gallon can in his right hand. He stooped for a moment and set the can next to the disabled vehicle and broke into a run.

Dartley poked the barrel of the MP5 through the doorway opening. He missed with his first two shots, then landed the third in the middle of the can, which exploded and blew flaming gasoline all over the Range Rover.

The doors opened on both sides and the occupants came pouring out. Dartley ignored the kids in their camouflage jumpsuits and bush hats. He watched for a tall, bony man in an officer's khaki suit with lots of ribbons and brass.

"There he goes!" Ibrahim yelled.

Then Dartley saw him too. The skunk must have crawled on his hands and knees out the far door and along the street. Now he had broken into a run, glancing back and keeping behind the cover of cars.

"Get out of here," Dartley said to Ibrahim. "Clear all your family away."

Dartley ran from the store. The bodyguards from the third vehicle had their weapons and were covering their president's escape route. They didn't see him coming. Not from a store almost next to them. They hadn't expected that.

He knew he had to take them with what was left in his magazine. Thirty rounds less the three he had fired at the can. He came at them on the run and fired from left to right, taking the first man with a single shot in the shoulder.

A short burst ran a line of holes across the midriffs of two others, and they fell hard, like mechanical targets on a range.

Things got messier with the rest. Dartley sprayed them wildly with bullets like a person spraying roaches from a can. He could not be sure how many he got, how many fired back or even how many just lay still and played dead. All he knew or cared about was that no one stood between him and the fleeing president.

He changed magazines as he ran. Hasan was quite a ways off down the street, running among the stalled, hooting cars. Dartley noticed that people who recognized their almighty president pointed in wonder as they saw him run for his life down the traffic-clogged street.

Dartley charged after him, running as fast as he could in the heat and fumes, holding the submachine gun in his right hand. It was perfectly timed. The car door swung outward just before he drew level with it, held steady by the driver's shoulder with one foot on the road. It caught Dartley all the way from the neck to the knees, as he slammed into it at a full run.

He picked himself up off the street, dazed and winded, then saw someone picking up the MP5 where it had flown from his grasp. Dartley drew his

Browning and shouted a warning. The man paid no attention. Dartley fired. He missed. The man scooped up the submachine gun and ran. Dartley fired twice more and missed each time. His left knee hurt, the breath had been knocked out of him and he couldn't shoot for shit! A car door could put an end to all that? Like hell it could. Dartley braced himself.

Hasan was still in sight down the street, going at a nice easy clip now, as if he were a marathon runner. Dartley set out after him, but immediately had to dive for cover as a burst of gunfire sounded behind him. The clown who had run off with the MP5 was now firing on him. Dartley showed himself and hit back with his Browning, drawing longer bursts of fire—until they stopped, the magazine exhausted. Dartley still had all the spares for the MP5 in his pockets. He ignored the gunman now and took off again after Hasan.

Hasan looked back over his shoulder and slowed down. He looked back again and stopped.

All Dartley could think was that Hasan had heard the pistol shots, had missed seeing him and assumed that the American was no longer in pursuit. True, Dartley was now running on the other side of the two columns of cars than where he had previously been. He kept low and close to the cars.

Then Dartley saw something else. Ahmed Hasan was talking with two uniformed cops, who would probably have stopped him anyway if he had tried to continue running. This gave Dartley time, and he used it to eat up the distance between him and his quarry. The two policemen were now looking back in the direction from which the president had come. They did not see Dartley until he was less than a hundred yards away. A pistol is not much use at that range, but Dartley blazed away.

He emptied the magazine without hitting either of them. He had to root in his pockets among the MP5 magazines to find his only other pistol mag. The police were zinging bullets off cars, almost touching his ears.

He emptied the new magazine at them, rapid fire, and brought both men down. Hasan was no longer with them or he would have bought it too.

Dartley saw him run into the entranceway of a building. Afraid to lose him if he stopped to pick up the downed cops' weapons, Dartley tossed away his empty pistol and went after him. His left knee was bothering him badly now, and he was not sure if he could manage a long chase through buildings and maybe over rooftops. Ahmed Hasan seemed to have nine lives.

Dartley laughed out loud when he saw Ahmed hiding behind some bushes at the back of the courtyard.

Dartley limped toward his prey. He was covered with sweat and dirt, his clothes were ripped, he was panting and he had no gun. Yet he intended to kill Hasan any way he could.

The president, seeing the American unarmed, emerged from the bushes with a combat knife in his right hand. He and the American stalked each other. It was clear to Dartley that Hasan wanted to play for time, jab at him and keep him at arm's length until help arrived.

Dartley pulled off his jacket, took a full MP5 mag

IAN BARCLAY

from one pocket and then wrapped the jacket around
his left forearm as a defense against Ahmed's knife
thrusts. He moved in, and each time Ahmed jabbed
at him with the blade he took it in the coat and
swung at the Egyptian's face with the magazine.

Blood soaked through his coat as time after time
the knife point found its mark in the flesh of his left
forearm. The pain only served to determine Dartley
even further, and he continued his attack until he
had Ahmed backed up against the rear wall of the
courtyard.

The mag's metal edges cut Hasan about the eyes
and one blow had already raised a huge, blue buise
over his left cheekbone. Hasan desperately drove the
knife with all his strength at his attacker. Dartley felt
the blade tear through the fabric of the coat a half-
inch beneath his arm. He let the blade sink to the
hilt into the cloth, then sharply twisted his arm
downward. The coat held the blade and twisted its
handle out of Hasan's grip.

Hasan jumped Dartley and knocked him on his
back. He tried to straddle him and choke him—but
suddenly released his fingers from the American's
throat. Hasan screamed in pain and his eyes rolled in
his head. He staggered slowly to his feet off the
downed American, who looked up at him with a
crimson-dripping blade in his hand. Hasan clutched
his stomach with both hands and half-ran, half-stumbled
across the courtyard to the street entranceway.

Hasan tottered out onto the sidewalk, then weak-
ened, and his hands dropped away from his stomach.
His belly was slit from hip to hip, and the contents of
his body cavity spilled out on the sidewalk at his feet.

312

Hasan wavered and fell face forward onto his own throbbing, glistening entrails.

The Light of Islam mullahs put their militias in the streets and the Cairo mobs fought them with American weapons and ammo which suddenly turned up in plentiful supply all over the city. The soldiers fought the police, and each side racked up impressive body counts. Fighting lasted into the early morning hours and did not start again at dawn.

When President Mubarak's motorcade left the American Embassy, he was greeted by joyous multitudes. There didn't seem to be a person left in Cairo who wanted to recall the bad old Light of Islam days.

Abdel Ibrahim insisted that Dartley attend the reception for the new president. Pritchett sent word from the embassy that he'd love to meet him. Dartley took a stroll and didn't come back.

The ticket agent at Cairo International Airport couldn't understand why Dartley was willing to wait six hours for an AirEgypt flight to New York via London, when for the same price he would only have to wait an hour for an Air France flight via Paris.

27 million Americans can't read a bedtime story to a child.

It's because 27 million adults in this country simply can't read.

Functional illiteracy has reached one out of five Americans. It robs them of even the simplest of human pleasures, like reading a fairy tale to a child.

You can change all this by joining the fight against illiteracy.

Call the Coalition for Literacy at toll-free **1-800-228-8813** and volunteer.

Volunteer Against Illiteracy. The only degree you need is a degree of caring.

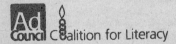

Ad Council Coalition for Literacy

Warner Books is proud to be an active supporter of the Coalition for Literacy.